MW01492398

PRAISE FOR WHISKEY AND WARFARE

"Every element of it just SANG. The story was *chef's kiss*. This book is truly special."

Sarah Chorn, author of *The Necessity of Rain*

"This is the story we all need now — filled with so much love and respect and genuinely fun adventure."

KD Edwards, author of *The Last Sun*

PRAISE FOR E. M. HAMILL

Dalí

"Told with raw emotion and fantastically rich world building..."

USA TODAY - *Happily Ever After*

Peacemaker

"...Tense, surprising science fiction that's thematically rich, sexually frank, and highly inventive in its cultures, technology, and dilemmas."

The BookLife Prize Critic's Report

Nectar and Ambrosia

"...So damn addicting. This book was fast, fun, and completely unique."

Bookworm Blues

WHISKEY AND WARFARE

A TEAM HUNTRESS FLIGHT

E. M. HAMILL

STAR
BARD
BOOKS

Copyright © 2024 by E. M. Hamill

All rights reserved.

No part of this book may be reproduced in any form or by any electronic or mechanical means, including information storage and retrieval systems, without written permission from the author, except for the use of brief quotations in a book review.

NO AI TRAINING: Without in any way limiting the author's [and publisher's] exclusive rights under copyright, any use of this publication to "train" generative artificial intelligence (AI) technologies to generate text is expressly prohibited. The author reserves all rights to license uses of this work for generative AI training and development of machine learning language models.

Content Warnings: *This book includes scenes of the funeral of a spouse, frank depictions of grief, violent warfare, and discussions of genocide/ethnic cleansing.*

DEDICATION

A nurse, an archaeologist, an ex-military intelligence analyst turned librarian, and a witch walk into a bar and get blended up with a healthy dose of space opera cheese ... What you get from that powerful concoction is this book.

It is a love letter to three people with whom I have been friends for the better part of our lives (I will not say exactly how long, but at least as long as Maryn and Jac!). I never made friends very easily when I was young, but I have somehow managed to stay in the orbit of some of the most amazing humans in the world.

So Reneé Ash, Ann Raab, and Lori Clyma-Lewis: this book is for you. You know the deep, dark secrets only lifelong friends can share. No matter how much life and geography might separate us, whenever we're together, the love and friendship stay exactly the same. I am so, so lucky to have you in my life.

If you see things you might recognize in this story, you're probably right, though no one character is based on anybody in particular.

Seriously. Nobody in particular. I swear.

You've always had my back. I'll always have yours.

In all phases.

CHAPTER
ONE

DR. MARYN ALESSI, former mercenary for hire and co-discoverer of *Calibotari andelessi*, found herself unexpectedly widowed. She was pissed as hell about it.

Most of the lingering attendees inside the tiny pan-denominational chapel wanted to express their sympathy in person, but Maryn would rather have had her teeth pulled without anesthetic than deal with more people by the time the formal observance was over. She fled as soon as she could, her closest friends following to cover her retreat down the aisle.

It was the cruel obverse of a wedding recessional. Like somber attendants, Colterrikor, Scylla, and Jac carried a few of the many flower arrangements that had crowded the floor in front of the plinth. Instead of her vibrant mate, a phantom ache like a missing limb occupied the emptiness at her side. What was left of Andelek lay cradled in her arms, condensed into a deceptively small but heavy rectangular box of ashes emblazoned with the seal of the Xyrian royal family.

Ze wasn't supposed to die before she did, goddamn it.

A celebrated adventurer and exobiologist, Andelek had only settled with her on this quiet planet because of what happened on her last mission. Now, a little more than two decades later, a virus native to Echo Four had decimated her mate's immune system in less than a week. It was unbelievable that so tiny a thing could end a life as exciting and meaningful as Andelek's. Unthinkable that it could rip away someone as important to her as ze was.

Echo Four's microfauna killed zem when no megafauna in the galaxy had ever come close. It was fucking unfair.

She winced, blinking at the brilliant sky as they emerged from the chapel. The Prime Galactic University president's hovering limousine waited outside to take her home, back to the institution-owned house she and Andelek shared.

Had shared. Maryn corrected the tense the way she'd begun adjusting everything in her inner dialogue over the last, horrible week. The same way she'd done when a member of her squad in the Artemis Corps wasn't there anymore. When they were dead, like Andelek. She had to pay attention to staying alive and pushing on.

Being practical didn't make it any less gutting.

Dr. Globney still talked with a group of academics who'd attended the observance. Professor Zill's weasel-like face kept turning in her direction as if he expected her to say something. Before the memorial service even started, the senior exobiologist had tried to talk to her about who would teach their classes next semester. She'd stared him down in disbelief until he backed away, stuttering his condolences. Maryn wasn't sure if her murderous expression caused his hasty retreat or the quiet, fanged snarl of her Boshi friend, Col, who stood behind her: six-and-a-half-feet of corded muscle beneath a sleek white pelt. Zill had probably remembered they used to kill people for a living. She doubted it was a sudden attack of remorse for his ill-mannered questions.

Her friends placed the flowers in a storage hatch behind the passenger compartment of Maryn's small electric vehicle and she set the urn beside them for now. Jac and Scylla enveloped her in a tight hug. Col wrapped her long, ivory-furred arms around all three of them.

This was the way they always embraced each other: as a unit, a knot of warmth and love, sharing memories mixed with laughter, or standing against past horrors. Frequent group subspace calls and text communications between meetups were a poor substitute for a satisfying tangle of arms and affection. It had been several years since all of them had been together on Echo Four. No matter how seldom the physical meetings occurred, whenever they reunited it was as if their lives had never taken separate paths.

"You are not alone," Col's soft voice reminded her.

Maryn swallowed to clear the lump in her throat, grateful for the love of her friends and their loyalty. "Thank you for being here," she said, stubbornly blinking away the burn in her eyes. "We're still meeting at my house, right?"

"Damn straight," Scylla proclaimed, her gruff voice hitched. She and Andelek had not been close, but the stoic pilot was uncharacteristically emotional during the service, as if she'd demonstrated the grief Maryn's current, spicy permutation of emotions would not allow her to feel. "Rampaging calibotari couldn't keep us away."

"We're bringing enough rain globe wine to kill one, in case any show up." Jac kissed Maryn's cheek, the familiar drift of vetiver clinging to her brown skin. The scent always brought out bright, noisy memories of the crowded market square where she had purchased the vial of perfume on one of their jobs.

When they pulled back from the hug, Col cupped Maryn's face in her soft, furry palm. "If you aren't up to it, we understand."

"Oh, no. There's no way in hell we are all on the same planet and we're not together." She glanced at each beloved face in turn. "How long can you stay?"

"I have taken a remote assignment for the bank for the next six weeks," Col said. "I am here as long as you want me, if I can be of help."

"We've got obligations to keep. We're trying to get jump clearance early tomorrow, but we're yours all night if you want us," Jac reassured Maryn, and turned to her wife. "Right, love?"

"You fucking bet." Scylla Merrow didn't look her usual self either, not in the severe black suit she'd worn for the funeral, her tattoos hidden behind full-length sleeves and pants. The buzzed haircut tipped with purple belonged to the person she knew and loved, but the stark white roots were new.

Something about losing Andelek made Maryn aware that none of them were young anymore. Scylla was older than her by almost a decade, but her body was still hard and trim. So was Jac Merrow in her sleeveless dress, bare brown arms strong and defined and her wild mahogany spirals tamed into a poufy knot at the back of her neck. She was put together from head to toe as she'd always been, even in battle. Maryn noted the deepening lines around her friend's hazel eyes, but to her, Jac was always stunning. Maryn figured she looked like twelve tons of shit herself, with grief and the mileage of fifty-four years she felt she didn't wear as well as Jac. Her body had gotten softer despite her daily workouts with Andelek, and in the last week … it wasn't important. She couldn't remember to eat half the time.

Dr. Globney waited for her near the door of the hovering limousine. Droopy Tridarian features and dark, fleshy ears made him resemble a sad-eyed canine, but his body language suggested he was resisting the urge to check his wrist chronometer. The university president had told Maryn that it was a tradition for tenured professors be driven one last time past the building where they taught before they were consigned to their final resting place. Since she planned to take Andelek's remains back to zer natal planet, she'd wearily agreed to the request.

"I will drive your vehicle home," Col purred, stroking Maryn's head. The Boshi remained as imposing as ever, fearsome to anyone who didn't know her until the incongruous, little-girl voice came out of a mouthful of fanged, catlike teeth. She showed no signs of age that Maryn could note, despite having been born sometime between her and Scylla. "We'll see you there."

The thought of her tall friend folding those long limbs into the tiny electric car brought a grin to her lips. "Thanks. This shouldn't take too much time."

Bidding a temporary farewell to the Merrows, she picked up the urn. Globney's chauffeur opened the door for her when she approached, and Maryn gave him a tired smile as she slid into the plush, cushioned seat.

"Thank you for indulging this ritual," Globney said as he climbed in beside her and signaled the driver. The door sealed behind him. She steadied the heavy casket against her when the vehicle rose on its air cushion and moved in a breathy exhale of forward motion.

When they reached the normally quiet campus, the outdoor common area teemed with students. A mob of young beings blocked the main thoroughfare, shouting something Maryn couldn't hear inside the soundproofed limo. Some held flashing holographic placards above their heads, polarized window glass turning the three-dimensional projections into flickering blobs instead of sharp images.

"What's happening?" she asked. "Is this a protest?"

"A demonstration demanding support for Qet's Khepran settlers," Globney told her as the limo driver angled a slow-speed crawl through the gathered students toward the eastern side of the university and its lecture halls. "There have been grim reports coming from media sources in the last few weeks about the Qetish unrest." The Tridarian's fleshy jowls wobbled as he shook his head. "Rumors of genocide. Someone who calls himself General Viltrux has overthrown the government and ordered the eradication of Qet-Khepran hybrids in the southern hemisphere."

"Oh, no." Horror blossomed despite the heavy blanket of control she'd relied upon to smother her reactions. "So much for the pretense of civil war, then. Has there been any talk of support for the settlers?"

"None I've heard. Galactic law prevents intervening in a civil conflict, of course, and so far, genocide is only a rumor. Ever since the privatization of mercenary corps, small colonies can no longer afford to pay for protection," Globney said, and glanced at Maryn. "I do not have to tell you so."

"No." Once upon a time, it had been Maryn's job to take fights like that. She, Col, Jac, and Scylla had been part of an exclusively female-identifying combat unit known as the Artemis Corps, which responded to far-flung colonies that were in danger or under attack—

for a price, of course, but the Corps had never turned down a plea for help. Not until they became a profitable enterprise, at any rate, and their handlers began to respond to money rather than desperate colonists.

"Are there still flights traveling to Xyri?" Globney asked. "The Pashni wormhole is dangerous right now. Viltrux's fleet is preventing Khepra from responding to the colonists. It's been classified as an active battle front. None of the commercial liners want to risk entering the Prime-side aperture until the fighting moves away from the star lane."

"I haven't heard anything as of this morning." That was one more source of stress she didn't have time for. "As far as I know, my flight still leaves tomorrow."

"You're certain you must travel now? It doesn't sound safe, and I know you are ..." Globney paused and amended what he'd been about to say. "You have an aversion to space flight."

That was an understatement. Maryn held a visceral terror of it. A bone-deep dread of the black after—

She clenched her fists against the memory, nails biting into her palms. "I have no choice." Her voice emerged with more edge than she intended. The royal family was respectful of Maryn's grief, and she loved her mate's parents, but their mourning rites lay rooted in tradition. "Andelek's remains must be returned to the soil of Xyri within two weeks of zer death in accordance with their spiritual beliefs. I only have six days left to get zem there."

"I see." She was thankful Globney didn't ask how she thought she'd do on the trip. Maryn had no idea. Hibernation wasn't an option for flights less than a month in duration. The medication that had been prescribed her when Andelek died allowed her anxiety to ebb long enough for a few hours of restless sleep each night, but she was sure it would be useless against the cold-sweat panic space flight instilled in her. Her palms grew clammy just thinking about it.

The curving road passed into a quieter, almost deserted area of campus. In front of the lecture hall where she and Andelek taught exobiology, a smaller, more sober crowd had gathered on the lawn.

She recognized a fragile, mothlike Dubasca, some young humans, and handsome, blue-skinned Xyrians as soon-to-be graduates who had attended the memorial at the chapel. There were just as many underclass students with them now, a mix of humanoid, oxygen-breathing species. As the limousine slowed to a crawl, then a stop, Globney lowered the tinted window on Maryn's side of the vehicle.

The Xyrians gave obeisance in deference to Andelek's royal status and knelt, bowing their heads. The Dubasca's feathery antennae rolled out and spread in a gesture of prayer. One of the humans crossed himself, the others standing in sober, respectful silence. Maryn nodded at the students and raised a trembling hand in thanks, touched by their regard for Andelek.

"Ze will be missed," Globney murmured. Maryn's heart swelled as the limousine moved forward again. This had been what she needed to know: that their students would remember Andelek and continue zer legacy, the study and preservation of the fascinating creatures which populated the galaxy.

Her newborn gratitude for Globney, a being Maryn had always considered a bureaucratic idiot, lived for exactly thirty seconds before he cleared his throat and killed it.

"My dear Maryn, I've been meaning to talk to you." He raised the window and shut out the roar of air. "We need to discuss your role at the University when Professor Zill takes over."

For a moment she could only blink, stunned. "When he … what? I thought since Andelek and I were co-professors, I would continue teaching these classes. I handled them alone whenever Andelek did field research off world."

"This is embarrassing." Globney had the grace to appear chagrined, his jowl pockets flushing a deep purple. "The board agreed to Andelek's contract stipulation we hire you both, but you have no official tenure here at the University, as ze did."

She'd known that, but she'd assumed … wrongly, it appeared. A helix of fire twisted inside, filling her with heat. "You're letting me go after twenty years?"

"Oh, no, certainly not. You are welcome to stay on as Malachi

Zill's adjunct professor if you wish. He is agreeable to that arrangement."

I'm sure he is. She counted to ten before she spoke again, the storm of her anger building from dust devil to hurricane. "Dr. Globney, the class is based on the curriculum Andelek and I developed together, which is derived from the research paper we wrote *together*, about the discoveries we made on Chrekem Seven *TOGETHER.*" Her voice rose and she hated how easily Globney got under her skin. This was why she'd preferred never to deal with him, hating his casual dismissal of human contributions to the research of older, wiser beings. Young Maryn, the fearless mercenary Andelek fell in love with, would have punched him in the face. This unattractive old woman encroaching on her territory was far less violent and too emotional for her taste.

"My dear Maryn—"

"It's DOCTOR Alessi," she grated.

"Yes. I know." He fidgeted beneath her basilisk stare. Maybe some of young Maryn was still there after all. "I'm sorry to have upset you. However, Professor Zill reminded me of his contract regarding tenure when it became clear Andelek's illness was ... well. His family is one of our largest benefactors. The generosity of Zillzanam Corporation funded many of Andelek's high-profile University research missions, as you know."

"I see." Her voice still quavered and she fought to gain a more controlled tone. "I presume he plans to teach the class using our curriculum?" Of course he would, the little rodent. Zill had always been resentful of her status.

"Andelek's research is the most up to date information we have on exobiology in the Shune Sector," Globney allowed. "Though, frankly, zer rather colorful person was the draw for many of our students. To hear about the discovery from Andelek zemself was inspiring, to say the least."

"Oh, yes, I know. I was there. For all of it." Heat built in Maryn's skull. If he wanted colorful, there were plenty of things she could say right now. It had taken her years to carve the decorative profanity and pithy sarcasm out of her soldier's vocabulary. She'd had to work hard to present her doctoral thesis without insulting the committee.

Her voice cut like shards of obsidian when she spoke again. "Thank you, Dr. Globney, for letting me know where I stand."

The weight of her angry silence filled the passenger compartment. Globney kept drawing careful breaths as if about to speak, then discarding whatever he was going to say with nervous, sidelong glances from bulbous brown eyes. Trapped with a human who might still be able to kill him six different ways, Maryn thought, as long as her trick knee held out.

She clutched the heavy urn against her for the remainder of the ride instead of succumbing to the urge to use it as a blunt instrument. The limousine slowed at a line of residential buildings. Her own vehicle was already in its charging station when the chauffeur drew up in front of her home. She didn't wait for anyone to open the door for her and fumbled at the latch to slide out of the cabin, an uncomfortable pressure building in her chest.

"Maryn … Dr. Alessi." Globney wavered between the door and the curb. She wheeled on him, and he stepped back as if he wanted to retreat to the safety of the vehicle rather than continue this conversation. "Professor Zill has a graduate student assistant who should be able to handle his requirements for the rest of the semester. Let me know what you decide when you return from Xyri. We will also have to discuss the matter of vacating university housing. There are lovely apartments on the other side of campus for non-tenured staff, and the rent is quite reasonable. But please, take all the time you need to fulfill your obligations to the royal family. Be very careful as you travel."

She turned her back on Globney instead of responding, unable to guarantee an answer without several of her favorite four-letter words. Striding down the path to her door, she slammed her palm against the scanner and the door moved aside with a meek hiss. She had just enough time to gently place Andelek's urn on the table in the entryway before the communications center on the wall gave three shrill beeps. Maryn peered at the displayed priority message out of habit.

DOCTOR MARYN ALESSI

PRIME QUARTER STARLINE REGRETS TO INFORM YOU THAT FLIGHT 2112 FROM ECHO 4 TO XYRI HAS BEEN DELAYED FOR ONE WEEK DUE TO DANGEROUS CONDITIONS IN THE STAR LANES. ALL FLIGHTS THROUGH KONECTHEDOT SECTOR ARE BEING RESCHEDULED. WE APOLOGIZE FOR THE INCONVENIENCE AND WILL KEEP YOU INFORMED OF THE NEW DEPARTURE DATE AND TIME.

Great. Just fucking fantastic.

She had no warning before her chest painfully convulsed. Deep, braying sobs of fury and humiliation hit her amid a grief so profound her knees buckled and took her to the floor.

Her friends were there, appearing out of nowhere as they'd always done in her darkest hours. She didn't remember being scooped up in furry arms and carried to the couch, only that Col cradled her like a child and hummed into her hair. Jac's cheek was warm on her back, a damp spot under Maryn's shoulder from tears, and Scylla sat at their feet with her head resting on Maryn's knee, swiping at her own sloppy nose and eyes with a handkerchief.

She slumped against her friends, exhausted, and wondered how she, ex-soldier of fortune and interspecies consort of a noble-born adventurer, had turned into a pathetic, aging widow in danger of losing her home.

"ZILL? You mean the rat-faced son of a bitch who bothered you at the funeral?" Jac was furious by the time Maryn was able to finish the story between hitched breaths and cold, fortifying gulps of rain globe wine. The dark curls making an escape from Jac's neat bun trembled with indignation. "I'll kill him for you."

The tangy bite of alcohol soothed some of the scratchy feeling the outburst left in Maryn's throat. Her tears had almost stopped, but the wound in her soul, no longer buried under shock and the mechanics of planning a memorial, sang with the hot-wire pain of an exposed nerve.

"It's my own damned fault I never negotiated a tenured contract after all this time." She rubbed her forehead against an ache that threatened to become a migraine, another reason she hated crying. "I assumed Andelek would live more than another century and I'd be long gone before it ever became an issue. I guess Globney did, too."

"Kissing the ass of people like Malachi Zill and his family. Corporate bastards." Scylla made a throaty noise of disgust, her muscular arms folded over her chest as she stood in the doorway. She'd changed from the suit into her customary shorts and a tank top, the colorful tattoo art collected on many worlds over her sixty-odd years bright against her arms and calves in the warm afternoon sunlight. A light breeze from the open portal ruffled her violet-tipped hair. "At least he gave you an extended leave, the condescending prick."

Maryn snuffled into a tissue. "Sorry. The crying is getting old. I can't seem to control it."

"I hear you," Scylla commiserated, her eyes on the blue slope of the mountains outside, her spacers' accent growing thicker. "Fucking waterworks all da time. It sucks."

"Goddamned hormones," Jac proclaimed with heartfelt condemnation. "I cried for three hours last week over a dead bird I found in the cargo hold." She regarded Col with an arched eyebrow. "What happens to your species as you age? I don't see you looking any different than the last time we got together."

"You can't tell?" Col stroked her furry cheeks. "I have more hair on my face."

"Don't we all?" Maryn gave a shaky laugh. "I look like I just hit puberty. I think my moustache is glorious."

"I have also developed lower breasts," the Boshi said, revealing her catlike teeth in a silent snarl of disgust.

"Mine are heading south too." Jac cupped her tits, staring at them in contemplation.

"No. Lower breasts." Col motioned to mid-abdomen beneath her tunic when it became clear they did not follow. "My second set."

All three humans stared at her with varying degrees of curiosity. "What are they for?" Scylla asked.

"In my society I would be expected to help nurse the litters of my children. If I had any." Col's furry ears flapped as she shuddered. "Mewling, damp little things. Why anyone would want them is a mystery."

"Ours turned out okay, and I didn't have to get cozy with anything but a syringe," Jac said with a laugh. "But I'm pretty sure Maya doesn't expect me to breastfeed our grandkids."

"Don't look at me. I got rid of the plumbing a long time ago." Scylla slapped her flat chest with both hands.

"How old is Maya now?" Maryn was chagrined to realize she hadn't asked after her honorary niece.

"Twenty-one. She finished her first degree and she's in medical residency on Telluride Station." Jac beamed with pride. "Her gene dads still practice in New Denver, so she's living with them. They've been trying to convince us to settle down there, where it's safe and boring, but we're not ready for that." Something Maryn couldn't name flitted through her expression before Jac's face softened. "She sends her love, by the way."

"Sweet kid. I owe her a graduation gift. What a lousy aunt I am." She sniffed and wiped her nose with a tissue.

"You're not."

"I haven't even seen her since she was six, when you came to visit."

"She gets it, Mar." Jac's voice was gentle but firm, trying to head off Maryn's slide into self-recrimination, but it was too much.

"I hate this. All of it." She balled up the soggy paper in her fist. "I can't stand the crying and getting fucking paralyzed by the thought of spaceflight. I have six days left to take Andelek to Xyri before the scheduled rites and I have got to pull my shit together. I could check interplanetary express freight pricing, I guess. They've probably raised the rates because of the war, but I can afford it."

Andelek didn't use the money the university paid zem, one of the benefits of being a member of a species with a life expectancy of two centuries, and whose family had made sound investments over millennia. They'd lived well enough on her pay. Twenty years of her mate's wages lay untouched in their joint account in the galaxy's most reputable bank, almost as if ze'd known she would need it one day.

Her eyes grew hot again. "But it just seems so wrong. Ze isn't a fucking box of supplies to be shuffled off world by a robotic pilot like so much cargo. But I don't know what else to do." Maryn made a frustrated noise as her voice snagged on the words. Tears came again whether she wanted them or not, and she swept the back of her hand over her eyes. "I'm running out of time."

"About that." Jac exchanged a long glance with Scylla before she continued, "We were talking. We want to take you to Xyri."

The warm burst of astonished gratitude faded against an electric-jolt corkscrew of anxiety drilling into her chest. Shame came next, as always, and self-disgust filled her mouth with a sour, acetic burn.

Maryn despised the inconvenient horror of deep space she'd brought back as an unwanted souvenir from her last mission. The fear of endless nothing crippled her. The mere thought of being unable to put her feet on solid ground and breathe air any time she wanted had kept her planet bound for twenty years. With Andelek beside her, she'd never cared.

"Are you sure?" she stammered. "It's such a dangerous flight plan right now. It won't complicate your business?"

"Nah. We're still freelance." Scylla shrugged. "Mostly private transactions. We're our own bosses." Her husky voice softened. "And you know the *Girl* would love to see you."

"I miss her too." *Golden Girl* was the well-loved privateer cruiser they'd pooled their end of tour bonuses to purchase when they left the Corps. The ship had been their home, their means of independence, and she had a definite personality. Its AI learning interface had picked up more human nuance with every mission until they treated it like a fifth crew member.

"The *Girl's* small enough she doesn't attract much attention on sensor sweeps. We need to go through Konecthedot system anyway on … business." Jac traded another secretive nod with Scylla, and Maryn wondered what they weren't saying.

"That is next to the front." Col wasn't fooled by the innocence act, her peridot eyes narrowed.

"Doesn't mean it won't be risky, but we can get you there in plenty of time for the remembrance rites." Scylla cocked her head and her deep brown eyes, so dark they were almost black, glinted with hope and mischief. "Whatcha think, Mar? We can make it a girls' trip if Col wants to tag along."

"Fuck yes!" the Boshi exclaimed in her sweet, breathy voice. "I have been bored out of my skull. I can work anywhere since CosBank gave me remote branch equipment."

What her friends offered was too generous to turn down. Not that they'd let her. She took a deep, steadying breath. "I don't know what to say, except—" she gestured helplessly. "Thank you."

Scylla gulped the rest of her wine, her enthusiasm building. "Konecthedot sector might be close to the front, but we haven't had any issues yet. It's less dangerous than anything we did when we were mercs. We've got two stops to make on the way, but after that, we head straight for the wormhole and Xyri. We can transport you faster without picking up passengers at every station like the star liners do."

"Globney said the Qetish fleet is blocking the Pashni." Maryn twisted her fingers together to keep them from shaking.

"They don't bother flights that originate anywhere other than Khepra, from what we heard," the pilot assured her, and amended with a skyward glance, "Leastways, not much."

"I haven't been off world since …" she faltered.

Terror. Black, endless space. Isolation. The memory threatened to overwhelm her already fragile composure.

"We know." Jac stroked her forearm.

Of course they did. They'd saved her life.

Young Maryn had been fearless and able to board a drop ship

after a weekend of binge drinking with her squad mates, ready to kick ass in zero gravity without a tether.

Where was that Maryn now?

"I suggest we leave sooner than later, before you talk yourself out of it." Jac sternly lowered her gaze to catch Maryn's, and she nodded. Her friend had known her for the better part of forty years, long prior to their Corps days, and was ruthless in pinpointing her propensity for overthinking. "I'll make sure we have plenty of alcohol and sedatives on board."

She managed a real chuckle at that. It felt good after the intensity of the last week. "My doctor prescribed some meds that should help me through the worst of it. I can pay you to offset the expense to your business."

"No need." Jac took her face between her hands. "It's what friends do, right?" She wiped away the tracks of Maryn's tears with her thumbs and kissed her forehead.

"Team Huntress rides again," Scylla's grin fractured the lines around her eyes into diamonds of glee, and she clapped her hands. "Damn, I'm excited about this!"

Well, shit, Maryn thought. *Now I have to go.*

A SLEEPLESS NIGHT LATER, Maryn debarked the shuttle at the spaceport at oh-too-fucking-early with a duffle of clothes and a crossbody satchel, the weight of Andelek's urn inside dragging at her neck like a proverbial millstone.

Why, why had she thought this was a good idea? There was still time for Jac and Scylla to take zer ashes to Xyri and give it to Andelek's parents. But the thought of relinquishing what was left of her mate to anyone, even her comrades, sent a stab of pain through her.

Besides, what would she do here? Pack up the remains of a life she and Andelek made together and move to a tiny apartment across campus? Spend the rest of her career second to that asshole, Zill? The option was even less attractive than space travel at this point and the mere idea stoked a cold, burning anger in her core she hadn't had the heart to acknowledge yet.

"Buck the fuck up, Alessi," she whispered to herself, and shivered in the pre-dawn chill.

"Did you say something?" Col asked, shrugging into the rucksack that held her stuff.

"No, just kicking myself in the ass," Maryn admitted. She lifted the duffle and slung the strap over her shoulder. "Where are we going?"

"Pad twelve." Col picked up the briefcase-sized computer array at her feet and gestured for Maryn to head to their left.

She could have recognized the ship's silhouette in the dark, but there was no need under the glaring corporate billboards looming over the apron where rows of personal spacecraft were berthed. Its gleaming, gold-tinted alloy reflected the harsh lights of the landing pad and the colorful advertisements for tourism, duty-free liquor, and spacecraft maintenance products. Despite her nerves, Maryn's mouth tugged upward in a grin as it came into view.

Her running joke with Scylla was that the ship looked like a pregnant blonde bat: round bellied and delta winged. The pilot staunchly defended the Caspian-built Astradyne cruiser as 'voluptuous'. Still, *Golden Girl* had been the most beautiful thing Maryn had ever seen as it streaked in to rescue her, just when she'd thought she'd die alone in the vast nothingness of space.

Scylla kept her star-faring baby in perfect repair, which made it odd to note the scratches and what Maryn thought was carbon marring the hull in places the reflective, heat shielded alloy should have protected. The ship was more battered than the last time she had seen it, but that had been several years ago. She glimpsed the pilot waving as they passed through the blinding pool of spotlight into the pad.

She reached up and touched the hull with affection. "Hello, *Girl*." The ship couldn't answer without her being on board or plugged into the AI's network, but Maryn imagined she felt a swell of recognition.

She pressed her palm against the vessel's outer skin, so many emotions coalescing through her she couldn't identify what they were.

A streak of discoloration on the plating grated her fingertips when she pulled her hand away. She paused to examine some of the rough, damaged metal as they neared the ramp. Beside her, Col cocked her head.

"I know energy weapon scoring when I see it," Maryn said. That it was still evident and Scylla hadn't yet scrubbed and sanded it away told her it was a recent thing.

"What kind of freelance cargo are they running?" Col's fangs bared in amusement. "Do you think they'll confess their schemes to us?"

"Eventually," Maryn sighed. "They always do."

Her feet came to an abrupt stop at the transition of concrete to ramp when she slammed against the invisible barrier of her fear. Sweat broke out under her arms and between her shoulder blades. A wild pulse hammered in her ears, fight or flight instinct screaming along every nerve. She realized she'd been standing there too long, shaking, and frozen in place, when Col touched her arm. "Are you alright?"

"You can do this," said another voice.

She looked up. Jac stood with her arm outstretched at the top of the ramp, her gaze filled with merciless compassion. "Nine steps. One at a time," she directed.

"This is ridiculous," Maryn groaned. "I've turned into a fucking coward."

"You haven't. We just need to help your brain remember the *Girl* isn't going to drop you. You've been with her on a hundred different trips, right? Not once has she let you down." She waggled her fingers in invitation. "We won't either, love. I promise."

"I know." Her white-knuckled hands clutched the strap of the shoulder bag. She forced one heavy foot to take the first step leading up to the belly of the *Girl*, then the other. Maryn made it into the corridor and Jac led her a short way forward so Col, too, could duck under the airlock seal and enter the ship.

"You did it, you badass." Jac's smile bathed her in warmth.

"Yeah." It didn't stop her from wanting to turn around and go right back, but Col operated the controls to retract the boarding ramp. The port closed, hissing as pressurized gas filled the airlock.

Too late to run now.

"You can strap into your usual seat up front or go to your bunk and burrow in there if it makes you feel more secure. Your choice, but the *Girl* wants to say hello when you're up to it." Jac beamed at Maryn, squeezed her shoulders, then bumped foreheads with Col. "Everything's in the same place. Welcome home, you two. I'm going to finish preflight checks with Scyll."

Despite her uneasiness, Maryn turned aft down the narrow, storage cabinet-lined corridor leading to the heart of the living quarters, Col close behind. The ship was the Merrows' only home and had gained more domestic touches than when Team Huntress was running privateer jobs. Magnetic holo frames of Jac and Scylla's wedding pictures and of their daughter Maya from birth to adulthood occupied many of the blank spaces on the white cabinet doors. She glanced at an image of herself and Col on the Merrows' wedding day, probably the only picture in existence of Maryn wearing cosmetics. Jac had insisted on a spa day prior to the ceremony, and even Col's claws were tipped in a pastel coat of lilac polish. Maryn hated makeup. It sweated off under battle armor, anyway.

The partition of the first sleeping cubicle, Jac and Scylla's quarters, was ajar to reveal an actual mattress and bedding set into the cubicle with sheets, blankets, and pillows tucked beneath sleeping harnesses to prevent them from becoming dislodged in microgravity. They'd removed the bunk's upper compartment since Maryn had last been on board, giving the illusion of an actual bedroom.

She skirted the round table and chairs welded to the gray deck. Muscle memory retraced the number of steps to the bunk that had always been hers, and she stopped at the third plane in the hexagonal walls. Col edged past her to the next cubicle, her customary space.

She pushed back the folding segments of the compartment door and ducked inside to crouch beneath the upper bunk. She lifted one side of the seat cushion to stow her duffel in the baggage space beneath. After a moment's indecision, she also placed the shoulder bag containing the urn among the pillows and blankets to secure it during takeoff.

Even though she knew what lay under it, she raised the other set of cushions. Two emergency environment suits were tucked into the storage locker, plugged into a hidden power source to keep them charged and ready. The nearest helmet faceplate gleamed from the recess and Maryn flinched at her mirror-distorted visage staring out of it. She swallowed hard and shut the compartment, turning away with half a mind to flee down the ramp to the certainty of air, and the heavy kiss of earth beneath her feet.

Col stood, waiting, patient, and blocking her escape route. "Do you want me to stay with you?"

"No, I'm fine. Go ahead." She cleared her throat. "Just give me a few minutes to convince myself that I'm not going to die."

Col squeezed her shoulder with furry fingers and left her there.

So many memories were made here. The familiarity bulldozed a path through her anxiety and hit her with another complicated flood of feelings. Maryn wandered over to the mag-locked door opposite her sleeping cubicle and peered through the glass into the dark medical pod, then into the narrow galley next to it. Everything was the same, just as Jac said, save that the mess table's display had been replaced by a newer model with state-of-the-art holographic tech.

Golden Girl could carry a crew of eight, but they'd seldom filled more than six bunks at a time. The cubicles were just roomy enough for two average-sized humanoids or one muscular, furry Boshi. The last bunk was dark with the partition shut. Even back then, they'd often used it for storage.

Andelek had started out in a separate bunk after hiring Team Huntress as zer personal security unit for the first trip into Shune sector. When ze and Maryn became lovers, they shared hers. White hot memories of making love in her cubicle with the partition drawn and the privacy noise screen set all the way to maximum sent a contraction through her pelvis. At least that part of her younger self had stuck around, much to Andelek's pleasure and her own.

Tears threatened again. She ducked into the steel-paneled lavatory to splash her face with cold water from the dispenser which reminded her she should pee before takeoff. She caught sight of herself as she glanced up from the head—why the fuck did they install a mirror facing the shitter, anyway? —and was horrified by the deep circles under her eyes. Silver graced her dark hair at the temples and glinted in the unflattering light. Sometime in the last nightmarish week, she'd become the spitting image of her gene-mother: crow's feet, worry lines, gray; everything. When the hell did that happen?

She cleaned her hands and exited the lavatory, caught in an indecisive waver between her bunk and the corridor leading to the cockpit. Her friends' voices drifted down the passageway: Scylla chattered away to Col as she prepared the flight computer for their journey, and Jac's answering laughter rang through the ship.

The sounds, like a beacon of comfort and safety, pulled her toward them.

CHAPTER
TWO

THE FIRST AQUAMARINE hues of sunrise colored the sky when she entered the cockpit and strapped in. Panels of blinking LEDs and holo emitters created a pre-launch light show as Scylla turned around from the pilot's seat to give her a happy fist bump and pass her a comm set. She settled the tech into the hollow of her ear and adjusted the band over her head before she spoke.

"Hello, *Girl.*"

"Maryn!" The ship's AI greeted her, its programmed voice as warm as if it was a being of flesh and blood. "It's so good to have you back on board. Where the fuck have you been?"

She snorted with startled laughter. Despite the stilted, mechanical interface the ship had in the early days, they'd always treated her like a sentient creature.

"We made some upgrades to her system, including the language and personality database," Jac explained, grinning. "She now has the ability to choose her own vocabulary."

"I hear that. I've been teaching at the university here on Echo Four, *Girl.* I'm sorry I haven't seen you in such a long time."

"I understand. I would like to extend my deepest condolences on the loss of Primetri Andelek, Maryn. Ze was my favorite client. It is my honor to carry zem home."

"Thank you." Her voice only wavered a little, and Col reached out to lay her hand over Maryn's where it lay on the armrest.

Rumbling vibrated the cockpit as Scylla began the engine warmup sequence. Younger Maryn had felt it as an almost sexual thrill, terrified and exhilarated by the anticipation of danger humming through her body. Now, her muscles stiffened; anxiety ran ice down her spine resulting in a convulsive shiver.

Col tapped her hand. "Did you bring your medication?"

"In my pocket. I want to see how I do without it." Her voice was too shrill.

"You don't have to impress anybody." Jac glanced back from the copilot's seat, her eyes soft. "We already know you're a hero."

A twinge of shame tightened Maryn's lips. She reminded herself Jac wasn't being condescending, groped for the vial, and slipped one of the pastilles under her tongue.

It dissolved in seconds and left a tingling, chalky residue which only hinted at the 'pleasant fruit flavor' advertised by the pharma-ceutical corporation, but it worked with speed on her over-reactive neurochemistry. Before *Golden Girl* lifted from the concrete pad, her pulse had slowed and the clenched muscles in Maryn's shoulders and back began to ease, even if her hands maintained a death grip on the arms of the jump seat.

She was on a ship which had never once let her down, she reminded herself. It was taking her to Xyri to fulfill her promise to Andelek's parents. She could do this. Right?

The brightening horizon lurched when Scylla turned the ship to face her allotted sector of sky and throttled up. *Golden Girl* moved eagerly toward the last, fading stars of morning as if rushing to join old friends. Maryn's body pressed back into the pads of her seat with the G forces of acceleration, constricting her chest and making it diffi-cult to breathe.

Panic did set in then, despite the medication. She squeezed her eyes shut and reached for Col's hand with desperate fear. Col's soft, furred digits gripped hers, her long thumb stroking the back of Maryn's hand in a soothing motion while the ship continued its ecstatic, upward leap.

With her eyes closed, the recoil of gravity's pull against her body told Maryn they'd broken away from Echo Four's bonds into freefall before the sound of *Girl's* engines throttled back. She cracked one eye to test her reaction to the ombré fade of blue and white atmosphere into sparkling, onyx space, cold and unforgiving, as it grew to fill the windshield.

The familiar confines of the *Girl's* cockpit held her in a warm embrace. Col's hand and the magic of pharmaceuticals kept Maryn precariously balanced on a knife's edge of the terror she'd developed after her near-death experience.

She could do this.

Scylla maneuvered the *Girl* into the taxi line of ships awaiting their turn at the jump ring. "We're gating to Farside, then we hit the black until our first stop. ETA forty-nine hours, seventeen minutes." The pilot grinned at them over her shoulder. "Plenty time for catching up and getting drunk once or twice."

"Breakfast before drinking," Jac admonished her wife. "I'm making Enutian waffles."

"Oh, yes please," Maryn said with shaky delight. Jac's waffles were the stuff of legend, crispy on the outside and full of fluffy, Enutian vanilla-laced cake on the inside. Under Jac's expertise, the tiny galley produced deliciousness no other ship's auto-chef could muster.

Without warning, a small, expensive short-hop coupe forged in reflective red alloy barged into the line of waiting vessels in front of them. Scylla swore as she throttled back. "Reduce thrusters and keep our distance, *Girl*." She whistled. "Damn, those new PanGemini coupes are pretty, pretty ships, but they attract the worst pilots."

"Rich assholes," *Girl's* interface agreed. "Permission to fire, Captain?"

"No, just let it slide." Scylla's voice held mock disappointment, and Maryn's eyebrows lifted.

"Fire what, exactly? I thought you were running cargo. Is *Girl* still armed?"

"Yes," the ship replied before the pilot could speak. "I still possess two Mark 3 energy cannons, 50 caliber guns, and a limited number of ballistic missiles."

"Well, that secret's out of the bag." Scylla glanced ruefully at her wife. "We might need to turn down her autonomy setting a bit."

"Missiles?" Maryn asked with a pointed stare at Jac.

"With the war, we can't be too careful."

"There is energy damage on the hull." Col cocked her head. "When did that happen?"

"A couple weeks ago." The pilot shrugged, her hands busy on the display. "Haven't been planetside anywhere long enough to work on it. Maybe we'll spend a few extra hours on Xyri so I can buff it out."

"What were you doing a week ago that required a full weapons array?" Maryn asked.

"Running cargo," Jac and Scylla answered in tandem.

"Right." She wasn't fooled. "I'm more concerned about *Girl's* road rage."

"I was attempting humor," the ship responded, and after measured pause, amended: "Mostly."

"All right, *Girl*, let's concentrate on the jump calculations." Scylla redirected the AI to business—unnecessary since the ship was more than capable of multitasking. Maryn settled back in her seat and exchanged a wary glance with Col.

Another wave of armpit-drenching anxiety built as the number of ships waiting outside the gate dwindled. The red coupe in front of them entered the U-shaped frame of the jump field. Distortion from the artificial wormhole shimmered, giving the smaller vessel an elongated, flat appearance as the gate's traffic control program reset coordinates for the vehicle. Instead of waiting for the gate to level out, the coupe hit its thrusters before the field was fully stabilized and disappeared in a flash of red.

"Somebody's in a hurry," Jac observed.

"Idiot's going to kill somebody on the other side, peeling out like that." Maryn clutched the armrests, tensing as the *Girl* counted down over the com. A jump from an occupied planetary system to Farside meant a jump into deep space. If the ship hit something passing on the other side, they'd be dead, or trapped until someone else came through the same gate.

The flame-lick of terror guttered and flared beneath her sternum.

She was escorting a dozen civilian academics from Echo Four to Andelek's research station on Babalu for a field study. Andelek and the crew of the Girl *were a few hours behind, having dealt with last minute red tape before they could break atmosphere.*

There was no way their transport pilot could have known an impatient ore-freighter captain was coming through the Tertiary aperture of an unmanned gate at the same time their little commercial ship approached from the Prime side. They had no warning and no chance to evade the oncoming juggernaut.

The cockpit sealed itself off after the nose-on crash, the pilots killed on impact. Under the scream of alert sirens and flashing lights, she activated the emergency beacon and got the terrified civilian passengers kitted out in their survival suits.

Maryn managed to don her own and made sure everyone else was strapped in before an explosive decompression sucked her into the void.

Without microgravity thrusters. Without a tether. Without a personal distress beacon or working radio, she discovered as she drifted farther away from the ship in a cheap-ass commercial environment suit never meant for space walking.

Hours later, she screamed herself hoarse, as if the rescue vessel taking the damaged vehicle with its passengers back through the gate to an occupied system could hear her. The undamaged freighter disappeared into the black and left her behind.

Alone. Stranded, and slowly freezing to death as the power pack in her suit dwindled to nothing.

"Breathe," Col whispered, her hand pressing Maryn's.

She obeyed, the deep inhalation a gasp.

"Damn, I almost forgot," Scylla exclaimed as she maneuvered the ship into the gate. "Tunes! We can't jump without tunes!"

"Yes, Captain," said the *Girl*. Familiar music blared through the cockpit.

Baby come with me, I'll fly you around
We'll reach for the stars, never leaving the ground
I'm your captain and this is my ship
Show me your galaxy, it'll be worth the trip

Maryn groaned in recognition of the old song. The band had been popular in their Academy days, and it hadn't aged well.

"Gah, no. That song's terrible," Jac protested, grimacing. "Play something else."

"Don't diss my tunes," Scylla argued. "Fine. *Girl*, bring up the queue from the Cali Nova job."

Different music filled the ship, and Maryn's watery smile grew wider as Scylla's head bobbed to the galloping beat of guitars, waiting for clearance to jump. The gate shimmered in the viewscreen as the intro to what they'd considered Team Huntress's official theme song blared from the sound system.

"Oh, I remember this!" Col began to sing the high falsetto harmony of the chorus.

Born to ride the solar wind
Bury me in the heart of a sun
My soul is chasing the star lanes
'til the Universe decides I'm done

Scylla belted out the lyrics as the countdown reached zero, throttling in a smooth, slow acceleration. The familiar tug of jumping built in Maryn's gut and snapped back like a rubber band against her spine as the ship was pulled through. Her pulse pounded as the silvery blur of transition waves obscured her view of the stars until they cleared to show a new field, endless points of light dotted thick with fuzzy galactic bodies beyond the curve of the gate.

The edge of deep space. Her adrenaline surged as if staring down something with teeth and claws. Once they left the frame, they were literally billions of miles from anywhere. Isolated. *Alone*, her brain screeched.

But she wasn't alone. Beside her, Col still sang counterpoint soprano to Scylla's baritone, and Jac was grinning at them, just like the first jump of dozens of missions when they were young and immortal. The sudden, sharp sense of nostalgia was overwhelming, and she raised her voice to sing the break with them, laughing in mild, giddy, hysteria.

Never going back to ground
Gonna live on stardust ale
Give me a chart to Adhafera
You can pull the lion's tail
Up in the black, forever we'll sail
She could do this.

"ARTIFICIAL GRAVITY'S UP," Scylla announced. Maryn's butt settled into the cushion beneath it with the slow, comforting return of her own weight.

"Just in time, too. I'm starving." Jac unbuckled the straps holding her in the jump seat. "Breakfast. Now. You want to help, Mar? Chef's assistant gets the first waffle."

"Hell yes." Relieved, Maryn disentangled from her restraints, glad for an excuse to escape the view of unending vacuum outside the windshield. She followed Jac down the corridor, steadying herself with one hand against the bulkhead.

Golden Girl didn't have full gravity—almost, but not quite. It was a change after the Earth-dense G's of Echo Four. She'd gotten used to it after two decades, and now her feet were feather-light on the deck. If she were honest, it wasn't much different than the way she'd moved through the last week after Andelek's death: off balance and easily set adrift.

Jac pulled the cooking iron out of a storage compartment: a Frankenstein's monster assembly she'd cobbled together from an antique iron waffle mold and high-tech hotplate elements. Cooking in reduced gravity was an art, but Jac had it down to a science. She set the appliance on the workspace to heat, tied on her apron, and pulled her tight brown ringlets into a thick, scrunchy-banded tail before she went to work.

"You've been close to the front." Maryn watched her assemble a mixing pitcher and ingredients. "Is it as bad as it sounds? Globney said Viltrux turned out to be a genocidal maniac."

"Are you sure you want to know? You can't unhear it." Jac glanced at her sidelong with grave regard as she opened a sealed compartment and removed two fresh eggs from their insulated cradle. "Sometimes I wish I could."

"Tell me. The media at home is sketchy. Echo Four sanitizes everything before it's released. The only way I can count on real news is through the university feed, and I haven't been there for a week." She shivered. "It'll help keep my brain occupied."

"What do you know about Qet?"

"It's the third Far-Prime world to be settled in the last hundred years. They stopped terraforming when they discovered the effect on its native animal life." Maryn shrugged. "I can tell you about the endangered herds of nomadic lizard elk that scrape their antlers against ore outcroppings, so they spark when they're fighting for territory dominance."

"That's cool!" Jac glanced up from cracking eggs. "I didn't know that. I meant its people, though."

She scowled at her. "Do I look like an anthropologist? I'd have to like people more to study them."

"Point taken." Jac discarded the shells into the waste system and wiped her hands. "Okay. What you need to know is this: Khepran settlers have been intermarrying with the original Qetish colonists for two or three generations. Mixed-humanoid individuals now outnumber the rest in the northern hemisphere. They call themselves Kheqet. The Kheprans revolutionized the mining operations in the north after they moved in, and it's a very lucrative business."

"What do they mine there?"

"Qetryllium." Jac measured out cups of flour from a collapsible silicone container. "It's a planet-unique element with a lot of the same uses as beryllium in the space industry. The northern settlement handles their own export business and relies on little help from outside. Qet is one of the few settled worlds in the far Prime with a self-sufficiency charter."

Hundreds of parent galactic corporations held a monopoly on supplies shipped to and from colonial holdings in the Prime quadrant of the galaxy, using subsidiary companies to funnel profits back to their home worlds. Qet having a charter like that meant very little interaction with the rest of the galaxy. "I'll bet big money hates it, since they have something unique."

"So do some of the Qetish, I guess. A splinter group in the government started to worry they weren't getting an opportunity to profit like the Kheqet and wanted to change the charter to allow corporate partners. Their faction hated allowing new immigrants into the colony charter in the first place and considers anyone of Kheqet descent a mutt. Viltrux broke from the rest of the government and formed his own regime, playing on the 'take Qet back for the Qetish' sentiment that's been festering."

Maryn made a sound of disgust. "The fuck? I thought the galaxy had moved beyond that shit."

"There were enough people who felt the same he was able to raise a private army and a small fleet."

"Oh yeah?" Private armies reeked of some corporation's interference. Maryn squinted at Jac while she whisked the batter. "How convenient."

"Isn't it?" Jac eyed her with grim approval. "When Viltrux seized power in the capitol, he rounded up anyone of mixed heritage in the city, mostly the families of Kheqet political representatives." Jac's mouth tightened into a hard line. "He ordered his troops to gun them all down, no matter how old or young they were."

"Fucking hell." Maryn couldn't process the kind of hatred it would take to kill children. The Artemis Corps had always protected colonists settling a new and sometimes barely habitable world from unfriendly trespassers, but never from their own neighbors.

"The Khepran home world tried to send help, but none got through Viltrux's defenses. The unarmed relief ships couldn't land

and were forced to retreat. Now they attack any Khepran vessels coming from the Tertiary side of the Pashni."

"And because it's framed as a civil war, it will be ages before any galactics care enough to debate intervention." Maryn slapped her hand against the counter. "Goddamn it. This is what we used to fight for."

"It's not all bad news getting out," Jac reassured her. "There is a strong local resistance headed by what's left of the previous government and the miners. Small transports are better able to evade the defense systems and they're evacuating as many of the Kheqet settlers as they can in groups. Xyri is taking in the refugees. Viltrux claims it's a violation of galactic statutes requiring neutral status in a civil war, but the Magnus Primetri politely told him to fuck off."

"That's what I'd expect from my father-in-law." Maryn let her mouth curve in a grim, satisfied smile before she drew herself up and rested her elbows against the counter. "But I know for a fact the Xyrian parliament won't even sneeze if it's going to interfere in galactic law. So how are weapons and supplies getting to the miners if the relief ships can't even go through?"

"Resistance ships, I suppose." Jac blinked at her, a guileless expression on her face, and laughed, holding up a floury hand in defense when Maryn eyed her. "Don't ask what you don't want to know, Mar."

"Why does *Girl* still have her cannons, and where the hell did you find missiles?" She leaned forward. "You've been taking fire. You are back in mercenary service."

It wasn't quite an accusation, but Jac's silence answered before she did. "We're independent contractors," she admitted. "There's an agent who contacts us when something needs to happen. For now, it's best we leave it at that. You know, plausible deniability and all." She pulled vial of amber granules off the magnetic rack of spices and utensils and waggled it with a lascivious smile. "Time for the good stuff."

The aroma of Enutian vanilla drifted up as Jac sprinkled it into the mixing bowl. Maryn closed her eyes and inhaled the earthy sweetness. It triggered an almost forgotten memory of something heated and extremely enjoyable, sending warmth to her cheeks.

"Mmm." Jac sighed. "Reminds me of the time we visited the pleasure exchange on Nataka. Everybody wore that vanilla cologne."

Maryn laughed. "God, I was just thinking about the couple who took me home. Her skin tasted like sugar cookies. I wanted to lick her from head to toe. She didn't seem to mind."

"I bet not. How did her husband taste?"

"Not quite as good. Like salted caramel. But he had other, very tasty attributes." She extracted herself from the remembrance. "This trip to Konecthedot sector. It's something your agent lined up?"

"Yes. But it's a code green assignment. We shouldn't have any problems." Jac winked as she whisked the batter. "Not like you couldn't handle it if anything did."

"Pssh." She sagged against the worktop. "I've gotten too soft."

"Bullshit." Gripping Maryn's bicep, Jac squeezed and left a faint, dusty white handprint on her sweater sleeve. "We're all a little fluffier around the middle, but you're still ripped as hell. I'll bet those underclass kids read the syllabus when you tell them to."

"I wish they did. And working out in a gym isn't the same as active duty."

"Well, you know the murphy gym is in the cargo hold. Knock yourself out." Jac's voice softened as she ladled the first scoop of batter into the sizzling iron and locked it down. The contraption began to rotate end over end in its cradle. "Like you said, it's good to keep busy when your brain works overtime, right?"

"Yeah."

Jac pulled a packet of meat out of the refrigerator. "How are you doing with the flight?"

"As long as I'm not staring out into the void, I think I can handle it." Maryn sounded surprised, even to herself. "I may not spend a lot of time in the cockpit until the viewport shutters go up."

"We'll go FTL after breakfast." Jac looked up from where she separated strips of bacon into a flat hopper. "How are you otherwise, honey?"

"Okay, at the moment." Maryn rubbed her forehead. "Tired. I might hit my bunk after we eat. I haven't slept much in the last few days because the house was too quiet. It's so strange. I never had trouble sleeping or missed the sound of Andelek breathing next to me when ze was away on a field study, but it's different now." She swallowed hard. "I know ze's really gone. Ze's not coming back this time."

"The energy ze put out into the universe was huge. You can't help but miss that." Jac's eyes were warm with empathy.

"No." Maryn smiled despite the gnawing sadness inside. "Larger than life and twice as sexy. Half our students had a crush on zem and the other half wanted to be zem. I was always a little insulted when I walked in to lecture alone and they deflated."

"Hey." Jac's admonition made her glance up. "Your name is on that paper too, and ze always gave you equal credit. Ze was so proud of your accomplishments. So what if Andelek was the proverbial Crocodile Hunter? I don't think ze ever thought to reach in between those jaws and teeth to swab a calibotari for a DNA sample." She wiped grease from her hands with a small towel clipped to the counter's edge and slid the hopper into its tray in the stove component. A flurry of beeps echoed the tap of Jac's lacquered nails against the instruction pad. "You're the one who figured out all the giant life forms in Shune Sector have a common ancestor to the dinosaurs on Earth. Andelek was too busy playing kaiju whisperer for the media drones. You recognized the calibotari's similarities to tyrannosaurus. Nobody else would have made the connection."

"I never thought a childhood obsession with dinosaurs would lead to a doctorate in exobiology." Maryn smiled. "I was a bad ass, wasn't I?"

Jac reached out and put her hands over Maryn's clenched fists where they rested on the counter. "Are, my love. Are."

"Not so much right now. I'm so fucking angry at Andelek." The words came out in a rush before she could stop them. "Ze wasn't supposed to die first. I thought we had another forty years or so before I ..." She swallowed hard to keep her voice from rising. "I know it's stupid to be angry, but Andelek promised ze would never leave me when I got old."

"The Universe isn't kind to promises. Col and I talked about that yesterday while you and Scyll took a nap." Jac's eyes puckered at the edges as if she were trying not to cry. "She said something that stuck with me. When we're thrown a wicked curveball, we're supposed to reevaluate what we're truly meant to do, or where we're meant to be. It doesn't tend use the kindest methods to put us there."

"Fuck the Universe," Maryn mumbled.

"Don't let Col hear you say it. She's convinced the energy we put out gets returned to us threefold. Everything seemed to work out for the four of us for a long time, didn't they? Luck. The Universe. Whatever it was," Jac mused, her forehead creased. "But life seems to be changing, or maybe my attitude is changing. I'm not sure. But I'm trying to focus on what I know for certain instead of the things I don't, and what I know beyond a shadow of doubt is that Andelek would never choose to leave you. Ze proved that once, didn't ze? And so did we." She pressed Maryn's hands between hers with a fierce clasp of affection. "No matter how much it sucks, we're supposed to be here right now, in this moment. Together."

"I don't know what I would do without you." Maryn freed one hand and interlaced it with Jac's so their fingers were tangled. "You've always been there to catch me or kick me in the ass when I needed it."

"Likewise. You've always had our backs. We'll always have yours."

She gave Maryn's hand one last squeeze and drew away to open the waffle iron, which had ceased its spinning cook cycle. Fragrant steam rose from the grid of an irregular brown square. Jac pried it off with a forked spatula. "First one is never perfect, so it's ours." She broke it and handed half the steaming cake to Maryn.

The first crispy, sweet bite melted her into an eyes-rolling-back-in-the head, sighing puddle of bliss. "God. These are more amazing than I remember."

"Yes, I can make a damn fine waffle," Jac agreed around chewing.

"Breakfast is the only thing I cook. I've gotten lazy. The autochef gets a workout but I've had it programmed to my specifications for quite a while now. It can handle the bacon all by itself."

Drawn by the increasingly seductive scent of food, Scylla and Col joined them, leaving the *Girl* to pilot herself for a short time. Scylla found a way to include alcohol despite her wife's warning and spiked the pitcher of orange juice with a small bottle of champagne she'd bought on Echo Four. "Mimosas!" she defended, pouring generous covered tumblers of the stuff for everyone as Jac gave her the stink-eye. "Mimosas are breakfast."

"Your liver hasn't screamed for mercy yet?" Maryn asked, amused.

The pilot scoffed. "It should be so lucky."

"To good friends." Col lifted her tumbler.

"Who know us well and love us in spite of it," Scylla proclaimed. Plastic thudded in a toast and they drank.

Maryn was surprisingly hungry and slathered her plateful of waffles with a glaze of butter. They didn't need anything else but the bacon, which she considered its own food group. Eating meat never bothered her, despite her chosen field and even though Andelek subscribed to the vegetarian philosophy of the Xyrian royal family. The truth was, most bacon was grown outside pigs now, and the real stuff could only be gotten from settled worlds raising actual, cloned animals from Earth's Ark stock.

"I found some old holos in the memory cache," Scylla announced after breakfast with a mischievous grin and tapped her fingers over the touchpad embedded in the table. A three-dimensional image spun into view above the surface, half of it blocked until she moved her plate.

"Oh, holy hell." Maryn gaped at the projection. A group of young humans and one Boshi, all in battle armor, jostled each other and smirked out of the holographic field. "Was that our first mission after basic training?"

"Yeah. Buncha FNG's who had no idea what they were getting into." Scylla's rough spacer's accent grew thicker. "You'se came aboard my ship with your shiny optimistic bullshit and I thought, damn, they gonna die. I signed up for my second tour right then so I could watch."

They snorted with laughter. Maryn and Jac had left the tenements of Chicago and its crater lake after their Academy graduation, both of them restless, eager to seek something outside the limited resources and opportunities of a healing Earth. They'd been lured by the Artemis Corps' reputation and its glamorous public image. Scylla had grown up on a space station, piloting almost as soon as she could walk, and joined the Corps for the love of flying high tech ships. Col enlisted to avoid being trapped in the socially enforced roles of her people, one of the few options available to those who did not fit into the narrow boxes of sexuality and gender Boshi society still clung to.

"God. That's Laynie, and Rover." Maryn peered closer as the loop repeated. "And Bishop? Damn, this is a blast from the past. We are so fucking young."

Scylla smiled and ran a finger over the next image, through the gun brandished across her chest. The holo flickered and restabilized. "I lost the gun on that mission, damn it. I liked that one."

"That's Mickey Trejo in the back, isn't it?" Maryn rotated the holo with a brush of her hand and pointed.

"The one and only." Jac snorted. "They should have been a salesperson, or a politician. Mickey could talk up a storm." She sobered. "Did they die on this drop, or the one after?"

"This one," Col said.

The hologram changed to a series of static images. She recognized the first one as soon as it popped up. It was of Jac, her face streaked with blood and dirt, hazel eyes looking right into the lens with an intense stare. "Oh, wow. That's the one you took that the Corps used as a recruiting tool, isn't it, Scyll?"

"Sure is." Scylla intoned in a deep, sonorous voice, "Join the Artemis Corps. You too can be hot, sexy, and deadly."

Their laughter rang off the bulkhead. "The number of human male applicants went up exponentially, if I remember," Col said.

"Completely missing the gender identification requirement in the contract." Maryn shrugged. "Earth doesn't teach enough mythology anymore, or they'd have understood Artemis only recruited female warriors."

The next picture was the four of them at a bar, just after Jac and Scylla became lovers. She noted the way her holographic image leaned away from their embrace, looking toward the camera with an indulgent, thin-lipped smile. "God, Scyll, I kind of hated you, didn't I?"

"You made passive aggression an art form."

Col booped Scylla's nose. "But you burrowed your way into our affections."

"Like a Gol Panedan heartworm," Maryn confirmed.

"See?" The pilot gestured in exaggerated rapture. "Poetry to my ears."

Maryn remembered being jealous and sometimes hurt when her best friend's attention and free time shifted to the gruff-voiced spacer. She and Col had become closer during that period, first lamenting their perceived loss of Jac, and then, unable to stave off Scylla's cheerful persistence, welcoming the pilot into their fiercely guarded circle.

"The four of us always worked," she admitted, glancing at Jac as she repeated the words her friend used earlier. "We survived every battle they threw our way. I hated it when you argued about my orders but what you guys ended up doing succeeded most of the time."

"You always gave good orders, Sergeant." Scylla snapped a mock salute. "Jac was just an asshole."

"Hey!" her wife scolded, and she laughed with them.

Their good humor faded with the next image. A war weary Jac, Col, and Maryn wore dress uniforms and stood guard over the remains of six fallen comrades. Palls emblazoned with the crescent moon insignia of the Artemis Corps were draped over each plinth. Beneath one of them was the officer Maryn received a temporary field promotion to replace.

Peloon. Of all the battles they'd fought, this was the one still haunting Maryn's nightmares. Their platoon was sent to secure a small, independent industrial colony against what the mission briefing described as 'pirates'. When they got there, they discovered they were outgunned and outnumbered by corporate raiders bent on taking possession of the factory. Pleas for reinforcements went unanswered. Most of their platoon was killed as well as almost all the civilians they were hired to defend.

Scylla disobeyed the Corps' orders and returned in the drop ship to evacuate civilian survivors and the remaining mercenaries. In the ensuing chaos, a wounded comrade was left behind. The pilot was slapped with a demotion and, ironically, Maryn received a commendation for assuming command of the battle after their lieutenant got her head blown off. The colony was lost to the corporate raiders.

"That's when we figured that they didn't give a shit about us or the colonies anymore," Scylla said. "They just cared about the money. More for them if there were fewer mercs to pay at the end."

Jac rubbed her eyes. "It was only five years. We all look so much older in that holo."

"A lot happened." Col pressed her furry hands together in front of her mouth, her head bowed. Maryn stroked her back in comfort, her fingers carding through the soft pelt.

"Young and stupid. We were mesmerized by the fantasy of the Corps without realizing the horror." Jac leaned her head against Col's upper arm.

"Stupidity, and the end of tour bonuses they lured us with." Maryn frowned. "They made certain the recruiting office didn't say how few survived until then."

The four of them met for drinks before returning to active duty from the funeral, growing concerns they had about the Corps' deteriorating core command too serious to ignore. An idea of forming their own security firm emerged that night. All they had to do was keep their heads down and survive the last seven months of their tour.

When their six-year commitment was up, they never looked back. The payout of their enlistment incentives—blood money if they were honest—got pooled to fund the means of their independence. A few years later, the Artemis Corps dissolved into a corporate mercenary unit.

In the next holo, their younger selves stood on the ramp of a shining, newly purchased Astradyne cruiser. "There she is, my baby," Scylla crooned. "My pretty *Girl!*"

"Am I still pretty?" *Girl* asked over the interface. "Prettier than the PanGemini coupes?"

"Of course you are," she reassured the ship.

"I know my operating systems are functional, but I was not certain if I have physically deteriorated like the four of you have."

Maryn's mouth fell open with a bark of offended laughter, and the pilot rolled her eyes with a long-suffering sigh.

"That was mean, *Girl,*" Jac scolded. "Watch it, or I'll uninstall those vocabulary upgrades."

"I am sorry. My programming does not include polite lies."

"Never did," Scylla agreed, grinning.

Maryn's breath caught when the next holo flickered to hover above the table. The figure in the image had zer back to Scylla's lens, but she knew zem at once; the long, silky fall of black hair pushed behind one pointed ear, graceful hands covered in delicate silver tattoos upraised to calm a nervous creature twice zer size with teeth longer than the gun Maryn held in the image. She wasn't looking at the beast, but at Andelek. The expression on her face was so full of admiration, longing, and outright lust that she couldn't help but laugh even though her eyes were wet.

"Oh my god. I think I'm drooling in that holo."

"You were in loooove," Jac said, drawing out the word. "We knew you were both goners. Ze looked at you the same way when you weren't staring at zem."

"Andy was something else," Scylla said with a half-grin.

Maryn tried to frown in admonition but her mouth refused and tugged her lips into a smile. "Ze hated it when you called zem Andy."

"Why'd you think I did it?" Scylla challenged.

"One of my favorite memories of Andelek was the night we got attacked by those mosquito-things from hell," Jac said. "We're all huddled in the gear tent watching them crawl over the sides like vampires trying to claw their way in, and ze brings out a fucking *sword* and starts hacking them in midair like a goddamned space elf."

"Zer love of kaiju did not extend to giant bugs," Maryn agreed with a shudder.

"I remember that!" Col bared her catlike teeth in a hiss of disgust. "It took three rainstorms to clean the gore off the shelter."

"We stood there cheering and calling out points for style." Scylla nudged Maryn. "I think you were ranking zer ass."

"Perfect ten," she confessed.

"I lost several of pints of blood before we discovered they were attracted to the standard repellents." Col shuddered, a ripple of fur from neck to lower back. "And then what did we find out they disliked?"

"Garlic," crowed Jac. "The whole camp smelled like my grandma's kimchi after that."

"I thought Andelek was a pacifist like most Xyrians until those poachers showed up on Chrekem Seven." Scylla shook her head in admiration. "Damn. Ze was colder than ice when somebody threatened zer giant babies."

Maryn shrugged. "The calibotari finished them off afterward. Ze was making sure they got fed."

Her laugh went ragged at the end, her breath hitching. There was a moment of silence, full of love and empathy, until Scylla bumped shoulders with Maryn and wiped her own eyes with her palms.

"So who's up for a round of poker this afternoon?" she demanded. "We gotta make some plans for entertainment."

"Are we going to do a beauty night?" Col asked. "I haven't had my claws polished in ages. The manicurists on Telera giggle and cover their mouths when I ask."

"Anything you want," Jac promised, standing to collect their empty plates. "I have plenty of the foam thingies that go between your pads to hold the fur back." She glanced at Maryn. "Do you want me to do anything, Mar? Eyebrows, nails?"

"I'll let you make me presentable for the funeral rites." She waved in the direction of her hair and face. "I know I look awful."

"Not what I meant," Jac said, swooping in to kiss the top of her head as she passed. "I just like pampering my friends."

After the cleanup, Maryn excused herself to her bunk and shut the partition behind her. The rumble of the ship's drive as it wound up for transition to superluminal speeds soothed her and made her eyes heavy. She opened the storage compartment and got out blankets, pillows, and prepared the bed. After a moment's hesitation, she the retrieved the satchel containing Andelek's urn, too.

"I'm still mad at you," she whispered. With the sleep harness pulled over her body, she hugged the bag close. She had time to wonder if she would be able to sleep before consciousness submerged beneath a dark river of exhaustion.

CHAPTER
THREE

MARYN WOKE to the blue-lit silence of the night cycle after an unbelievable twelve hours. She took a quick turn in the cleanser, knotted her hair back after she dressed and shrugged into her cardigan against the shivering chill of space.

Emerging from the head, she glanced down the quiet corridor leading to the cockpit. The FTL shutters were closed over the windshield, so she went that way. Col sat in the copilot's station. A set of prayer beads made from polished meteorite chunks moved with soft clicks through her furry digits and a meditative hum vibrated deep in her throat. She looked up as Maryn approached and eased into the pilot's seat.

"We left food in the galley for you." She folded the strand into her palm with a muted rattle. "Scylla and Jac went to bed four hours ago."

"I can't believe I slept so long." Maryn sat in Scylla's usual place. "What about you? Aren't you tired?"

"I am. I did some work and now, I need a nap." The Boshi yawned, showing all her teeth and a curling pink tongue.

"What are you doing for the bank now?"

"My official designation is Concierge Accountant for CosBank's biggest Prime quadrant clients. I call it glorified customer service to beings I would like to invite to kiss my furry ass." Col's bifurcated upper lip lifted and crinkled her nose in her version of a human smile as Maryn chuckled. "While I am traveling, I agreed to do some auditing of colonial accounts. It has become the way for corporations and other unscrupulous entities to launder galactic credits."

"A lot of that going around?" she asked.

"More than anyone knows." Col yawned again. "The *Girl* has everything under control, of course. Are you sure you will you be all right if I sleep?"

"I'm good, really. Thanks."

Col stroked Maryn's cheek with one fur-backed hand as she passed her the headset. Sharp canines bared in another fearsome yawn, she wandered out of the cockpit and disappeared. Maryn put on the comm headset.

"Status report," she requested.

"Good evening, Maryn. All systems operating within parameters, save for a slight decrease in the starboard engine's output. I have compensated for that. Scylla plans to have it overhauled the next time we visit Manny on Cinderfall."

She smiled in recognition of the mechanic's name. "How is my favorite squid?"

"Larger. I estimate Manny's mass has increased by one point oh three times," *Girl* advised. "He is the only one Scylla and I will allow to make critical repairs."

"Where are we in the flight plan?"

"We are approaching the edge of Konecthedot sector." The heads-up display brightened the cockpit in verdigris ghost light. A gold tracking dot cruised the navigational chart with its imaginary boundaries. "Thirty-five hours, eight minutes, and forty-four seconds remain on the clock before we reach our first destination, and then on to the rendezvous point."

"Rendezvous with who?"

"The party receiving the cargo we will take on at our first stop."

The *Girl* had learned to be cagy, Maryn thought, or she'd received orders from the Merrows not to be specific regarding the flight plan. "I just assumed we were going to the trade hub after we took on cargo."

"The meeting will now occur in open space per the agent's instructions."

That didn't sound suspicious at all. Her friends were hiding something and Maryn wanted to know what it was. She changed the subject, knowing she could get nothing out of the *Girl*.

"Any ships in the area?"

"None within my sensor range."

"Good."

Silence fell again. Her stomach made a loud noise in the emptiness of the cockpit, and though she didn't feel hungry, she knew she needed to eat something.

She found the food they'd left for her in the galley, a salad of cheese, greens, and fruit. Jac had stocked up on fresh and frozen foods on Echo Four. They'd be eating a steady diet of prepackaged stuff after a couple of days, so it was best to enjoy the perishable groceries while they lasted. Maryn grabbed the food, filled a water ration bottle, and went back to the cockpit.

Her enthusiasm for the meal went from apathy to interest after a few nibbles. All the vegetables were grown in Echo Four's terraformed soil, varieties from Earth and other settled worlds. The savory cheese was not from home, though, nor the tart, purple fruit which burst between her teeth in tiny juicy explosions. Andelek would have loved the salad.

The thought brought an unrelenting sting to her eyes. She sniffled through the last bites of her dinner before sweeping her hand over her lids in a futile attempt to stem the tears. Setting the container aside, she buried her head in her hands in the sapphire twilight of night watch where no one could see but the *Girl*. The fierce ache of Andelek's absence threatened to turn into a full-fledged crying jag.

She didn't want that, even though the grief counselor at the medical center had warned her that it was to be expected. She needed to find something to occupy herself. She'd left her mobile university database at home. She didn't even have assignments to grade, she realized, and lobbed another resentful javelin of thought at Malachi Zill and his two-faced campaign for her job.

"Are you all right, Maryn?" The interface conveyed a sympathetic tone to the words. If she hadn't already known the AI before the upgrades, the ship sounding so human might have creeped her out. "Your vital signs are showing stress."

"Yeah, *Girl*. I'm okay. Just sad and angry."

Was even that the description for what she felt? There were countless gears to the intricate clockwork of emotion spinning inside her. Grief. Loss. Anger, less now at Andelek for leaving her, and more with herself for the predicament she faced at the university. Fear: now, that was heavy gear ticking away in her chest, one that had kept her grounded for over twenty years and boomed in her ears louder than ever as the future stared her down with pitiless, unblinking eyes. She had no idea what she would do after they reached Xyri and fulfilled her promise to the royal family. She wasn't too old to start over, but thinking about it made her so fucking tired.

"Get a goddamned grip, Alessi," she whispered.

"Maryn," *Girl* said in her ear. "I found something in the holo cache I think you should see. May I play it for you?"

She wiped her eyes again and sniffled. "What is it?"

"A message from Primetri Andelek to zer parents, while we were searching for you after the accident."

She stilled. She'd never seen any communications from that time, delirious from radiation exposure, hypothermia, and dehydration during the mad dash for the nearest hospital on Echo Four. Andelek and her friends took turns cradling her in the medical pod to keep her from screaming in terror as she drifted in and out of sedation. "All right."

Andelek's three-dimensional image flickered into life, so damned beautiful it made her heart ache. Long, glossy black hair; symmetrical features. The Xyrians as a species were attractive, and ze had been especially so, at least to Maryn. Ze hadn't changed in the two decades they'd spent as life mates and lovers, with zem well into middle age by Xyrian reckoning. It bothered her at first, aging while ze stayed the same, but Andelek had scoffed when she said as much and kissed the lacework of lines at the corners of her eyes, the grooves beside her mouth, promising Maryn would never be more beautiful to zem than she would be tomorrow, until the next day, and the next.

The silver tattoos on zer forehead and hands marking zem as a member of the royal family shone against zer cobalt skin as ze spoke in a quiet voice, dark eyes full of pain. *Thank you for your kind words of comfort, my parents. I know how difficult this is, and I cannot imagine what Jac, Scylla, and Col must be feeling. But all of us know our beloved Maryn is one of the toughest, most intelligent forces in the galaxy.* A faint smile crept over zer lips. *If anyone can find a way to survive, it will be her. We have six hours before the power pack in her environment suit will no longer be operable and we must abandon hope. Until then, we will not stop searching, though authorities have already quit after what appeared to us a perfunctory scan.*

Were our positions reversed, I know Maryn would refuse to give up unless no possibility remained. And should we not locate her in time — zer throat worked against a swallow, and Andelek's smooth contralto voice trembled. *You expressed your concerns when I first told you I was in love with a human because of the difference in our expected lifespans. I knew it would be difficult to face, but I never thought it might be so soon. For all my adventuring, I am not as strong as she is. I will never be the same, for she has enriched my existence in ways I did not know possible. Therefore, I will not give up. When we find her, I will treasure every moment I have with her. If we do not, I must carry on when mourning is done, as she undoubtedly would. She would expect no less of me. I will contact you when I know more.*

The holo flickered and disappeared. Maryn's tears ran slow and hot against her cheeks. "Thank you, *Girl*." Her voice quavered, but a cool relief began to grow in her chest.

"I hope it did not add to your sadness."

"No. I think it was just what I needed to hear."

EVERYONE FELL into their old routine aboard ship without discussion. Jac and Scylla had the day watch, and Col the evening. Maryn continued to take midnight to morning. They all met for breakfast and dinner between shift changes, reminiscing about their privateer days and catching up. The Merrows remained evasive about their business ventures, though Scylla let slip a few things that convinced her beyond a doubt their exploits were not conducted through legal channels.

They took turns using the fitness equipment in the cargo hold, a compact set of hydraulic resistance weight machines and a micro-gravity treadmill Maryn harnessed herself into. The art-grav was less damaging on the cardiovascular and skeletal system than zero G's, but not the same as planetary gravity and still required regular exercise twice a day to compensate for the difference. Running allowed her to turn off her brain and just sweat. The ache of working out in space was different from the surface; kinder on her knees, perhaps, but she ached in places she hadn't remembered there were muscles. Something else she hadn't missed was the daily ingestion of Calci-Quik, a thick white paste meant to keep her bones strong and sound, which had all the taste appeal of a mouthful of bitter, minty glue.

The near-absent humidity of manifold-generated oxygen aboard ship was the same it had ever been, playing havoc on her nasal membranes and giving her a terrible case of dry mouth. Maryn drank plenty of water but despised the fact she had to pee more frequently. Oh, well. Today's coffee was tomorrow's coffee, as the old saying went. She was doing her part for the reclamation system.

She'd awakened from her post-duty sleep cycle, jostled out of slumber by the intermittent engine burns of the drop from FTL, and wandered into the cockpit with a container of high octane, over-caffeinated coffee. Despite the falling sensation in the pit of her stomach when she glimpsed the white-spangled starfield outside, Maryn couldn't help but stare in horrified fascination at what lay ahead. It seemed to be a small pulsar flashing rainbow colors, but no star she'd ever seen changed rhythm in rapid, stuttering semaphore patterns like that.

"What the fuck is it?" she muttered in horror, cupping her hands around the warm beverage. "Why is that star having a seizure?"

"Zillzanam Station," Jac said. "It opened about fifteen years ago after the Far-Prime worlds were settled. You think it's bad from out here? Wait until we're up close. It's like hell had a marketing team."

"Mmf." She sipped her coffee with a grimace. "Sounds charming." She paused as her sleep-fuzzy brain connected some dots. "Did you say Zillzanam Station?"

"Uh huh." Jac glanced up. "Why? You can't have been there before, right?"

"No." Globney had told her Malachi Zill's family owned the corporation. She didn't want to pour salt in that wound yet. "We're not spending money there, are we?"

"Not one credit." Jac smiled. "I promise."

Scylla was busy talking to the station's flight tower, so Maryn wandered back to the table and its holographic display. "*Girl*, can you show me data on Zillzanam Station?"

"Do you want the propaganda or the real information?" the ship inquired.

"Both, I guess." Propaganda was useful to see the public face a corporate entity affected, and where it was contradicted by facts collected through unbiased data retrievals.

She flinched when smiling humans appeared in the holo above the table: eating, gambling, dancing, shopping, and having sex to bright, cheerful music. "Oh, god, no. No, it's way too fucking early for this. I changed my mind. Text only."

What she got from the data was that Zillzanam was a typical corporate giant, complete with its own mercenaries to protect a vast empire of interests throughout the galaxy. It had no fewer than twenty thousand sub-corporations tied to its bottom line. The space station hung in the center of a web of transportation lanes, each leading back to Zillzanam from outposts and planets where their goods were sourced and out to the newly settled parts of the galaxy. It was in direct competition with the galactic trade hub and twice as popular: its flashy, crowded promenade catered to travelers on commercial liners as a connecting terminal to intergalactic passenger flights, bludgeoning them with holographic advertisements for shiny, duty-free shops and personal services. One could have a haircut, get laid, and afterward have a meal prepared by a five-star chef.

Maryn had an ingrained distrust of companies with mercenary troops after Peloon and a separate conflict known as the Steel Union Rebellion. Corporate soldiers battling a company's employees to ensure the owners got a bigger profit contradicted everything she'd fought for. Every corporation spun their private armies as 'defense against piracy', but she knew better.

She had been aware corporations funded some of the university's field programs, including Andelek's, but never liked it. Big discoveries meant big sponsors with money to burn and a need to hide their more predatory actions behind philanthropic gifts. Her academic brain understood that the university relied on donations from wealthy citizens and lucrative organizations. Andelek had bankrolled zer own research when ze hired Team Huntress, one of the benefits of being rich. But independent, university-backed studies to confirm the data were imperative after she and Andelek wrote their paper and blew stuffy exobiologists' minds with the unexpected results. The thought still made her smile vindictively.

Col, fur rumpled with sleep, waved at her as she wandered out of the head and down the corridor toward the cockpit. After another jolt of coffee, Maryn was more prepared for social interaction and joined them in the cockpit.

"Mornin'." Scylla's growl made the word more a complaint than a greeting.

"Just in time," Jac said. "We're getting ready to dock."

The station's flashing lights and holographic billboards spelled things out now, inane advertisements and travel updates.

IRULAN COSMETICS FOR ALL BEAUTIFUL BEINGS

THE NEW PANGEMINI COUPE AVAILABLE HERE! FOUR EXCLUSIVE ALLOY COLORS

NOW OPEN: FREE-SWIMMING BUFFET FOR OUR AKEBRIAN TRAVELERS

ACTIVATE FREQUENCY 8675.309 FOR INTERGALACTIC FLIGHT INFORMATION. ALL FLIGHTS TO THE TERTIARY QUADRANT VIA THE PASHNI WORMHOLE ARE DELAYED UNTIL FURTHER NOTICE.

"We listened to the infodump. The Pashni's still open, but no commercial liners are going through," Jac told her. "Nothing's changed as far as we can tell."

They were making reasonable time according to the clock, but Maryn didn't want to endure the crowds or the greedy avarice of the space station's consumer orgy side. "How long are we staying?"

"It's a quick transaction," Scylla assured her. "In and out."

Rather than the outer docking facilities for tourists, they headed for the darker interior of the ring-shaped construct where cargo ships docked, illuminated by fewer headache-inducing light displays.

Without warning, a reflective, purple-alloyed coupe cut across their path in a ridiculous wide turn from a deep, white-outlined bay topped by the double infinity logo of a PanGemini dealership. "Fucking Christ in a sidecar!" the pilot swore. "Gotta be some morons out for a test drive. They need to dial it down if they can't handle the speed."

"How do they tint the alloy those colors?" Col asked. "It's so shiny. I've never seen anything like it."

"Some new proprietary process." Scylla shrugged. "The rest of the industry is desperate to get their hands on the formula. The color is in the metal and doesn't fade from radiation exposure. Even Astra-dyne's only got gold and silver."

"They're still not as pretty as me," *Girl* sniffed over the headset.

"Has he contacted us with the platform number yet?" Jac frowned at her wife.

"I pinged him as soon as we were in range. Don't worry, he'll get in touch when he can."

Maryn's suspicion spiked when *Girl* announced, "I transmitted our response to the docking beacon using the alias we were provided. It was accepted without delay. We're in."

Col bounced in her jump seat and asked with glee, "Is this illegal? Are we doing something unlawful?"

"Definitely not on the books," Scylla admitted.

A deep voice crackled over the com. "Sorry for the holdup. Seven A. Cameras are off."

"Roger. Seven A." Scylla piloted the ship to the darkest area of the ring docks. The pressure door opened on a bay with no lights inside, and the *Girl* auto docked in the narrow space with subtle employment of the ship's directional thrusters. Magnetic clamps on the landing gear made a booming sound as they met the deck. The loading bay door closed behind them, still in pitch darkness until a pair of headlights appeared in front of them.

"I'm lowering the cargo ramp," Jac said to their unidentified contact.

"I have three for you." The voice from earlier was back. Maryn thought they sounded to be male, and younger than any of them. Most people were, nowadays, she thought with a mental shrug.

"That's not as many as we expected. Was there a problem?" Jac questioned.

"It's all I could transfer before the system threatened to scream bloody murder."

"We don't want to put you at risk. Some is better than none. Thank you." She tapped the panel in front of her and a holographic image from the *Girl*'s aft camera rotated into view.

The headlights belonged to a robotic lifter running on a magnetic track, a pallet held between its forks. Three rectangular cases, each the size of a coffin, were shunted into the cargo bay with efficient speed. As soon as it cleared the ship, Jac raised the ramp.

"You sure you won't get in trouble?" Scylla asked their faceless contact.

"Nah. The corporation won't miss these. They've been in the warehouse for years, waiting for the price to go up again so they can tack more on the tag. At least with you, I know they'll go where they're needed. The handlers have already hacked the database to change the inventory count. The transfer location changed again because of ongoing situations in Konecthedot. I'm sending it to you now."

"Great work. We'll blow out of here quick so we don't give 'em any reason to be suspicious."

"I hear it's turning ugly out there. Be careful."

"Roger that."

Scylla released the magnetic clamps and hovered out of the bay with expert piloting. Once outside, she set an unhurried course for the outer ring of the station.

"Transmitting second alias." *Girl's* pause seemed drawn out this time, and Maryn found her pulse hammering in her ears until the ship confirmed, "Accepted. We are clear to depart."

"Outstanding. No problem with the codes this time. They're getting better," Jac remarked to her wife.

The transaction had taken less than fifteen minutes from docking to departure. Maryn was impressed, though somewhat alarmed at the whole process. But if they were stealing from Zillzanam Corporation, she approved, even if it was petty. Only a hint of accusation tinged her words when she pronounced, "You are smugglers."

"And very good ones, it seems," Col added.

"Don't ask," Jac sing-songed, just as Scylla breathed in a way that sounded like a prelude to spilling her guts. "If we're stopped, the less you know the better."

"Are we going to be arrested on our way to Xyri? I don't think the Magnus Primetri will appreciate bailing me out in time for Andelek's funeral rites." Maryn narrowed her eyes at the Merrows when Scylla flashed a look that said *help me* at her wife prior to answering.

"Oh, no. We wouldn't have brought you if we thought that could happen. It's all good."

Right, Maryn thought.

"I'll secure the cargo before we hit FTL." Jac unstrapped from the seat harness and floated down the corridor.

"Do you need assistance?" Col asked, all innocence.

"No, I've got it. Back in five," she called, already halfway to the common area.

"How about some tunes?" Scylla suggested, and without waiting for anyone to answer, said, "*Girl*, cue up the Faraday job playlist."

Music blared through the cockpit, cutting off conversation as the pilot pretended to be busy calculating her flight plan. Maryn swapped eyerolls with Col behind the pilot's turned back. Neither were fooled by a lame distraction intended to make it difficult to ask questions. From experience, she knew Scylla would be the first to crack under pressure.

The music was excellent, regardless.

MARYN'S fourth midnight watch was scheduled during a bland sector of space with no asteroid fields or nebulae to avoid, and she found herself on the verge of terminal boredom. She worked out in the cargo hold beside the crates they'd taken on at Zillzanam Station, which Jac had covered with a tarp and strapped down under tight webbing. Maryn circled them multiple times, looking for clues, but any identifying marks were hidden and her investigation yielded no information to what was inside.

There was only so much to do. Maryn had already lost several hands of poker to Scylla and Col, and after a couple of shots of whiskey, allowed Jac to tear out her eyebrows one by one until her friend's sadistic urge was satisfied. Then she'd let her polish her nails with clear lacquer, though she'd drawn the line at toenails. Col now sported pale pink claws on each of her four appendages but was still in possession of all her eyebrow fur, which Maryn thought was unfair.

She used to pass the time on watches like this reading, indulging a lifelong fascination with dinosaurs and dragons. If she wasn't geeking out over kaiju or studying for an upcoming mission, she would listen to recorded books by writers of fantasy whose imaginations boggled her mind, taking her to places which never existed. Jac had always teased that Maryn fell in love with Andelek because ze was a space-elf who chased dragons. And ze was. And she had; oh, she had.

But in her grief-fogged state, she'd forgotten to pack her digital library when she left home, along with the outfit she had planned on wearing for the memorial rites. There was nothing to be done about her books until she got back to Echo Four, but she thought she would have time to buy or borrow suitable white funeral robes when they reached Xyri.

She turned those thoughts aside before mourning seeped in and washed out the foundation she was trying to rebuild. It was better to stay busy, like Jac suggested. Maryn toggled the heads display to see where they were, but she could only watch the gold dot representing their ship crawl through grid lines for so long until her mind strayed back to the reason she was here.

"Maryn? Would you mind performing a maintenance item?" The *Girl*'s interface was a welcome distraction from the tedium.

"Absolutely not," she said.

"The CO2 filter is past due for change. With four humanoids on board, it has just reached a critical threshold. Life support is not yet compromised, but it is approaching the red."

"You bet." She padded down the corridor and opened the manifold's maintenance hatch, flush with the deck. "That's odd. Did Scylla forget to do this?"

The ship didn't answer immediately. "Yes, I believe so," it said at last. Maryn frowned. For Scylla to fail to heed a critical system warning was unheard of.

"That's not like her."

"No, it is not," the *Girl* agreed. "But I have been programmed to provide periodic reminders. You just happened to be on watch."

"Huh." Maryn let it slide. "Are the supplies still where they used to be?"

"Yes. Third cabinet, second shelf."

She retrieved a new filter from the corridor storage area and lowered herself into the narrow space, crouching to unclamp the connectors and slide out the old carbon dioxide filter unit. She replaced it with the new one, reconnected the tubing, and groaned, hauling herself out of the crawlspace and shut the hatch. She discarded the dirty filter in the waste system to be recycled.

They had passed the intangible border delineating Konecthedot sector two days ago. Jac's new coordinates from their contact at Zillzanam Station indicated a point in open space off the usual star lanes. They were to meet the other ship and transfer the cargo before they headed for the wormhole. Maryn was uncomfortable with the idea, not only because it added almost half a day to their travel, but because it seemed risky. Jac assured her it wasn't the first time they had done this, and knew the expected crew were trustworthy.

The *Girl* was flying through disputed territory now. Viltrux's fleet patrolled the lanes closest to the Pashni, trying to prevent the Kheprans from interfering in its so called 'civil war'. She decided it would be wise to catch up on developments she'd missed. The university subscribed to all media sources in the galaxy; Maryn tailored her personal feed to receive accurate reports condensed in a weekly digest. However, she hadn't retrieved it while holding her dazed vigil during Andelek's illness and death.

"*Girl*, do you have any reputable information about what's happening on Qet?"

"Certainly. I'm afraid the latest news download I performed was on Echo Four, and the media there is very tight-assed." Maryn couldn't suppress a grin, unable to disagree. Echo Four's galactic news coverage was tepid at best, so neutral in focus it was barely news at all. *Girl* continued, "Scylla and Jac have an anthropological summary and archived stories. The most recent data I have from trustworthy sources are several days old."

"Let me see the summary first."

What was occurring on Qet occurred on Earth more than once in past millennia, horrific genocide of marginalized groups by authoritarian leaders who held fearful sway over their nations. Their home world had not yet recovered from slow-healing generational wounds, but now advanced together as a cooperative species on their small, crowded planet. When they took their first tentative steps into the galaxy, they had discovered a universe of neighbors living in societies as gloriously varied and fucked up as they were.

The indigent humanoids who had first settled Qet were clustered in Shene, the capitol city on a warm, southern continent, and a smaller city called Tenent in the rugged, colder northern hemisphere where the mines were located. In the south, their primary industry was agriculture, fresh produce grown in the small planet's rich volcanic soil. The settlement charter was clear that Qet was to be a self-sustaining colony and avoid corporate entanglements which would detract from its ability to remain independent.

The original colonists were a species slow to reproduce, bearing one child or none during their lifespan unless aided by science. A past administration welcomed the Khepran settlers, a similar humanoid species from a dangerously overpopulated moon. Viltrux's ultra-conservative faction in the colonial government had balked at allowing colonists from other planets due to what Maryn interpreted as speciesism. Their worst fears were realized with a successful and fertile integration between the two groups in the north.

Rumors of genocide filtered out a few weeks after the fall of the old government with the arrival of Kheqet refugees on Xyri. The news archive was comprehensive in terms of sources, and brutal in its honesty, yet none of the sources was able to explain how Viltrux was able to raise an army when his faction was a minority. By all accounts, the majority of the Qetish planetary defense troops still supported the deposed chancellor in exile.

If it wasn't corporate interference, Maryn would eat her newly polished nails and let Jac paint her like a clown. She fucking hated corporate mercenaries, the indelible memories of Peloon and the Steel Union Rebellion etched in scar tissue.

Maryn surfaced half the night later from her deep dive into the media when her stomach growled in the silence of the cockpit. Crew change and breakfast were only a couple of hours away, but she had forgotten to eat.

She finished what Jac left out for her and drank more water before having to pee again. She was cleaning her hands when *Girl*'s alert tone sounded over her headset. "Maryn, I'm picking up something unusual on the long-range scanners."

"On my way." She padded up the corridor and strapped back in. "What've you got?"

"A large debris field in the star lane which was not previously reported," the AI said. "No asteroid belts exist in this sector, and the chart was updated less than seventy-two hours ago by a passing freighter. I suspect it may be war detritus."

"I thought the war hadn't come this far." A frisson of something she couldn't name shivered down her spine, and Maryn pulled her shapeless cardigan close. "Put it on screen."

The three-dimensional representation of the obstacle spun in space, each tiny fleck of light representing a solid object which could punch through the *Girl's* hull if she went through it in FTL. "Can we go around it?"

"Aye. Calculating a new course to avoid the debris and its predicted trajectory." A line skirting the field branched off from the current path on the heads-up. "It will add an hour to our journey. We will still make the rendezvous within the allotted time and will arrive on Xyri four hours prior to Primetri Andelek's funeral rites."

Less time to spare than she'd hoped, but it was good enough. Maryn settled back to read more of the news articles until a faint signal keened in a rise and fall of plaintive electronics, like a cry for help. Her head snapped up. "Is that what I think it is?"

"Asteroid fields don't send out distress beacons," *Girl* confirmed.

"Oh, no." Panic started behind her breastbone and tried to spin its way up her throat, but she fought for composure, her palms damp with sweat. The heads-up showed the ship was adjacent to the debris field, well out of range, but ... "There may be survivors," Maryn breathed.

She couldn't leave anyone out there, like she had been.

Her heart sped up with—dread? Excitement? She wasn't sure, but adrenaline flooded through her and her nerves quivered with antici-pation. "Drop out of FTL, rescue protocol. I think you need to wake everybody up."

CHAPTER
FOUR

"I AGREE," *Girl* said crisply in her ear. "All hands, prepare for emergency deceleration sequence." The announcement shattered the stillness of the ship, blue night lights paling to yellow, then white.

Maryn secured her water bottle and empty food container in a compartment beneath her chair and silenced the warning on the instrument panel as forward-facing thrusters roared into life. The initial drag pushed her away from the seat to strain against the harness. If *Girl's* summons didn't wake everyone, that certainly would. Moments after the first braking maneuver, the Merrows appeared, yawning but alert.

"What's going on?" Scylla ran her hands over her head and raked up purple-tipped spikes.

"We're approaching the coordinates, but *Girl* detected a debris field where one shouldn't be," she answered, and quickly unbuckled the safety harness to slide out of Scylla's chair. "It's not on the charts. The spread suggests it isn't a natural asteroid swarm. Then we started to pick up an intermittent distress beacon." The faint digital wail over the comm repeated as if on cue. "There it is again."

"War debris?" Col had padded up behind them and slipped into her jump seat.

"*Girl* and I think it's possible there are survivors."

"If it's a battle site, we won't know what side they're on," Scylla warned.

"Does it matter?" Maryn arched one eyebrow as she buckled in.

"Well ..." Jac sighed submission as she slid into the copilot's chair. "It might."

Col hummed deep in her throat. "There is more to your free-lancing than you've told us, isn't there?"

"Maybe a little bit," Scylla admitted. "Everybody's strapped in, right? I'm turning off artificial gravity. Emergency deceleration maneuver in three ... two ... one."

Maryn's body strained against the harness as Newton's law displayed itself more assertively this time. The *Girl*'s programmed rescue protocols kept them in wide, but ever-tightening circles near the source of the distress signal. The braking process took more than an hour until the ship slowed enough to drop into sub light engines, and Scylla turned them toward the beacon's coordinates.

"Jeeze, the spread is massive." Jac whistled as she took in the radar display. "That's got to be more than one."

"The war made it to the sector sooner than you thought," Maryn confirmed.

"Whatever this is had to have happened within the last few hours." The pilot's hands flew over the instrument panel. Steel shutters over the windshield retracted into their pockets, and they all stared in disbelief at the carnage revealed in front of them. "What the living fuck?" Scylla whispered.

The slow-spinning bulk of a fragmented spaceship loomed ahead, a hull lined with dark, empty windows. Flotsam drifted around it in an expanding corona.

It was impossible to miss the bodies floating among the wreckage.

"There's a marking on that piece of hull off starboard. Can we magnify it?" Maryn asked.

The *Girl*'s camera zoomed in. On the battered panel, the unmis-takable logo of a stylized star flashed over and over as it rotated slowly away from them.

"It's a Khepran transport." Dizzy horror made Maryn's thoughts spin for a moment before something in her mind dropped into place with a sharp, decisive click, and warrior Maryn emerged, cold and angry. "That was a passenger vessel."

"They were probably carrying refugees." Rage burnished the edges of Scylla's voice. "*Girl*, take high resolution images from the fore and aft cameras. Make sure you capture the insignia. We need to get this on record. They wouldn't have had the shields or firepower to stand up to a warship. Damn those bastards to fucking hell. Where's the beacon coming from?"

"The signal is not from the transport. It is from a Qet registered intersystem ship," *Girl* answered. "It matches the one we were supposed to meet. It's coming from a cluster of wreckage off starboard."

"No," Jac breathed, and Scylla slammed her head against the cushioned headrest, a profane oath hissed through her teeth.

"Scan for survivors," she told the ship.

Maryn closed her eyes for the endless fifteen seconds it took to complete the survey. "Two humanoid life signs," *Golden Girl* confirmed. "It appears they tried to launch a life pod before they were destroyed, but it didn't clear the tube. It's still there."

"This is officially a rescue mission," Scylla announced.

Jac glanced at Maryn. "You remember how to work the retrieval arm? I need to prep the medical pod in case we have casualties."

She unstrapped. "Are the claw controls the same?"

"Yes. They've gotten a little sticky on extension, but you'll figure it out," Jac started unbuckling, too.

They shifted without further discussion, like they always had. Col, too large to operate the hydraulic arms, drifted to the copilot's seat as Jac and Maryn propelled themselves through microgravity down the corridor to the crew quarters using handles welded in the bulkhead. Jac powered up the glass-fronted medical pod while Maryn unsealed the hatch in the floor. She pulled hand-under-hand down the ladder and shut the airlock behind her before she descended into the small control center outside the cargo hold.

"Power switch, pressure bleed, external video, status green," she whispered as she punched buttons on the console. A set of robotic grabbers unfolded from their resting position in the hold's overhead. Her ears popped as the bay vented its atmosphere in preparation to open. She pulled the harness from the bulkhead and tried to slip her arms into the hydraulic controls, but her sweater caught on the piston joints.

"Shit." Old lady clothes were not practical for rescue missions. She discarded the sweater, her undershirt offering no resistance to the chill of the tech as she slid into the frame. The heads-up display projected on the booth window, showing the debris field outside as hydraulic claws spread in an echo of her movements. Her finger joints complained, stiff when she flexed in the mechanical gloves, but the response from the gear was as intuitive as she remembered.

"Are you in position, Maryn?" *Girl* asked. "We are about to match the speed and rotation of the wreckage. I am opening the cargo bay."

"I'm ready."

"We're in position." Scylla's voice came over the headset. She squinted at the display as the external floodlights played over twisted metal. The ramp began to descend, letting the void in. A cold sweat broke out over Maryn's skin at the sight of interminable space.

I'm inside, not out there, she reminded herself. She tried to train her attention on the heads-up instead, but her eyes refused to focus. "*Girl,* adjust the holo projector for plus three distance and magnification."

"Setting display for granny glasses," the ship responded.

"What did you say?" Maryn blurted.

"That's what I call it. *Girl* does too, now," Scylla said over the comm.

Her eyes finally cooperated. The blasted hull of the ship spun beneath them and she caught sight of the cylindrical life pod, projecting part way out of the tube from which it had been launched.

"I see it. Match trajectory and rotation." She extended her arms. The hydraulic limbs reflected her movement. "There's a piece of debris jamming the life pod into the tube. I can only see one of the retrieval cuffs on the pod. It's twisted the wrong direction. Bring us more to port."

"Roger. Correcting speed and rotation." Scylla said. The stars outside spun in a dizzy arc, drawing Maryn's gaze to them, and she blinked sweat out of her eyes. "How's that?"

The other cuff was in view. "Good for now." She reached for the near cuff and clamped hydraulic fingers around the handle. The other limb extended but she met unexpected resistance before she could use the claw to grab the metal rod jamming the tube. "The right arm is stuck."

"You have to punch a little to unstick it," Jac told her over the headset. "It's got shoulder issues. *Girl*'s getting old, like us."

"I beg your pardon," *Girl* said, offended. "I'm younger than all of you. It's not the age. It's the shit you've put me through."

Maryn carefully retracted her arm, swiveling, and extended her fist with more momentum. The joint popped and the robotic manipulator extended the rest of the way, the metal hand slamming against the lifeboat. "I probably just scared the hell out of whoever's in there." She wrapped the claw around the junk pinning the capsule into the tube and pulled back. The rod moved but refused to let go. "It's not going to budge without a little force. It might just pull the wreck with us before it releases. How big of a problem is that?"

"Big," Scylla admitted. "A huge section of the transport is drifting toward us faster than I hoped. We won't be able to move out of the way fast enough lugging that behind us and I don't want the *Girl* smashed between 'em."

"If we leave the life pod here, they're going to be smashed instead of us," Maryn snapped. "How long do we have?"

"About two minutes until we have to disengage."

"Just like old times," Maryn muttered. "All right. Give me a minute. Be prepared to move away as soon as it comes loose."

She wrapped one hydraulic claw around the tow handle, the other on the obstructing debris and pulled. Both shifted in the tube and stuck again. "Come on, you bastard," she grunted, throwing her weight against the hydraulics. The cylinder slid out another foot, not even halfway out of the launch tube.

Her thigh muscles burned with the effort as she leaned backward in the arm controls. She staggered when the cylinder suddenly slid free, and the hydraulic claw jerked the life pod forward too quickly, banging it on the ramp of the cargo bay.

"Damn it, I'm really rattling whoever is inside. I hope they're strapped in."

"Make it fast, Mar," Scylla said. "That wreck's getting too close."

Maryn gritted her teeth and clamped the other claw on the opposite tow handle. She carefully drew the vessel into the bay and deposited it hatch side up on the deck, not as gently as she would have liked. "Got it. Go!"

Impulse engines fired, treating her to a fresh, terrifying sight of wheeling stars and drifting wreckage as the bulk of the shattered transport plowed into the remains of the smaller ship and drove it toward the *Girl*'s stern. "I said go, go, go!"

"There's a lot of debris. I'm pedaling fast as I can!" Scylla yelled.

"Pedal faster!" The cargo bay port began to close and she kept a hydraulic grip on the life pod as it skidded for the opening with the force of acceleration. The wreck outside began to disintegrate into smaller pieces before the port shut out Maryn's view of the tumbling wreck. She lowered the life pod to the deck and stowed the robotic arms back in their overhead compartment.

"Resume pressurization," she told the ship on a trembling exhale. "How are their life signs?"

"Stable, but showing some stress," *Girl* reported. "So are yours."

"Yeah," she agreed. "As soon as I can breathe, open the control room airlock."

Maryn slipped out of the harness and winced, rubbing her neck and right shoulder before she put her sweater back on, chilled from contact with the machinery. A few minutes later, the indicator on the airlock door turned from red to green. Pressure seals hissed when she punched the controls, and the port swung into the bay. She launched herself from the port frame toward the battered pod.

The handle of the vessel's escape hatch burned cold to the touch. Maryn swore, shaking her hand and rubbed her frost-nipped palm. The seal on the hatch hissed with escaping air. Somebody on the inside was making their way out, so she floated backward, hovering, as it slammed open.

She froze, staring down the business end of an energy pistol.

"WHOA, WHOA. YOU'RE SAFE," Maryn reassured the wild-eyed being behind the gun, holding her hands up to show they were empty.

Tousled dark red hair almost obscured hard damson eyes rimmed in black lashes. Golden skin shaded from bronze at the hairline to pale topaz at the chin, and a trickle of red-brown blood seeped from a mottled bruise on their right temple. She was not certain of gender but from her research recognized them as a Kheqet hybrid.

"*Kas nim pidoq?*" the being spat. The pistol never wavered.

She didn't speak Khepran fluently without a translator patch, but Maryn thought it meant, *Who are you?*

Jac floated into the cargo bay from the open hatch, and the hybrid swiveled the gun to her. She held up a soothing hand and said in Gallingua, the common galactic tongue, "Dair, don't shoot my friend. She just saved your life."

Surprised, Maryn processed that Jac knew this being as Dair relaxed and slowly lowered the weapon, tucking it into a thigh holster strapped against their close-fitting, insulated body suit. The scalloped edge of one ear, pierced with several glittering rings, was just visible beneath the floating tumble of waves. They asked in the same language Jac had spoken, "Where is Scylla?"

"Piloting the ship," she answered. "There's a Boshi on board, so don't freak out when you see her. Do you need medical attention?"

"We got tossed a little, but we're fine. Have you found the other pods? They should be transmitting on the same frequency."

Maryn's heart fell. She and Jac exchanged a glance. "We didn't receive any other signals. How many?"

"Two more," Dair's voice broke on a note of desperation. "Two in one of them, three in the other."

"Scyll, any more distress beacons?" Jac asked over her headset.

"Negative," the pilot answered. Jac shook her head at Dair, her lips tight.

"No," the Kheqet breathed, a stricken look flitting across their features. "We have to be sure."

"*Girl*, can you help?"

"Rescanning the wreckage for debris matching life pod schematics," *Girl* stated.

"I'll make a quick loop around the wrecks," Scylla informed them over the headset. "We can't stay long. Sensors are picking up a frigate in the quadrant. If they're not friendly, we don't want them to notice we're here. I've already finished calculations for the rest of the trip to Xyri."

"Who else was on board?" Maryn's insides lurched.

"Three more refugees, my pilot, and his brother." Dair's expression crumbled, then rearranged to a neutral mask. They leaned down into the pod and spoke softly. "It's all right. You can come out."

The upper half of a topaz-skinned face peeked above the rim of the pod's hatch, bright, frightened eyes belonging to a much smaller being.

"*Vo tatra Rinana?*" the child's voice piped in question.

Grief shadowed Dair's face, so fleetingly Maryn almost missed it before a bright smile took over. "We'll catch up with your family later. Come on, little one." Dair pulled them free of the pod. Maryn guessed the kid to be no more than five years old and also a hybrid Kheqet, dressed in a similar insulated body suit.

"Look, humans!" Dair said, giving the kid a bounce as they picked him up. "Isn't that exciting? You've never met their species."

The child nibbled on their chubby golden thumb and regarded them with a wary expression.

"Well, hello there," Jac said in a bright voice, and the boy shyly turned his face into the older being's neck. "Let's take you up to the berth deck where it's warm."

Dair smiled down at the child. "This is Zeddi. He probably needs to use your waste system by now."

"Oh, let's not wait then." Jac waggled her eyebrows at Maryn.

"Hold on." Dair moved toward the pile of cargo secured at the stern. "Are those the guns? Only three crates?"

"Ah. Yes. We'll talk about that later." Jac shot a furtive look at Maryn. "Will you show them where the head is? I'll wait here until we know about the other pods."

She stared daggers at her, then blinked and smiled with false brightness at their new passengers. "Sure. Follow me." She pulled herself back into the control room and opened the overhead hatch, shooting up through the tube. Dair followed, Zeddi clinging to their back. Maryn showed them to the lavatory and flipped the switch to convert the toilet from flush to vacuum. "Is he familiar with the process? It's a little different in zero gravity."

"Zeddi's an expert by now," they assured her. "Thanks."

She left them to it. Col joined her in the common area a few minutes later as she waited for them to come out. "Is everyone all right?"

"Yes, an adult and a child. They appear to be Kheqet refugees. According to them, there were more refugees in other pods."

"We found no other life signs," Col told Maryn in a hushed voice, and glanced at the closed door of the lavatory. "Scylla is anxious to head for the Pashni. We are to secure the passengers as soon as they are out of the head. Did they say what happened?"

"Not yet." She lowered her voice to a whisper. "The crates in the cargo hold? They're guns."

"Guns?" Col's icy green eyes widened and the Boshi glanced over her shoulder as Jac emerged from the ladder tube, shut the hatch, and sealed it.

"Can I leave you and Col in charge back here?" Jac asked and she pulled herself toward the corridor. "I need to talk to Scylla. Have them take the far-left cubicle when they come out of the head. It's been modified. Then strap yourselves in. We're going to haul ass out of here."

"Yeah, sure." Maryn answered. The double beep of deactivation sounded over their headsets as Jac floated into the cockpit. "I guess we're not included in the conversation," she noted.

Col cocked her head with a puzzled *mrrr* sound. She opened the partition to the end sleeping unit and they both paused to stare.

Curtains draped all four walls, stiff fabric shot through with glittering threads. The material's close weave was peppered with hair-thin wire. It produced an electronic signal meant to disrupt external sensor sweeps and prevent an accurate assessment of life signs inside the vessel. Maryn had seen something like this on one of their past missions. It was used to hide trafficking victims on board a kidnappers' ship.

Oh, yeah. Jac and Scylla had a lot to explain.

"More secrets?" Col frowned, sharp canine teeth just visible behind her lips.

"They're going to have to come clean sooner rather than later." She turned toward the sound of the lavatory door as Dair and Zeddi appeared. "Everything work out all right?"

"It sucked my poop down," the kid announced in Gallingua, surprising them.

"That's ... good," Col said. Zeddi's dark eyes grew round at the sight of the Boshi.

"Furry," he whispered, and reached for a handful of Col's pelt.

She took a step back to evade him. "We are about to transition to FTL. Maryn will show you where to strap in."

She led them to their cubicle and turned down the jump seats at the head of each bunk and made sure they were safely secured before she and Col followed suit in their own quarters. She toggled her headset. "All right, *Girl*. Everybody's ready."

"Acknowledged," the ship responded. The engines began to wind up almost immediately—Scylla was in a hurry to get out of there. By the time her butt sank into the cushions twenty minutes later, Maryn had worked up a simmering kettle of pissed off and was determined to find out what the fuck was going on. She got out of her cubicle and grabbed a couple of fluid rations before she poked her head in to check on their guests.

"Are you okay?" she asked, giving them the water.

"We're fine." Dair answered, their voice quiet. Zeddi was leaning as close to them as he could manage while restrained in the jump seat, his small hand tangled with theirs.

"You can remove the harnesses, but don't leave the cubicle. We have to sort some things. It's not safe for you to move around yet."

"Understood." Dair still eyed her suspiciously.

"There are blankets and pillows under the bunk if you need them. I'll be back in a few minutes." She drew the curtain and closed the rolling partition.

Col had already emerged from her quarters and stood at the mouth of the corridor. "Is it time to grill their asses?" she asked sweetly.

"Hell yes." Maryn stalked toward the cockpit. Hushed voices stopped at the sound of their approach. Scylla's guilty expression vanished behind her headrest as she hastily turned back to the instrument panel. Jac regarded them with a resigned nod.

Maryn leaned against the bulkhead with her arms crossed. "All right. Who's going to talk first? Because I've worked myself into a full rage, I just need you to point me at a target."

"I surrender," Scylla erupted in relief and turned her chair around, hands raised. "What do you want to know? I can't stand keeping secrets from you."

"Then start talking."

"We're working with the Kheqet resistance," Jac confessed. "We've been transporting weapons and supplies into the northern settlement ever since the reports of ethnic cleansing started. We usually find cargo runs that give us legal reasons to be in the sector. Ships originating somewhere outside Qetish space have to produce a valid reason to be there." She swallowed, her gaze dropping to her lap and her twisted hands. "We were having trouble getting permission to gate jump to Konecthedot because of the increased fighting here. Flight control finally approved it when we told them we were transporting the Dowager Consort and the remains of Primetri Andelek to Xyri for zer funeral."

Those words punched Maryn in the gut.

"You were using me and"—her voice broke—"and Andelek as an excuse to be in this sector?" A slow-burning flashfire worked its way up her chest to her face, a painful mix of betrayal, hurt, and acrid fury.

"We would have been here anyway, but without a cover story. I'm so sorry." Jac reached for her, and Maryn flinched. Her friend's expression crumpled with remorse. "I swear to you, we were going to come clean as soon as we thought it was safe. You and Col would be able to honestly deny any knowledge of our activities if we were detained and questioned."

Maryn blinked against the burn of angry tears. "Or you could have told me the truth from the beginning."

"We should have." Scylla squirmed under Maryn's gaze, her hand raking through her spiky hair. "We didn't expect this. We were supposed to load the weapons into Dair's ship and keep going. We had no way to know the war moved this far into the sector."

"If they've expanded the front, who is in control of the Pashni wormhole?" Col posed the question, the thin edge of a crystal razor in her delicate voice.

"When we left, it was still open, but held by Viltrux's fleet," Scylla assured her, but doubt clouded her expression. "We need to reach Xyri and then regroup with Dair's cell. The fuckers are taking out unarmed refugee ships and executing witnesses. This takes their war crimes to a whole other level." She glanced at Maryn. "What do you think the Magnus Primetri will do?"

"I don't know." This had been an act the Xyrian parliament would not be able to ignore, despite the planet's obsessive neutrality. She understood that. She could even understand Jac and Col's involvement in the resistance. But the knowledge her best friends had—had *used* her—scraped a bloody furrow in her already fragile composure, brittle against the anxiety of being in deep space and the nagging sense of emptiness left by Andelek's death. "Right now I don't care. I need to be alone for a little while."

Maryn wheeled around and stomped down the corridor. She wore her fury like a billowing, self-righteous cape and their guilty silence followed until she climbed into her cubicle, slammed the barrier shut, and jerked the headset away from her ear. The privacy field hummed into life with the punch of a button, insulating her from outside noise and prevented the scream she muffled with her pillow from being overheard.

She folded into a ball, too hurt to cry, too angry to forgive, and so goddamn tired. She closed her eyes and took deep breaths through her nose, out through her mouth.

It was refreshing to feel something besides anxiety and grief, even if it was rage. Trust Jac and Scylla to bring out the strongest of her emotions. They'd pulled shit like this before, staunch believers in the adage that it was better to ask forgiveness rather than permission—like the time they liberated seven cases of expensive Tridarian whiskey from an employer's private warehouse without Maryn or Col's knowledge.

It had been damn good whiskey, though.

In wartime, she adhered to the *don't ask* philosophy too, especially when their squad's actions conflicted with their commander's orders, sparing collateral damage but achieving the same success. This was different. Wasn't it?

Her sigh wobbled when it came. She pressed her hands over her eyes to soothe the building ache behind them. What they'd done had crossed a line, maybe for the right reasons, but was still a slap in the face. Maryn couldn't decide why it hurt so badly: because they'd lied, or because it looked like they didn't trust her enough anymore to tell her the truth.

Who was she, now? A loose end to be tidied up at the university. A retired mercenary, getting too old to be of any use in a fight. A widow and part-time friend to these comrades who were once her entire world.

None of that was entirely true. She knew it, even felt guilty for allowing this indulgent wallow in self-pity. Because she wasn't sure what the answers were anymore, she let the lonely fire of resentment keep her warm for a while.

CHAPTER
FIVE

JAC WAS FEEDING their passengers when Maryn emerged from her pissed-off cocoon, confident in her ability to function as a reasonable human. Zeddi devoured a leftover waffle under Col's hyper-vigilant attention. The Boshi seemed to think the kid was going to turn feral and go for her throat, but at the same time stared at him in fascination. Maryn slid into a seat and with a cool, silent nod, accepted the sealed mug of coffee Jac placed in front of her like a peace offering. The cup clicked against the magnetic rim of the table. She held it between her hands and let the radiant warmth seep into her cold fingers.

"What happened?" Maryn asked Dair as they picked at the last of the fresh fruit. The Kheqet hesitated, glancing first at Jac, who nodded in encouragement.

"You can trust her. She was our squad leader back in the corps."

Dair took in her baggy sweater, the dark circles under her eyes, and her disheveled, graying hair with a dubious expression. She couldn't blame them for their reluctance. The younger being answered,

"Our pilot received a distress call from the refugee transport before we were in range, about an hour out from our rendezvous time. This evacuation ship left the camp a couple days ago and we were bringing another family to it. The vessel was at stop when we got there. A frigate was parked off their port bow and they just ... destroyed the transport." Dair's voice was dull with remembered horror. "When they detected our ship, they turned their guns on us as we tried to run. They didn't even hail us."

"Clearly, they did not want witnesses," Col growled.

"Did you see any markings on the frigate? Qetish insignia? Corporate logos?" Maryn asked.

"There wasn't an opportunity to look, but none of Viltrux's fleet is marked. They're black with a reflective black stripe down the side. The planetary defense force only had three ships, and they were destroyed when the government was overthrown." Dair watched Zeddi reach for Col's furry arm with his sticky hand, and he giggled when the Boshi flinched and gave him the side-eye. Their voice dropped to a whisper. "We barely had enough time to get in the life pod before our ship exploded. It mustn't have been possible for the others. His parents, his infant sister, and my crew."

Maryn's eyes became wet. This poor kid's entire family was gone, snuffed out in one vicious instant. She pushed away the thought to prevent turning into a blubbering mess, her emotions still on a hair-trigger, and motioned to the pistol strapped to Dair's thigh. "You're pretty comfortable with a gun. You're a soldier?"

"Planetary defense force. In the capitol, before Viltrux started killing our people." The being ran a hand over their smooth, ombre-shaded face. "Now, I guess I'm Zeddi's guardian until I can get him to Xyri."

"I would have thought you'd known him a long time." Jac smiled, leaning on the counter between the galley and the mess table. "He seems attached to you. You're good with kids."

"Latched on to me the second he came aboard." Dair turned a fond gaze on Zeddi. "He's a charming little guy. I have ... I had ... younger siblings." They swallowed. The shadow of loss melted Dair's expression into brief, fluid vulnerability before resolidifying into a blank and unyielding mask. "My mother was one of the

Kheqet representatives in the government. I was wounded in the first skirmish and got evac-ed to the resistance base up north. But my family was killed in Shene."

There was nothing to say that could ever impact Dair's pain. *I'm sorry* wasn't enough. She floundered a moment, knowing that platitudes were useless, but still feeling she should say something.

Zeddi chose that moment to yawn over the remaining crumbs of his waffle. Col raised her arm, startled, as the child climbed into her lap and leaned against her chest. The Boshi stared at Maryn in a silent plea for help and cradled him like a bomb.

"Poor baby. He's exhausted," Jac noted with a smile. She turned her head to regard Dair as well. "So are you."

"I'm fine." Dair sat up straighter, but the dark, purplish shadows beneath their eyes were evident. "Just give me something to do."

"Nothing to do until we reach Xyri. It's hours yet before we get to the Pashni. Why don't you both get some sleep?"

Dair started to protest but yawned as well and conceded without a fight. They collected Zeddi from Col's lap (the Boshi seemed reluctant to hand over the now-sleeping child) and disappeared into the shielded cubicle. Jac waited for the partition to slide closed, then met Maryn's gaze.

"I know you're angry with me, but we have to tell the Magnus Primetri what happened," she said with quiet urgency. "This was an unprovoked attack on innocents. They aren't even pretending it's a civil war anymore. We have got to get the word out that a corporation might be involved."

Still nursing the complaint against her treacherous friends, Maryn prickled at Jac's use of *we*. "There's no proof. Without markings or documentation, they only have our word to go by. I don't have that much clout."

"My friends, have you forgotten my remote assignment?" Col said, her eyes bright as she drummed her hands against the table. "I am researching colonial accounts. Money trails. I can search through CosBank data for large amounts of credits coming in or out of Qet's banking system."

Jac shot a considering look at Maryn. "Qet shouldn't have any dealings with corporations other than mining transactions because of their charter."

"If we find items with a corporate account attached, perhaps we can identify it." Col rubbed her furry hands together. "I can't upload a new set of accounts until we reach Xyri, but, oh! Tactical accounting sounds like fun!"

Maryn couldn't help but grin at her enthusiasm. "I should be able to get Dair an audience with Lekere—my father-in-law—after the funeral. They can tell him firsthand what happened, but you know it's not a decision he can make alone. The Xyrian parliament has final say, and their history on this kind of thing is not very encouraging. I'll send a message updating our arrival as soon as we're out of the wormhole. How far behind are we?"

"Only four hours. We will still arrive before the rites." Jac started to say something else, thought better of it, and continued instead, "You were up all night. You need sleep too. Hopefully, the rest of the trip will be as uneventful as we planned. We'll wake you up when we make the transition unless you'd rather sleep through it."

"No. Have the *Girl* wake me up." She got to her feet and moved toward the cubicle.

"Mar ..."

She held up a hand and kept walking. "Allow me to be petty for a while."

"Yes. Okay." Jac began to collect dirty utensils and the untouched coffee, her eyes downcast. Col rose to help clear the table but gave Maryn a nod of solidarity as she passed.

She had never been able to harbor a grudge against Jac for long, but she was going to fucking milk this one as much as possible.

"MARYN?" A quiet voice roused her from dreams of being held in warm arms, a kiss pressed to her temple.

"Andelek?" she murmured in sleepy confusion. Her hand

collided with the padded wall of the cubicle and the dream evaporated. "Sorry, *Girl*. Are we approaching the Pashni?"

"Yes. We are about to initiate the drop from FTL. Scylla is turning off the art-grav." The AI paused. "Were you dreaming?"

"I think so."

"I apologize for interrupting."

"Thanks." Maryn breathed an uneven sigh. She struggled out of the blankets and turned down the jump seat from the head of the bunk to prepare for the change in velocity.

Tomorrow would bring Andelek's memorial service. She touched her limp, sleep-wrecked bun and realized it had been a couple of days since she showered. The sonic cleanser was good for many things, but not washing her hair. There would be time to do an actual hydro-wash before they reached the wormhole. She wanted to be somewhat presentable for her royal in-laws, though they would never comment on her appearance. As planetary kings and queens went, Lekere and Nadele were laid-back beings, save for their gentle but unyielding insistence on Andelek's return to Xyri.

The swooping sensation from the sudden absence of gravity hit like a wave. The initial deceleration pressed her back against the cushions, subsiding with the gradual decrease of the prescribed burn from forward thrusters. She waited until the maneuver was complete and freed herself from the harness. It would be half an hour before the next speed reduction. She fished for clothes beneath the bunk and scrabbled for a comb from her bag, then bundled her stuff together and emerged, blinking, from the dim cubicle into bright, day-cycle lighting.

She heard murmurs coming from the direction of the cockpit: Jac and Scylla, with Dair's voice lifted above theirs. She navigated toward the lavatory. To her surprise, Col's quarters were open. She and Zeddi were strapped into opposite sides, the bunks pulled down to join in the middle as hers had been. In the foot of space between them, a battleground emerged as toy representations of the kaiju she and Andelek had discovered snarled at each other, courtesy of Zeddi's enthusiastic play. Andelek had once gifted the set to Scylla as a joke, stating ze understood it was tradition for all human pilots to have dinosaurs on the bridge.

"These calibotari live in the northern hemisphere of Chrekem Seven, and the pseudosaur lives in the marshes of Rune," Col was saying, another toy creature in her hand. "They don't really fight, you know."

"These ones do!" Zeddi proclaimed and rammed the calibotari's head against the pseudo-saur's side in a plasticene collision, then made them both jump to attack the second calibotari in Col's hand with savage roars and chomping noises.

Col looked up and met Maryn's amused gaze as she passed, but the expression on her friend's furry countenance held no plea for rescue, only bewilderment at the child's faulty logic.

She gave her a thumbs up of encouragement, retrieved a packet of water from the ship's rations, and dragged herself into the lavatory. Stripping off her dirty clothes, she stuffed them into a cage on the bulkhead with her clean set on the outside and slipped her bare feet under the anchor points in front of the toilet. She strapped on and deployed the suction to perform her necessary bodily functions while she washed her hair—one learned to economize activities in deep space, and those habits came back without much thought.

She glimpsed herself in the mirror, wondering for a second time what the fuck had they been thinking when they installed it across from the toilet. Her body was still trim thanks to her fitness routine, and in zero gravity, everybody's tits looked perky. Familiar twists of healed skin traced her abdomen and flank: a knife thrust that almost took out her left kidney, and a scar which resembled a crescent moon beneath her navel. Her squad had joked about that one, about Sergeant Alessi being so devoted to the corps even her scars looked like their seal. That shrapnel had taken out any chance of natural reproduction at age twenty-four, leaving nowhere to reattach the organs she'd had removed and preserved upon enlistment as most other recruits did.

There were furrowed gouges on her back, hidden at this angle, remembered in the tightness and stretch of rough tissue over her left shoulder blade. A trio of claw slashes heralding her first foray into exobiology traveled down her right calf. Her friends had their share of scars too, the marks where they cheated death more times than they could count. So had Andelek, wearing the story of claws and teeth in zer skin.

It was the new, invisible crater in the center of her chest that hurt more than any other.

Released from its elastic band, Maryn's hair surrounded her head in a spiky, dark halo, and she tugged the comb through it to work out the snarls. She'd kept it short in her mercenary youth, and considered cutting it again, but what was the point? She'd only be in space a few more days. She opened the valve on the water pouch and worked the fluid right into the strands to minimize the escape of tiny, spherical drops before scrubbing her scalp with the no-rinse soap from a dispenser on the wall.

Squeezing the remaining water into a cloth, Maryn washed with the same no-rinse solution before releasing the vacuum on the toilet seat to finish the PTA bath. A towel from the storage rack beside the mirror dried the excess and she bundled her damp hair into the absorbent material while she dressed, shivering in the chill.

With fresh clothes and clean hair, she felt less likely to bite anyone's head off. She put the used towels in the bin for reprocessing and took her soiled clothes back to the cubicle before she foraged for breakfast.

There were packets of food in the galley designed to be consumed and digested in microgravity. She slid one into the warmer for thirty seconds, grabbed another water ration, and took them both back to the cubicle to strap in, leaving the partition open. She donned her headset but peevishly kept the conversation channel closed. With a few minutes to spare, *Girl* broadcast the second deceleration warning through the ship's comm.

The hot cereal packet, spiked with cinnamon and diced fruit, wasn't terrible. Getting her fiber in microgravity was important to bowel function, she reminded herself as she sucked the gruel through the one-way valve and flattened the plastic pouch from the bottom.

Having your ass sealed to a vacuum toilet was bad enough without being constipated. She still had dents from this morning. It hadn't been something she had thought about much when she was young, but older Maryn had to keep tabs on it.

When she emerged from her cubicle to recycle the pouches after the second burn, she was greeted by Col and a giggling Zeddi as they watched an ancient anime classic at the holo-table. *Attack on Titan* was not a kid friendly show, but the child was in ecstasy, his dark eyes wide with fascination.

Dair floated down the corridor, their golden features creased with frustration. Jac followed close behind.

"We're approaching the Pashni," Jac advised, giving Zeddi an cheerful wave. "Initial sweeps say we're alone, but we're a couple of minutes out of sensor range."

"Come on, little one." Dair held out their hand with false brightness. "Time to strap in."

"I have to poop first," the kid announced, unclipping the belt that held him down at the table.

Dair exchanged a concerned glance with Jac. "Can't it wait?"

"No." Zeddi whined, both hands going to his clenched butt as he hovered above his seat. "It wants to come out."

"I remember those days with Maya. There's not much we can do about it," Jac relented.

"You have to go very fast," Dair said and tugged the child toward the lavatory door.

"I can do it myself," Zeddi gave them a determined glare. He pushed them out the door and shut it behind him.

"Independent little cuss," Maryn remarked.

Without preamble, *Girl*'s interface crackled in Maryn's ear. Across the table, Jac and Col stiffened too as the ship warned, "Sensors are picking up a frigate. It appears to be the same one we detected leaving the debris field."

"Pull back the sensor sweep," Scylla barked over the com. "Are they aware of our approach?"

"I don't know how they couldn't be. They are at full stop in front of the wormhole," *Girl* stated.

The pilot swore under her breath. "Is the kid still in the head?"

"Our flight manifest only lists four passengers. We need to hide two humanoid life signs right now in case they scan us." Jac pointed to the insulated cubicle, meeting Maryn's gaze with a sharp nod. She understood.

"What is it?" Dair, without a headset, demanded.

"A frigate, maybe the same one. Col, you're going to have to handle Zeddi," Maryn ordered as she grabbed Dair and pushed them toward the curtained quarters. They shook free from her grip, glaring, but complied.

"I don't know what to do with a defecating child," Col protested, her voice rising to a panicked pitch.

"You'll figure it out," Jac called over her shoulder as she launched herself up the corridor.

"*Girl*, put the common speaker in Dair's quarters so they can hear, too." Maryn dived in beside Dair and yanked the glittering curtain closed, sealing the magnetic clasps. She directed Col, "Make sure he turned on the vacuum in the head. We don't want floaters."

"Floaters? What—Oh, that is revolting," the Boshi objected.

"We are being scanned," the ship announced. "They're hailing us."

"This is the frigate *Raging Fire*." The voice over the comm was already confrontational. "Do not approach the wormhole or you will be treated as hostile. What is your business here?"

"*Raging Fire*, this is the Caspian-registered cruiser *Golden Girl*. We are enroute from Echo Four to Xyri on a time-sensitive passenger run." Jac was cool and efficient but managed to sound bewildered. Only Maryn's long acquaintance with her recognized the tightness beneath the words.

"What is the nature of your passenger run?" Suspicion dripped from his transmission.

"If you're going to use me as an excuse, now's the time," Maryn barked into the headset. Jac picked up the baton.

"We are transporting the dowager consort of Primetri Andelek and the Primetri's remains to Xyri for zer funeral rites."

"Transmit your flight plan and manifest at once."

"Transmitting."

There was a delay. One minute stretched into two, then three.

"What does the ship look like? Any identifying marks?" Maryn asked.

"No insignia, which you'd expect if it were a pirate fleet," Jac responded. "It's in great repair. Black alloy with a reflective stripe. Top of the line. That says a lot of money. I doubt they're your average, run of the mill mercenaries."

"We don't think so either," Dair agreed. "His personal soldiers wear plain armor with full helmets and visors. We don't know if they're Qetish at all. None of their military vehicles have identifying numbers or symbols."

"Pirates are proud of their colors. It has to be a corporation that helped him overthrow the government," Maryn declared, convinced. "But they don't want to advertise."

The unnerving silence stretched into ten minutes. Then fifteen.

"What the fuck is taking so long?" Scylla rasped over the internal com.

"They know," Dair pronounced, their voice muffled by the insulating curtain.

"How could they?" Maryn spoke with a steadiness she didn't feel.

"They could have taken the captain or some of the crew to interrogate before they destroyed the ship." Dair took shallow, rapid breaths. "They might know where to find our camp."

"Stay calm," she said in the most neutral a tone she could manage and raised her hand as a transmission crackled.

Another officer took the place of the first. "What heading did you take from the jump gate at Echo Four?" This one's voice, composed and silky, sent up warning signals for her. They sounded more like a board member than a fleet captain.

"To Zillzanam Station and then to Konecthedot Sector," Jac answered. "Just like it says on the flight plan."

"How many passengers on your ship?"

"Four. Three humanoid, one Boshi."

"You performed no unscheduled stops or detours?" they inquired.

"We were forced to detour around an uncharted asteroid field passing through the sector." Jac's innocent act was flawless and made Maryn huff a soft laugh despite the tension.

"And I assume your ship's computer would show this should I board and review it myself?"

"Over my dead body," *Girl*'s interface whispered over the headset.

There was no hesitation in Jac's reply. "Yes."

They all knew it wasn't true.

"One more question, *Golden Girl*. Why are you armed?" The soft, menacing inquiry sent a chill down Maryn's spine.

"We're a decommissioned privateer vessel, *Raging Fire*. But one can never be too careful," Jac answered.

"Indeed. Prepare to be boarded, *Golden Girl*."

Dair's stricken gaze met Maryn's, a brief terror transmuting into resignation, then the emotion drained from the younger being's eyes, replaced by cold calculation of the odds. Their hand drifted to their sidearm.

"Sir, in order to meet the Magnus Primetri's timetable, we are on a strict flight plan." Jac's steely voice objected. "We are already hours behind due to the unplanned detour."

"I'm certain the Magnus Primetri will understand," they replied with mocking courtesy.

If their actual transponder records in Konecthedot sector were brought under direct scrutiny, it wouldn't hold up. Dair and Zeddi could not be found, nor the three crates of guns in the cargo bay Her consort status wasn't powerful enough to deter the frigate from acting, but she had to try.

"Let me talk to them," Maryn said.

"Channel open," *Girl* replied.

"*Raging Fire*, this is Dr. Maryn Alessi, Dowager Consort of

Primetri Andelek, and I do *not* understand," she barked, allowing a sharp edge of distress to color her words. "I promised the Magnus Primetri my mate's remains will be there in time for zer funeral rites, which begin in less than twenty-four hours, and ..." She gave hormones and grief full rein and burst into convenient, but genuine tears. "I demand you let us continue our flight plan unmolested!"

Girl continued to broadcast her sobs over the comm. She hoped they were effective because she hated this. Once she broke down, she was afraid it would be a while before she stopped. In microgravity tears and snot tended to float everywhere.

The destruction of a ship carrying the remains of a high-born member of the royal family and a living consort, however low-ranked, could be an incident with interplanetary consequences. Even the Xyri couldn't turn their other cheek against that. The frigate still might not hesitate to destroy the *Girl* and everyone on it to hide their war crime.

The silence was embarrassing as well as nerve wracking. Her sobs went on, and just as Maryn feared, she couldn't stop. At last, the exasperated, original officer snapped, *"Golden Girl,* you may approach the wormhole. *Raging Fire* out."

The *Girl's* engines surged. "Col, are you and the kid secure?" Jac called over the headset.

"Affirmative. There are no floaters."

Maryn laughed over her tears with a high-pitched edge of hysteria. Dair eyed her in trepidation as if she was a complete madwoman.

"We're approaching the Pashni," Scylla said. "Prepare for threshold distortion in five ... four ... three ... two ..."

The sensation of breaching a wormhole's gravitational field was never one of Maryn's favorite experiences. White noise filled her ears, and it was as if her body were being stretched thin, heart pounding against the strain of moving blood through vessels pressed flat. Her lungs were desperate to draw breath with the weight of a mountain on her chest. It only lasted seconds but cured her sobbing fit. Hard to cry when she couldn't manage the required lungful of air.

The sweet relief of zero gravity returned within a few seconds.

Once the rushing sound cleared from her head, the leftover hitch in her breathing from the crying jag seemed too loud in the insulated bunk. From Col's cubicle came the faint sound of a frightened, weeping child.

"Zeddi's never been through a wormhole before," Dair said in a low voice, and Maryn waved them on.

"It should be safe now. Go on," she managed to say.

She tried not to take offense at the younger being's relief. Dair unbuckled their harness and propelled themself through the curtains, a few floating, spherical tears following in their wake.

Maryn shrugged off the straps of her restraint and took another moment to collect herself, wishing she had something to blow her nose into. Damn, she was a mess.

Jac appeared as if summoned, drawing the curtain aside. She launched into the bunk and wrapped her arms and legs around Maryn in a tight, zero gravity hug. She laughed wetly and hugged her back as they drifted above the cushions, surrounded in a constellation of salty droplets.

"I'm sorry," Jac's voice was muffled against her chest. "I'm so, so sorry."

"I'm still pissed at you."

"With good reason. I hate that you were forced to display your grief like that, and it's my fault."

"It made them uncomfortable enough to let us go." Maryn horked back snot with a disgusted noise. "Nobody wants to deal with a hysterical old lady."

"Stop saying that. If you're old, so am I. I reject your reality."

"I do feel old. I feel like a fucking afterthought. To Dr. Globney and the university, even to you. Tell me the truth. Would you and Scylla have offered to take me to Xyri if it hadn't been a good excuse?"

"Of course we would have." Jac had the grace to not sound offended. "We argued about whether it was too dangerous to bring you this way. Scyll thought it was, but I held out. We never wanted anything we're involved in to put you and Col in danger. I didn't tell you everything from the start, and that was wrong. But I thought if you'd known ..."

"I would have talked myself out of space travel yet again. You know me too well. I hate you."

"You don't hate me," Jac murmured into her neck. "You love me."

"Always have, always will. But I'm still pissed as hell."

"But look at you. You aren't terrified. You rescued two survivors of a war crime in deep space without falling apart, and you just faced down a mercenary frigate with the power of fucking hormones." Jac brushed tears away from Maryn's cheek. "Old ladies don't do that. Well, maybe the hormone part, but not the rescue. Only bad asses."

"I guess I did." The realization spread through her like sunlight. She hadn't touched her meds at all since they left planetside—she hadn't even *thought* about them during the frantic scramble to retrieve the life pod. She'd leaped into action like young—

No, like Maryn would have.

But thinking about what happened sent a lance of ice through her heart. The destruction of the refugee ship was a war crime, only one in dozens if not hundreds of atrocities Viltrux and his soldiers had committed against the Kheqet hybrids. Families like Zeddi's and Dair's, whose futures had been ripped away due to unbridled violence fueled by ignorance, fear, and what was beginning to stink of greed.

Xyri's staunch neutrality couldn't stand, not with these horrors happening here and now. And Maryn, damn it all, was in the best position to plead their case.

CHAPTER
SIX

THEY MADE planetfall ninety minutes before the rites were scheduled.

Xyri loomed in the viewscreen, a palette of red granite mountains streaked with snow, lush forests painting swathes of green and deep purple across a horizon slashed by a shard of glinting sapphire ocean. The relief of reaching an oasis after the long, dark desert of space gave the muscles in her neck and shoulders a sudden, loose feeling, releasing the tension she'd held over the last six days.

Xyrian military ships waited in orbit and fell into formation around *Golden Girl* as she broke atmosphere. A precise, authoritative voice emerged over the comm system.

"Consort Maryn Alessi, this is Flight Leader Katalin. Welcome to Xyri. Have your ship follow us. You will land at the Magnus Primetri's private estate rather than the spaceport." She imagined she heard reproach in those words but was put at ease when ze continued in a warmer tone, "It is our honor to escort you and Primetri Andelek to zer ancestral home."

"Thank you, Flight Leader Katalin." A sob threatened to punctuate her response. Col squeezed her hand.

Maryn and the whole team had visited the estate before. They picked up Andelek there after ze had hired them as security for zer first intensive field study of the Shune Sector. She had campaigned for that contract via subspace communication, geeking out in an embarrassing display over the recent discovery of Shune's megafauna, which she'd been following because *dinosaurs!* Andelek told her later they got the job because she fascinated zem with her extensive amateur knowledge of Earth's prehistoric fauna. She'd only babbled on that way because the charming being on the other end of the call was already something of a celebrity, a dashing royal adventurer, and she was fangirling.

On their first mission, they'd fought off poachers and the swarm of huge bugs bent on sucking them dry. Between it all, Andelek started teaching her exobiology, an excuse to spend time together. And then they had discovered the calibotari. Andelek's recording drones captured it all on holovids, beamed out in serial form across the galaxy to a rapt audience of billions. The scientific community was still reeling over what the shared DNA connecting Earth's dinosaurs and the Shune sector's megafauna might mean.

Their escorts brought them in low over lush foothills behind the planet's largest city; the bulk of the metropolis lay hidden in plum-shaded foliage, only a few buildings visible above the canopy. The parliamentary arena where Andelek's remembrance ceremony would take place bloomed like a strange white flower among the leaves. Xyrians lived in harmony with the flora and fauna of their ecosystem, a lesson hard learned by past generations who had almost driven their home to the brink of unsustainability, like Earth had been. An alliance between humanity and their peaceful galactic neighbors provided them with the guidance to heal their own wounded planet. Earth was still recovering, and the serene beauty of clear skies and abundant plant life on Xyri proved it could be done.

The sprawling house belonging to the Magnus Primetri and his family was visible only in glimpses of windows and flashes of stone walls through the trees as Scylla landed the *Girl* on a fan-shaped private pad beside their state vessel. Maryn unstrapped as Scylla began to cycle down the engines and run through the landing checklist.

Through the windscreen, she caught sight of a group of beings standing outside a nearby ground vehicle, waiting for the engine wash to cool before they approached. Andelek's father Lekere stood at the front, his sapphire skin shining against white mourning robes. Everyone in the assembled party was wearing the same color.

"Oh, shit," Maryn said, stricken. "I forgot to pack anything white. I thought we'd make it here in time for me to find something in the city."

"Hang on. I got you, boo." Jac unstrapped and disappeared down the corridor at a jog. Maryn followed her and retrieved Andelek's urn from the space beneath her bunk. She set it on the table as Jac rummaged in a narrow storage cubby and removed a thin, hard-sided garment case. She unsnapped it to reveal a white tunic paired with flowing slacks in the same icy shade, and an ivory dress.

"Our wedding clothes. I think the suit will fit well enough. Scylla was thinner then. The pants should only be a little short on you."

Maryn stripped off her baggy sweater and cargo pants and slid into the borrowed outfit. The slacks drooped on her hips but their fullness made up for the inch of ankle showing. The tunic hid the loose waist and settled around her with only a hint of bagginess in the shoulders. It would do.

Jac unbraided Maryn's ponytail and ran a brush through her hair, then twisted it into a neat sable knot at the back of her neck, binding it with the stretchy band she'd removed from the original mess. She stepped back and surveyed Maryn with a critical eye. Her expression softened and she smiled.

"You look perfect."

"Thank you." She swallowed and picked up the urn. "I guess I'm ready."

Dair and Zeddi were peeking out from behind the curtains of the insulated bunk, interested in the whirlwind of making her presentable for a royal funeral.

"Wait here, please," Jac told them. "We have formalities to attend to."

Scylla was already at the door, extending the ramp. The scents of chlorophyll, earth, and water collided like a wave of life as Maryn took a deep, steadying breath. She descended with Andelek's urn cradled in her arms until her feet met solid ground, the pull of planetary gravity as heavy as her heart.

Lekere's dark eyes crinkled as she met his gaze. She hadn't been back to Xyri with Andelek since they took their consort vows, crippled by the ridiculous fear she'd allowed to direct her life for so long, but they had often spoken with her royal in-laws over subspace calls. Maryn adored them. Andelek's older and younger siblings stood behind their parents, three tall beings as beautiful as her mate had been. She did not know them as well, but they, too, had always treated her with affection.

Beside Lekere, his consort Nadele made a tiny gasp of pain as she caught sight of the burden Maryn carried. It was the sound of a mother realizing her child was truly gone, and Maryn's eyes overflowed again, unable to bear it.

"Magnus Primetri. High Consort." Her voice broke as she stumbled over the words, the damned tears tracking a hot course down her cheeks. "I've brought Andelek home. I'm so sorry."

Lekere stepped forward and placed his hand on the urn. His other arm enfolded her and drew her in. With Andelek held between them, she wept—controlled this time as she and her father-in-law sagged against each other in their mutual sorrow. His eyes were wet, too when he pulled back to look at her. The lacelike silver tattoos across his forehead glittered in pale sunlight, his long, black hair streaked with white.

"Maryn, my daughter by the love of Andelek. I know this was a difficult journey for you." He brushed the crest on the box of ashes with his cobalt fingertips. "Thank you for returning our child to the soil of zer natal planet."

Nadele deposited a soft kiss against Maryn's temple as she joined the small huddle and rested her trembling hand on the urn. For a moment the container of ashes was held between the three of them before Maryn relinquished the casket to Andelek's mother. She carried it to her surviving children, who surrounded her, supporting their mother, and touched the urn containing their sibling until it was encapsulated by loving hands.

Lekere looked over Maryn's shoulder and smiled. She turned to see her friends standing at attention at the bottom of the ramp, an honor guard for Andelek's return.

"I remember you. Jacqueline, Scylla, and Colterrikor, isn't it? Be at ease." They relaxed into parade rest. "Thank you for braving the Pashni to bring my child and zer consort home. We did not know things had deteriorated so badly until we received your message."

"There are things we have to tell you, Magnus Primetri," Jac murmured. "We have two Kheqet refugees on board we rescued from deep space in Konecthedot sector. It is the primary reason we were delayed."

"I hope you will meet with them tonight," Maryn said. "The story is not good. You need to hear it."

"Indeed?" Lekere's gaze sharpened a moment before he nodded. "They are safe here. We will share a casual meal later, and you are all welcome. I will send someone to guide you."

"We would be honored, Magnus Primetri." Col placed one furry hand over her heart.

Lekere drew Maryn toward the knot of family making entrance into their state vessel. "Come. We will fulfill the rites and then return Andelek to the soil. Zer death will sustain new life for our planet."

THE ROYAL FAMILY'S vehicle passed hundreds of somber Xyrians who knelt beside the route as they passed, an echo of the remembrance performed by the university students. Andelek had been well known for zer exciting life, and the people had followed their Primetri's adventures with as much fond indulgence as there had been real scientific interest among galactic academics. Maryn and

Andelek's love story had even been a subject of wistful romantic speculation for a while.

But for a Xyrian to die so young was nearly unheard of, and she suspected it was viewed as an unthinkable tragedy. On Earth, it would once have been a circus of media coverage and demands to capture the grieving family on camera for the consumption of prying, curious viewers. She was thankful Xyrians had no use for that kind of tawdry spectacle. Zer death was handled with the gravity it deserved.

Maryn's part in the ceremony was brief. As Andelek's consort, she carried the urn behind Lekere and Nadele but in front of zer siblings as they entered the building. The parliamentary chambers, a vast, circular room draped in mourning white, were filled with as many beings of political and academic importance as citizenry. Lekere took the urn from her and placed it upon a plinth at the center of the room. A hooded priest, his blue skin laced with the white tattoos of their planetary spiritual practice, took over then and the family was seated together in a small, private nave. Nadele held her hand and leaned her head against Maryn's as both wept in silence.

The priest spoke of Andelek's love and reverence for nature and the cycle of life, for the creatures that coexisted on their planet, and the beings and fauna with whom the Xyrians shared the galaxy. All were tangled in the vast roots of an ecosystem which could not be measured, and of which the Xyrians considered themselves a caretaker. Andelek had embodied that philosophy by discovering and teaching how all life throughout the universe was interlaced.

To her surprise, Maryn's part in the discovery was mentioned by the officiant. He painted her as a kindred spirit to Andelek who also recognized how all life was intertwined, and how their love for each other had been a symbolic representation of this philosophy.

She was touched, though her face heated as she reflected with a small smile through the tears. There was nothing metaphorical about how they'd fallen in lust, then mutual respect and friendship, and finally, deep love. Andelek, with zer longevity, had at first proceeded the manner of a Xyrian courtship, often decades long. Maryn, a warrior, knew life was short and hadn't hesitated to express what she wanted. Ze proceeded with more urgency after ze realized Maryn's life was fleeting by comparison.

Their relationship was far from perfect: Maryn was coarse at times, snagging against the silken etiquette Andelek had grown up with. Ze was often exasperated with her quick temper, especially when it came to university politics, and she hated it when ze would apologize to others for her behavior as if she were a child. That argument usually followed them home for a couple of days. But their common interests and love were as real as such things could be. They would eventually talk it out and making up with each other was almost worth the fight.

At last, the formal observation was over. They retrieved the urn and drove back to the estate.

"Will you continue to teach when you return?" Nadele and Maryn were arm in arm as the family walked beside a crystalline lake. A forest of stately trees stood where previous ancestors had returned to nourish the planet, silver-barked ghosts beneath the gloaming shift of red-blue leaves and white blossoms.

She winced. "There are … complications at the university." She thought about it a moment. "I don't know if I even want to, if Andelek isn't there."

"May I say something you might not wish to hear?" Nadele posed the question with soft hesitance. Maryn glanced at her, trepidation building in an uncomfortable knot behind her sternum.

"Of course."

"My child loved you so. But," she said, "ze never pushed you to face your fears or tempt you away from Echo Four. It was a gift of love, but one which may have had unintended consequences."

"I know." She swallowed hard against the guilt she'd been fighting for two weeks. "If Andelek hadn't settled on Echo Four with me, ze might still be alive."

"Oh, no. Not what I said, my darling. Ze would have lived only half a life without you beside zem." Nadele touched her head to Maryn's in comfort. "I meant, unintended consequences for you. Ze created a life where you would never have to make the choice to leave. It seemed to me Andelek held you back out of love because ze was afraid of losing you."

Stunned, Maryn thought about what she'd said. Echo Four was a safe place where she didn't have to face anything that terrified her, full of entertaining distractions and rich with resources. "I never thought I could gate jump again," she admitted. "Space isn't as comfortable as it was before the accident. But bringing zem home was important. It was bigger than my fear."

"Holding proof of my concerns," Nadele agreed. "When presented with the need, you overcame it without difficulty. I am afraid Andelek may have unintentionally kept you from healing out of zer desire to protect you."

"I let zem." Maryn pushed away a stray lock of hair which had escaped her bun to float in the gentle wind. "I didn't push myself either. I allowed the expectation of a trauma response to keep me away from spaceflight. And now?" She frowned, trying to find the words. "I'm appalled at what's happening on Qet. I feel called to do something, and I'm terrified. I'm so much older than I used to be. It seems strange to think I might still be useful."

"Older." Nadele laughed, a whispery, musical trill. "Oh, my dearest daughter of love. You are barely over half a century old. In our eyes, you are just beginning to live."

Andelek's remains were interred beneath the roots of a sapling in a private, familial observation of remembrance. White was not a practical color for digging and planting, but no one cared, streaked with grass and mud and tears, feet bare against the cool ground.

Maryn made a silent promise to have Scylla's wedding clothes professionally restored, kicked off her shoes, and dug alongside Andelek's siblings, scooping out handfuls of earth. It was a primal, satisfying thing to have soil under her fingernails and create her mate's final resting place with her bare hands, only the first cuts in the turf created with a small, sharp-bladed trowel. While they worked, zer siblings and parents shared stories of zer mischievous childhood that she had never heard before and set her laughing with them.

At last, they spread the gray pebbles of Andelek's ashes against the bottom of the grave and tenderly placed a silver-barked sapling's root ball on top of it. The network of tendrils searched through the dirt, wriggling, stretching as they found stable footing and dug themselves in. Maryn scattered the first handfuls of soil over the roots, and then all of them added more, patting it in to support the young tree as it stilled and settled into its new home. Nadele gave the new planting its first water, as she'd given her child zer first sustenance at birth.

They returned to the estate house, a rambling structure at the foot of the mountain. Its stone and wood construction fit seamlessly into the landscape, using as few artificial building materials as was practical. Most of the house was the same on the inside, natural materials and light sources wherever could be managed, but with the unobtrusive integration of required technology.

She and the family changed out of their funereal whites into comfortable, everyday clothing. The dirt-crusted clothes she'd borrowed from Scylla were taken to be cleaned with the family's robes and she was loaned a floaty, sand-colored gown to wear which must have belonged to Nadele, more transparent than Maryn might have worn but more than acceptable by Xyrian standards. She was glad she hadn't removed her tank top and boxer briefs during the quick-change onboard *Golden Girl*.

They gathered in an open-air dining alcove, the long, recessed table crowded with a delicious spread of fresh-picked fruits, warm vegetable dishes, bread, and cold salads. Jac, Scylla and Col were already there, seated beside Dair and Zeddi on the cushions. They stood when Lekere and his family entered the room. Nadele greeted Maryn's friends with affectionate embraces and then turned to the Kheqet pair, her eyes filled with compassion.

Jac introduced the younger beings. "Magnus Primetri, High Consort, this is Argowin Dair, and Palinoko Zeddi."

"Welcome to Xyri, and to our home," Nadele said. "May it be a refuge of peace."

"I apologize for intruding on your family at such a difficult time." Dair bowed their head, but they were almost quivering with pent-up desperation to get to the matter at hand.

"Our daughter tells us it is a grave situation. Under the circumstances, I cannot imagine not hearing you out." Lekere turned his gentle smile on the child. "And who is this young one?"

"I'm Zeddi!" he announced. "I'm four cycles old. I have a sister who was just born. Her name is Rinana."

Nadele glanced at Maryn, who shook her head in sorrow. Dair swallowed hard as their gaze carved away and down. The High Consort understood and held out her hand to the boy.

"It is so very good to meet you. Shall we sit and have some lunch?"

Lekere and his family were enchanted by Zeddi. The child was soon chattering away with their youngest daughter, who was born a few months before Maryn and Andelek entered their consort bond. Melika was still considered an adolescent and was not yet tattooed with the royal family's emblems.

Col sat beside Zeddi, having warmed to him in a way that made Maryn stifle a grin as she exchanged a mirthful glance with Jac. For someone who'd decried children as 'damp, mewling things', Col was becoming as doting as any grandparent might have been and fed the kid the best tidbits from her own plate.

Each dish had a significance to the family or to Andelek. Maryn had known ze loved *sheli*, clusters of bright yellow, grape-like fruit which tasted of creamy lemon. The family grew them on the estate. Radek, during the planting of the new tree, had told a story of when he and Andelek were young, how they had lain under the shady vines and eaten sun-warmed fruit until they were sick.

The casserole she nicknamed Xyrian quiche, Andelek's favorite comfort meal, was a heavy, delicious combination of cheese, colorful vegetables, and eggs. Maryn had learned to make a passable version with local varieties available on Echo Four, but the subtleties of nonavian eggs, and native squashes and root vegetables gave it a different flavor.

Zer middle sibling, Kanaran, was genderless, as Andelek had been. Ze played peekaboo across the table with Zeddi and distracted him while the others discussed the terrible event in Konecthedot sector after the meal. When Dair told him of the star liner's destruction, a horrified silence fell over the group as Scylla flicked up the holographic records from her PDD. The graphic images of debris and bodies revolved in the air above the device.

Lekere and Nadele's son, Radek, was eldest and the presumptive heir to Magnus Primetri, the hereditary head of an otherwise parliamentary government. He was a great deal like his father: brilliant and possessed of a fierce desire to protect their planet, but he lacked some of the playfulness his parents and other siblings displayed, perhaps out of self-perception of what a leader should be.

"We received word the refugee ship did not arrive as expected." Radek's generous mouth was clamped in a tight line. "We assumed they were forced to take another route to avoid the front."

"The Pashni is the front, now," Scylla told him. "It's patrolled by a frigate called *Raging Fire*. They stopped us and threatened to board, but the fact we were carrying Primetri Andelek's remains and the Dowager Consort saved our asses. I mean our butts." She flushed red and amended, "Saved us. Sir."

"*Raging Fire* may have taken prisoners before they destroyed the transport." Dair's voice strained against despair. "Their log would have the coordinates of our camp in the mountains. There's a final evacuation planned in a few days when conditions will be favorable enough for us to get another ship in and out of the northern hemisphere and the last of the refugees to safety here on Xyri. I have to go back and warn them."

"They are actively hunting them." Kanaran breathed, zer stricken gaze following Zeddi as he climbed into Col's lap. "Father, we cannot continue to remain neutral in this conflict. Our defense ships must accompany the refugees."

"The parliament fears that by sending fighters, we will invite the war into this sector," Lekere said in a tired voice. Maryn had the impression they had discussed it many times, and the sinking weight of hope lodged in her throat.

Beside him, Radek agreed. "Not only that, but if our fleet is compelled to fire upon Qetish ships to protect the transports, we are taking sides in a civil dispute against galactic laws."

"With all due respect, we are beginning to suspect this is not a civil war," Maryn interrupted.

"Please explain." Lekere regarded her with a troubled expression. Maryn nodded at Scylla, who flicked up a blurry holo image of the frigate that had detained them.

"Sorry for the poor quality, but we had to be sneaky about it," the pilot said.

"The *Raging Fire* has no Qetish markings. No identifiers," Maryn pointed out. "Dair tells us the military equipment and soldiers Viltrux commands also bear no insignia of any kind. Their ships are well maintained and up to date, which says money. If they were pirates, the ships would be barely spaceworthy and garishly painted. We've seen this kind of thing before in the Artemis Corps. We believe these are corporate mercenaries and not Qetish citizens."

"Do you have proof of this?" Lekere's gaze flickered between the humans and Col.

"I work for the largest bank in the galaxy, Primetri," the Boshi told him. "I have just begun auditing the data which I hope will show suspicious financial activity in Qetish colonial accounts linked to corporate money laundering or bribes to Viltrux and his faction."

"So there is no evidence at this time," Radek clarified.

"Not yet. But this is what we used to do, sir," Scylla was in earnest, her weathered face as serious as Maryn had ever seen it. "We've seen pirates and small mercenary outfits, and that's not what this is. I feel it in my gut."

"We cannot risk violating our neutrality on feelings alone," Radek began, not unkindly, but Dair gave a guttural cry of frustration.

Everyone looked to them as their fist crashed against the table, and Zeddi jumped, a startled whimper escaping the child's lips. He cowered in Col's lap, her arms going around him in comfort and she purred a soothing, low note as he buried his face in her fur.

"The time for neutrality has passed!" Dair drew themself to attention under the somber eyes of Lekere. "They destroyed an unarmed transport ship full of refugees and murdered my crew and passengers because we witnessed their crime. It was only because of Jac and Scylla ..." Dair's gaze rested on Maryn and they amended in afterthought, "and the Dowager Consort that Zeddi and I escaped the same fate. They are murdering my people. My family is dead! What more needs to happen for you to get involved?"

Radek began to answer, but Lekere raised his hand. His son settled back and let his father speak.

"Other worlds have always looked to us for a haven, or to foster unbiased negotiation." The Magnus Primetri rubbed his forehead, his fingers tracing the silver lines in his skin. "Truly, no other recent conflict has been so barbaric as this. Perhaps it is time to alter our stance. But it is a question for our people, not one I can make on my own. Too much is at stake. We will release a galactic statement condemning the destruction of the refugee ship and call parliament to assemble for an emergency vote."

Politics. Maryn's optimism guttered and went out.

"How long will that take?" Dair demanded. "Weeks? Another month before the debate and arguing is done? We're bringing in a transport to evacuate the last colonists in only a few days. I thought you were their monarch."

"I am sorry." Lekere regarded them with sorrow. "I may be the planet's leader, but my position is built on the trust of my people that I will listen to what they have to say. To do anything else would make me as much a tyrant as Viltrux. We have been down that path before. It did not end well."

Dair closed their eyes, despair written in the lines of their face. "I have to return to Qet. My people need me. And we need help."

"We will leave as soon as we're able," Jac assured them, and turned to Lekere. "We've been working with Dair and the resistance to transport weapons and supplies to the freedom fighters and ferry out as many Kheqet colonists as we could at the beginning, but ours is a small ship. We can't possibly carry enough people out to make a difference. There's only two of us."

"Three." Col looked up from where she cuddled a sleepy Zeddi against her chest, his fingers winding in her silky fur.

"Four," Maryn added and blinked in surprise. She exchanged a glance with Jac, whose expression glowed with approval.

"It occurs to me, should we wish to do so, we do not need the parliament's permission to privately fund an independent contractor to escort the refugee ship." Nadele's eyes, wide and innocent, turned to her daughter-in-law. Maryn cocked her head, not daring to let the spark of hope flare yet, but her admiration for Nadele began to shine and prepare a place for it to rekindle.

"Mother!" Radek scolded, but Lekere raised a hand to stop his protest, his eyes glinting with grave mischief at his mate.

"Wait, my son. There is precedent. After all, Andelek hired a certain privateer company to protect zem in zer endeavors," Lekere mused, his gaze locked with Nadele's. "Of course, we must do it anonymously."

"Of course," Nadele murmured.

"You cannot be serious." Radek's looked between both parents in disbelief, then to Maryn, pleading, "Sister, would Andelek want you to put yourself in danger?"

With a faint smile, Maryn said, "I think you know the answer to that. Andelek wouldn't let innocent beings of any species suffer if ze could help."

Radek sat back, his brow furrowed. His gaze didn't leave Maryn's until he nodded, and sighed, "You are correct."

"There would be a risk." Jac tapped her fingers on the table, considering the offer. "If we were detained, your involvement might be suspected." She glanced at Maryn. "*Raging Fire* knows who she is."

"Then you'd best not be captured," Lekere said with dark humor. "Tell us what you need in order to escort the ships."

Triumph swept Maryn in an unexpected rush, and Dair's eyes widened in cautious relief.

Scylla grinned at her wife, and then at Maryn and Col. "To provide cover against a frigate?" She rubbed her hands together with anticipation. "We should talk about things that go *boom*."

"What about Zeddi?" Col stroked the drowsy child's hair with her massive hand. Nadele smiled at her.

"He is welcome to stay with us while we search for his family among the refugees already here."

Maryn realized belatedly that she was a privateer again.

EVENTS HAPPENED after dinner with dizzying speed. Scylla's shopping list of 'things that go boom' could not be filled on Xyri without undue questions from the planetary militia, but Lekere established a generous (and anonymous) galactic credit line for them, keyed to Maryn's biometrics, which would take care of their expenses. Jac assured her she and Scylla had a long-standing relationship with a supplier who could obtain what they needed, no questions asked.

Dair had connections in the resistance and the government in exile. A flood of outraged messages came back to *Golden Girl* in response to Dair's communique regarding the destruction of the refugee transport, but containing equal relief Dair was safe and sound after the attack on their own ship. Maryn suspected they were a bit more important to the movement than she'd initially believed.

Dawn painted the sky with broad strokes of citrine and pearl when Scylla started her pre-flight checks. Maryn found herself drawn back to the mirror surface of the lake and the mist-veiled grove of trees. She sat beside the sapling and rested her hand on the mound below the slender trunk. It shivered under her touch as its roots settled deeper into the earth.

"I know you're out there, somewhere." She gazed at the still-dark horizon opposite the paling skyline, a scattering of bright stars still visible against the encroaching sunrise. "I've been thinking about what your mother said. That you protected me because you were afraid of losing me. We always knew how short my life might be compared to yours, but neither of us suspected this. I wasn't prepared. It was the only thing you couldn't protect me from."

She exhaled a laughing sob which crumbled into uneven pieces, her eyes wet. "But I think I'm going to be okay. I don't want to be safe when there are people who aren't, people I might be able to help. I have to try. I think you would understand. You always believed in me even if I didn't when it came to academics. Now I have to remember how to believe in the person I used to be. Jac's right—she was pretty badass. I think she's still around."

Maryn sniffled and wiped her eyes before she climbed to her feet, working out the stiffness in her legs. She touched one of the delicate branches, smooth bark beneath her fingertips. "Until we meet again, love. I'll visit your tree the next time I'm in the neighborhood and see how much we've both grown."

CHAPTER
SEVEN

MARYN'S EYES were open when they left the atmosphere, though she pointedly did not watch the jewel-toned morning get smothered back to sleep by thick, star-splattered darkness as they breached the edge of space. Instead, she studied sector maps on a PDD to re-familiarize herself with the star lanes between Xyri, the Pashni wormhole, and Qet.

"What's the plan if *Raging Fire* is still waiting outside the Pashni?" she asked as they ate breakfast around the table, a meal supplemented by fresh supplies from Xyri and still-warm pastries Nadele had given Maryn as they said goodbye. The flaky crust nestled a cheesecake-like filling, sweet and dense, topped with lime-bright berries.

"We jump to FTL as soon as we're clear of the distortion effect," Scylla answered with confidence. "They'll barely know we're there before we hit it."

"Your ship is distinctive." Dair frowned, picking at their pastry. "They're going to recognize us."

"That's what happens when you're as pretty as me," the ship said. Maryn smiled despite her misgivings.

"Damn straight," Scylla agreed. "We aren't gonna wait around to see if they ask us to dance, Dair. It'll be fine."

The pilot didn't appear worried, but Maryn shivered when she thought about racing out of the aperture like that. It wasn't the same as speeding out of a high traffic jump gate, but without re-checking their immediate flight path, a hasty acceleration still held increased risk for collision with another ship in the star lane, or an asteroid drifting through the sector.

"After we visit our friend, we set course for Qet and go through the back door," Scylla continued, talking through her flight plan.

"The back door?" Col inquired.

"It's an old jump gate the resistance put into play." Jac looked up from her yogurt. "You can't find the receiving end without an invitation and coordinates. It terminates inside the planet's ring system."

Maryn's almost-quiescent anxiety woke with a startled yelp. "Oh, it fucking does not."

"Yes." Dair frowned at her. "It has a fixed location on one of the large bodies in the outer disc. The moonlet's orbit brings it over the northern hemisphere every eight days. Small ships like this are almost undetectable and read like debris or meteorite activity. We use it for arms and supply shipments. We have no alternative. It's the only way to avoid detection by Qetish planetary radar."

Maryn stared at them in disbelief for how anyone could think a jump gate in the fucking middle of a planetary ring full of obstacles was a good idea, until Jac nudged Maryn's arm and mouthed, "Breathe."

She inhaled and exhaled in measured increments, counting down. "Right. What kind of weapons do you have in the locker, and what is in those crates?" She turned her mind to preparations.

"We've got four Sivad guns and half a dozen sidearms of various origin," Scylla said. "The crates contain three pulse rifles and ammunition. We were supposed to receive twelve cases, but our contact was going to be compromised if he transferred more. Here's the wish list Dair and I came up with."

She pulled up a document on the holo table. It was enough weaponry to arm a platoon, which was reasonable, but Maryn's eyes widened at some of the other items. "An RPG?"

The pilot shrugged. "I'm out of grenades."

"How often do you need grenades while running cargo?" Col's eyes narrowed.

Scylla grinned. "You'd be surprised. Besides, you know they're fun."

"Conceded." The Boshi's sharp teeth flashed as she grinned back.

"Planning a ground assault, are we?" Maryn was certain that hadn't been mentioned in the same conversation as escorting a refugee ship to Xyri.

"The transport will land and dust off on a very short timetable, about four minutes. If our location has been compromised, we'll need the means to cover them on the ground as well as in flight." Dair made a harsh sound deep in their throat and regarded Maryn with hard eyes. "Are you sure you're up to this?"

Maryn's face grew hot with annoyance, but she bit off her reflexive reply and stared at the younger being with narrowed eyes. It was a valid question, she decided, though Dair was testing the limits of her patience.

"She has more battle experience than you," Scylla bristled, but Maryn held up her hand.

"No, they're entitled to an answer. I haven't been running drills and combat simulations for the past twenty years." She met Dair's gaze. "I understand your reluctance. You haven't seen me at my best in the last couple of days. I know I'm rusty. But believe me, if I didn't think I could contribute something I would have stayed on Xyri, so give me a fucking break."

Dair stiffened, their eyes smoldering. "We're talking about the lives of more than two hundred refugees. I think Jac and Scylla can handle it, but I don't know you."

"You have yet to question my assistance," Col remarked, one fang visible beneath her curled lip. "Is it on my teeth alone you have decided I am a worthy ally, and Maryn is not? I'm a fucking accountant! A damn good one, too. I have been out of active combat as long as she, and I am five years older." She sniffed, offended, and examined her polished pink claws. "Humanoids always think I'm a wild animal because of my appearance. It's hurtful."

"I ..." Dair ran both hands through their hair, clutching the sides of their head with a harsh sigh. "That doesn't make me feel any better about my own judgment. I'm already questioning every decision I've made in the last week."

"Of course you are. You lost your entire crew and three refugees, and you haven't had time to process it." Jac leaned forward. "You're exhausted. I know you haven't slept more than a couple of hours since we found you. Tired is stupid. You need to get some rest."

"Besides, your list of allies is pretty fucking scarce. Maryn got you a personal audience with the Magnus Primetri that might change the direction of this war. A little gratitude might be nice," Scylla snapped at Dair and concluded in a rising voice, "Accept the help we're offering, go take a nap, and stop being an asshole. You're on my ship, so that's an order!"

The younger being's face flushed to a ruddy orange from anger or embarrassment; Maryn wasn't able to tell which. Dair swung their legs over the bench and stalked off to their sleeping cubicle, slamming the partition closed behind them. The hum of the privacy barrier tickled Maryn's eardrums a second later.

"You good, Scyll?" Jac regarded her wife with weighted concern in her eyes. "That was harsh."

"They pissed me off." Scylla shoved away the crumbs of her breakfast and stood. "I'm going to double check calculations for the gate jump." She stomped down the corridor. Heavy metal blasted from the dark cockpit a moment later.

"Wow. That's her angry music." Maryn cocked her head. "Is she okay? Menopause got her too?"

"Not quite." Jac began to collect the empty food containers and put a lid on Dair's unfinished breakfast. She glanced up briefly, such profound sadness in her eyes that a wave of foreboding crested in Maryn's chest. "We aren't the only ones starting to feel our age. Scyll's having a rough time of it and Dair's not helping. Go talk to her, Mar. I'll finish here."

"I will assist." Col cupped the stack of dishes in her enormous hands and passed them through the partition to Jac. Maryn stood, then, as an afterthought, tapped at the screen.

"As long as Lekere is footing the bill, we should add battle armor. If we're going in for a ground assault, we're going in with our asses covered."

"Affirmative." The *Girl* added the items to the list.

Maryn padded up to the cockpit. It was illuminated only by *Girl's* amber eye and the glow of Scylla's PDD, the pilot's expression storm-lit and thunderous. She slid into the copilot's seat, wincing at the volume in the small area.

"Is Dair worth the Screaming Dolphins' greatest hits?" She raised her voice to be heard over the crash of drums, bass, and guitars and the cetacean lead vocalist.

Scylla snorted. "They think they know everything. They can't be twenty-five cycles old."

"Now who's being ageist?" Maryn raised an eyebrow at her. "We thought we knew everything back then, too."

"At twenty-five, we already lived through four years of our mercenary tours." She stabbed her finger against the PDD where she calculated the jump. "We weren't kids anymore."

"Neither is Dair, no matter how much of a pain in the ass they are." Maryn's lips curved in a sad smile. "*Girl*, will you turn down the music so we can talk?"

"No problem," the ship responded. "The shrill squeaking makes my circuits feel weird." The volume decreased to a more tolerable level.

Scylla stared at Maryn before she exhaled in a harsh puff of air and tossed the data device on the console. "You're right. Dair's not a kid. They've taken on a huge responsibility and they're doing pretty goddamn well for someone who lost their entire family in a purge. I can't fathom what headspace they're in. I just hate getting reminded we're not young anymore. My body does that every damn day. My knees hurt. My right shoulder doesn't move in certain directions after that shrapnel I took on Sokanit and it hurts like a motherfucker if I don't take anti-inflammatories."

"I hear you. The knees are a bitch. All those hikes in powered armor carrying an energy pack on our backs took their toll. But I don't feel any different in my head," Maryn confessed. "I know I'm chronologically fifty-four, but I thought there'd be some kind of … I don't know. Some kind of level up where I feel wiser or gain more gravitas. All I have is less patience for stupidity and an increased number of bathroom trips."

"I know, right? Whoever sold us on that fairytale oughta be court martialed," Scylla grumped.

"You've seemed a little more emotional than your usual self. Everything okay?"

The pilot looked down in her lap and picked at the cuticle of her thumbnail. "Did Jac talk to you about me yet?"

Maryn's gut twisted at the note in Scylla's voice. "About you? No." Her friend nodded and didn't look up. Sudden fear ran a cold finger down the back of her neck. "What is it?"

"I didn't want to bother you with it so soon after losing Andelek, but you're already noticing stuff. It's getting harder to hide. My last physical examination turned up issues. They said there's degeneration in my brain, what they call 'spacer's rot' in the pilot's guild. Probably early dementia brought on by repeated exposure to cosmic radiation."

"Oh. Oh, Scyll." Maryn couldn't even think. A black hole opened in front of her and she fought the pull of despair. Not Scylla. She couldn't lose her too.

"Right now, it's only manifesting as emotional outbursts, memory glitches, and confusion. Worse some days than others, but I take drugs to help with that. After a while, they won't work anymore. But the neurological symptoms are already making my reflexes slower."

Scylla glanced up at the pale, glowing eye watching over them. "It's one of the reasons we upgraded the *Girl*. She can practically fly herself without me in case I start to forget important things like raising the shields or initiating life support systems. She did more of the flying than I did when we picked up Dair."

"I have your back, Captain," *Girl* said, and Maryn was certain she heard affection in the ship's artificial voice.

"Oh, Scylla." Her voice failed her, lips icy with shock. She struggled for words. "Does Col know?"

"Jac told her before we left."

Maryn's sorrow and denial built into an explosion of anger. "Fuck!" She slammed her fist into the arm of the jump seat. "It's not fair."

"Maybe not, but I'll play the cards I got dealt. I wouldn't trade one minute of my life." She hesitated, and amended, "Well, maybe a few of them we spent on Gol Paneda, but—" Scylla smirked at Maryn's wobbly laugh. "I have the finest woman in the galaxy for a wife, a daughter who's smarter than both of us, the two best friends anyone could ever have, and the greatest ship ever built."

"Damn right," *Girl* said.

"I've been blessed by the stars. Can't ask for much more." Scylla glanced at the shielded windscreen. "Maya and her gene dads are trying to talk us into retiring. They want to take care of me, but I refuse to sit around and let my brain run out my ears. I was born in space, and it's where I'll die. Jac promised I'll meet my maker out here on my own terms when the time comes. Make sure you hold her to it."

"I will." The promise burned in her throat. "It'd better not be anytime soon. I don't think I could handle it right now, not that you have any say in the matter."

"I still have time. Doctors predict five years unless they come up with a miracle cure to arrest the degeneration. They can do a lot of stuff, but they still can't repair long term radiation damage." Scylla reached for Maryn's hand. "I'm okay, Mar. It'll be a while yet before things get gnarly. Jac and I have it set up and she knows when I want her to pull the plug if I can't make the decision on my own. Until then I'll be out here, doing what I love." She put her other hand over Maryn's and gripped it tight between hers before she withdrew. "I'm so fucking glad you're with us right now."

"Just like old times," she said, but couldn't suppress the uncertainty in her voice.

"Well, now with more meds," Scylla deadpanned, throwing up jazz hands, and Maryn snorted with agreement. The pilot's teeth flashed white in the dim, citrine light. "You doing better?"

"Staying busy. Like I told Nadele, this is bigger than me. I can't go back to Echo Four with its sanitized media and pretend nothing's happening. I've seen it with my own eyes." She set her jaw. "The rest of the galaxy needs to fucking wake up and take notice."

"That's the Maryn I know and love." Scylla picked up her PDD and turned back to the jump calculations. "Don't you dare start treating me any different. I'll kick your ass off my ship at the next port."

WITH DAIR HIDDEN in the insulated bunk, Maryn and Col took their places in the cockpit with Scylla and Jac as they approached the end of the Pashni. Tension wound Maryn's shoulders into knots as the *Girl* throttled back their momentum and opened the shields. The distortion effect of the passage was clearing enough to see stars and black space on the other side, but she knew the ship's sensors would be unable to pick up anything until they were outside the wormhole.

The physical discomfort of transition hit them, and as it subsided, the viewscreen looked out on hell.

"Shields to maximum! Evasive maneuvers!" Scylla yelled as a corsair fighter streaked past the nose of the ship. Maryn was thrown hard against the straps of her seat as *Golden Girl* careened starboard.

They'd emerged into an active battle.

Snub-nosed Khepran ships harried unmanned fighters with missiles and streaks of argent energy blossomed from their cannons.

Drone sentries lined the corridor in front of the wormhole, weapons firing outward toward the violent encounters between the robotic fighters and the Khepran ships.

Raging Fire lay at the end of the deadly hellmouth, waiting like a predator for anything emerging from the aperture.

"Shit! Khepra's trying to break through!" Scylla shouted.

The closest drone gun swiveled toward the *Girl*.

The ship rocked with the blast against its forward shields. Robotic sentries turned in succession to target the perceived threat coming out of the wormhole. Maryn's heart pounded, her palms damp with sweat as the ship lurched with each new assault. They couldn't hold up for long, but on either side of the corridor the battle between the anonymous fleet and Khepran fighters raged in conflagration for control of the Pashni.

"Maryn! Col! Take out the drones!" Jac shouted. Maryn obeyed without thinking. She pressed the release on her jump seat and swiveled the chair to face the port gun controls. The console in front of her flared to life, a u-shaped handle emerging from the bulkhead. Crosshairs formed over the globe on the heads-up display as her hands gripped the familiar handles of the weapons arm. Her thumb pressed the firing mechanism and held it down as Scylla swept the ship through a gauntlet of unfriendly fire.

Energy beams from the *Girl's* ventral cannons seared metal and Maryn witnessed the white-hot fire of her energy cannon pass through the engine of an unmanned fighter chasing a piloted Khepran craft on the other side of the deadly corridor. The ship spun away and exploded into shards of metal as its Khepran opponent streaked away unharmed.

"Shit!" She'd joined the battle raging outside the corridor, and it would draw so much more unwanted attention. "I just took out one of the unmanned ships and picked a side. We need to get out of here now!"

"Thirty seconds until FTL jump," the ship replied. "The frigate is in our way."

"Everybody hold on." Scylla dodged a chunk of debris.

The *Girl* advised with a hint of urgency, "There's a stupid fighter on our tail. They must have seen what Maryn did."

"It was an accident!" she howled.

"They don't appear to care, Maryn!" The pilot rolled the ship in an ascending spin.

"They're still following us," Col reported.

"We're going to have to make a statement," Jac said as the frigate loomed in the windscreen.

"Got a choice one in mind." Scylla punched it. "This is gonna happen fast. *Girl*, be ready to make the course correction as soon as we're on them. All shields to forward."

"A collision course?" Maryn yelped.

"Trust me! Now shut up, I have to concentrate. Count it down, *Girl*."

"FTL jump in five … four …"

"Their targeting system's locked on," Col said as metal shutters began to close over the viewport.

"I got it!" Scylla snapped.

"Three," *Girl* said at the same time. "Two."

"Missiles fired," Col shouted. Maryn's heart lurched in her chest as the frigate's port side filled the narrowing view in the cockpit. Energy weapons burst against their forward shields, and missiles streaked toward the *Girl's* metaphorically bare ass.

"One!" Scylla's muscular arms shoved the yoke forward and dove beneath the *Raging Fire's* hull, passing so close Maryn swore she could make out rivets in the blur of its shining black skin before the protective panels rolled closed over the viewscreen.

An explosion, then another rocked the ship. A sharp spin to starboard made Maryn close her eyes in expectation of being ejected to drown in the frigid, airless sea of space, and feeling strangely calm about it.

"Course corrected. Making jump to FTL." *Girl's* crisp artificial voice said, and the air was stolen from Maryn's lungs as their velocity increased without the usual care in acceleration, slamming them all back into the padding of their seats. "We are clear of the battle."

"Holy fuck, dear," Jac wheezed. "That was some statement."

"Ha. Still got it," Scylla clutched her chest. "Great job, *Girl*. Any damage?"

"Nothing major, Captain. The explosions were the fighter's missile impacting their hull, followed by the fighter itself."

"Did we blow them up?" Col inquired.

"We aren't that lucky," Jac said. "It could be bad if they are corporate and report back."

Dair's voice came over the com. "What the fuck was that?"

"Only a little skirmish," Scylla said. "We tried to blow up the *Raging Fire*."

"And Maryn committed an act of war against them, so there's that," Col added sweetly.

"It. Was. An. Accident," she repeated through gritted teeth.

Silence, then: "You engaged the *Raging Fire*?" Dair's words dropped out one by one, as if they weren't sure what they'd heard.

"Well, yes, but." She drew out the words in a sigh. "I also might have shot down an unmanned fighter."

"Couldn't be helped. We got spit out right into the middle of a battle for the Pashni," Jac informed Dair, and then asked: "Do we know who was winning?"

"I estimate the number of Khepran ships matched the unmanned fighters. I would need more data to extrapolate a potential outcome," the *Girl* replied. "But we may have influenced the outcome in favor of the Kheprans."

Scylla glanced up at the ship's interface. "ETA at Anubis?"

"Twenty hours, six minutes."

"All right. Let's pin down our wish list and send it to my contact." The pilot rubbed her hands together in anticipation. "I want that rocket powered grenade launcher."

"Wait a minute." Maryn leaned forward, her mouth opening and closing in disbelief before she found the words. "Did you say Anubis? As in Bee Arturio?"

"Um. Yes. Yes, I did." Scylla's lips pressed together. She didn't meet Maryn's gaze.

"The last time I knew, Bee still wanted to kill you," she accused.

Jac made a see-saw motion. "They worked things out. Sort of."

"Does that mean she's forgiven you for leaving her on Peloon?" Col's furry eyebrows lifted.

"Yeah, no. Don't mention Peloon," Scylla shook her head.

"Great," Maryn breathed. "Just great."

CHAPTER
EIGHT

ANUBIS WAS a rough place in Maryn's smooth memories of their privateer days. It was a desert planet on the surface, but generous underground water reserves ran beneath the rocky crust, the surface aquifers controlled by rival gangs. The outpost settlement where Bee Arturio trafficked weapons remained unaffiliated with more civilized systems, free of pesky trade laws, sanctions, and corporate interference. One could buy anything there if they had the credits. The anonymous account set up by her royal in-laws would give them carte blanche in the stalls of the open market, and credibility in the less public areas where the real business happened.

"She still in the same place?" Maryn asked Jac, her voice muffled by the cowl protecting her mouth and nose from the grit blowing across the arid landscape. The *Girl* and a dozen other ships huddled on a rocky apron behind a sail-like outcrop of rocks near the water filling stations. The grimy little town that had sprung up around the market was veiled by the dust storm. She adjusted the goggles to fit over her eyes and could just make out the sharp edges of structures half a kilometer away.

"Bee's come up in the world a little since you were last here." Jac glanced at her, hazel eyes bright under her own goggles. "She's not in a stall anymore. She has her own saloon with the real stuff set up in the back."

"Huh." She'd never liked Beatrice Arturio, and dealing with her was not in her top one hundred's list of a good time, even when they were in the Corps together. She would have preferred to stay on board with Scylla and Dair, but Lekere had registered her biometrics alone for transactions on the new credit line. Short of cutting off her thumb and putting it in stasis, her presence was required—though Jac might impress Bee if she pulled a severed thumb out of her pocket to make the transaction.

Her head ached from the braid securing her hair close to her scalp instead of her normal messy bun, and her fingers kept brushing the sidearm strapped to her thigh. She'd borrowed a flak vest and leather jacket from Scylla for this outing. Her cardigan wouldn't provide any sort of protection against blades in the rough lanes of the black market; besides, what few clothes she'd brought with her from Echo Four were hardly mercenary in style unless she were a rogue librarian dealing in rare, expensive book trafficking. Appearance counted for a lot in mercenary circles. If she looked like someone's auntie toting an energy pistol, they'd just laugh before they shot her.

Their small group wore their weapons openly and bypassed all the forward-facing displays of avarice protected by canvas-shrouded awnings and hard-sided tents. The town was bigger than she remembered, a grid of streets spreading out from a water tower in the epicenter. Sandwiched between Jac and Col, Maryn glanced at the wares offered in the street. Nothing much had changed. Drugs. Small weapons trade. Some very shapely blades caught her eye. She paused for a second to stare in covetous interest before Col prodded her to follow their friend and they headed for the darker alleyways and crannies.

Their way cleared without much trouble, not due to steely-eyed Jac, who barged ahead with a purposeful stride, but because of Col. The Boshi wore her body language as armor, her fangs and narrowed eyes lost behind her own cowl as she brought up the rear like a towering, furry bodyguard. Jac made a straight line for one of the doors in a cramped alleyway guarded by hatchet-faced mercenaries in battle gear.

"What do you want, Grandma?" One of them sneered behind an acrylic face shield as his gaze lingered on them with dismissive impatience. "The bar entrance is one street over."

"I'm not here for fucking knitting club." Jac took a step closer, stared up into the young being's eyes, and said in a frigid voice, "Why do you think I'm here, you little shit? I sent your boss a message. She's expecting us."

"And don't let Bee catch you calling her Grandma." Col loomed over the guard and pulled down her face covering to reveal her snarling teeth. "She's older than we are."

The guard blinked first and gulped. "Yes, ma'am. Sorry. Orders are that all business goes through the front now. One block that way. Second building on your left."

Jac favored him with a scalding glance before she turned and they made their way out to the dusty street, the wind buffeting canvas awnings with crisp whipcracks the closer they got to the corner.

"Not a problem, is it?" Maryn asked in a low voice.

"No. Her bar's not one of the worst places here, but it's still plenty rough enough." Jac turned the corner of the street, lined with several buildings on either side. Maryn noted couple of brothels and half a dozen bars, most with clusters of hovercycles or short-range transport pods parked in front.

They headed for the building the guard had indicated. It was a two-story building, and Maryn had a sense of déjà vu. Its planked sidewalk and balconied upstairs recalled something out of Earth's Old West, down to the loitering crowd of glowering human mercenaries and other unidentified beings whose faces were hidden in deep, shadowed hoods. She ignored the glances of malevolent curiosity as Jac threaded them through the bodies and into the establishment.

Maryn pulled down her cowl to take in a lungful of air: cool, filtered, and delicious. She moved her goggles up to the top of her head. Col pulled her hood off and shook the dust out of her furry ears, a plume extending from the rapid motion of her head.

Bright, musical siren calls of gambling machines and loud voices bludgeoned her ears after the relative white noise of wind outside. The bar's tables were full of the same kind of crowd gathered outside on the sidewalk. Synthetic alcohol was dispensed by robotic bartenders rolling along a track atop an actual, polished wooden bar. The real stuff was locked up in full display behind the counter and retrieved when an order was made by a singular human attendant wearing an old fashioned, ruby-hued brocade vest over a white, long-sleeved shirt with a black garter on his left bicep.

The saloon's theme didn't end there. An ornate stairway at the back led up to the second-floor balcony, the AI-manned podium at the balustrade marked by a rotating hologram with a stylized, spinning red umbrella: the galactic union symbol for professional sex workers. Some inebriated humanoid tried to make a break for the stairs without interacting with the holographic concierge and was felled by the buzzing arc of the electrified force field which protected the landing. He fell in a smoking heap to the floor and two tablehops dragged him into an alcove behind the stairs.

"Nice." Maryn watched the scene with approval. "Bee supports the union."

"She's still got her standards," Jac agreed.

"How do we contact her?" Col took in their surroundings.

"Let's start with the bartender." Jac nodded at the human, who couldn't have been much older than Dair. They shoved their way through to a space at the wooden counter and waited until the garnet-vested bartender caught sight of them and made his way down.

"Afternoon. Welcome to Miss Bee's," he said. "How may I help you?"

"We have an appointment. The name's Merrow."

"Ah." His eyes widened. "I've been instructed to give you a drink on the house while you wait. Please have a seat."

Exchanging wary glances, they eased into the bar stools. The young human came back with three glasses. He set them up on the bar and went to the spirits behind the secured wall. His palmprint unlocked the partition, which slid upward and let him pluck out a bottle before it descended.

He presented the alcohol with a flourish. "Peloonish whiskey. Twenty-eight years old."

Oh, shit, Maryn thought. That was a rather pointed reference to their shared history with Bee and could be interpreted a myriad of ways, most of them unpleasant.

"Thank you." Jac smiled as the young man poured a finger of liquid in each.

"Only the best for Mom's Corps buddies," he allowed with a sunny grin.

Maryn blinked. "You're Bee's son?"

"Yeah. Happy to meet you. I'm Gabriel." He looked nothing like their old comrade, but that wasn't unusual, especially if Bee had chosen a surrogate parent and her genetics hadn't factored into his conception. His features were sharp and masculine, with bright blue eyes where Bee's were as black as her soul. Long blond hair was tied back in a neat ponytail, which hung to his narrow waist. He was a pretty young man.

"Good to meet you too. I have a daughter about your age." Jac lifted her glass, and Maryn and Col followed her lead. "To our hostess."

Maryn hoped it wasn't poisoned, but the way he smiled in pleasure at their toast made her feel more at ease. She took a careful sip. Her trepidation was forgotten as the whiskey made its way over her tongue in a smooth, golden flood, prickling her nostrils and creating a lovely heat all the way down to her stomach.

"Oh, that's delicious," she murmured. "The citrusy notes are divine."

"A connoisseur," Gabriel said, impressed. "Would you like a double?"

"Thank you, but I should pass. I need to be sober for this meeting," she admitted.

"Mom's almost done with the last client. Give us a few minutes to clean up and she'll be right with you," he informed them.

Another disturbing turn of phrase, but Maryn was willing to let it pass until Gabriel's eyes narrowed, distracted by a commotion in the row of gambling machines. A tall, mothlike Dubasca with tattered antennae was slamming all four spindly fists against a slot machine which had just paid the house with the last of its credits. As the being picked up a stool and began to swing it at the machine, Gabriel cross drew an energy pistol strapped at his side and fired once in a quick, economic motion. The Dubasca crumpled to the floor, and the stool clattered to land beside its still-twitching body.

The same unobtrusive table hops carted the corpse away to the under-stairs. The roar of conversation, momentarily silenced by the bark of Gabriel's pistol, returned in building waves.

"Sorry about that." He shrugged and holstered the weapon. "House rules prohibit destruction of property. I'll be right back."

"Understood," Jac reassured him as he moved away. She raised her eyebrows at Col and Maryn.

"Seems like a decent kid," Maryn hazarded over another sip of her whiskey. It was excellent stuff.

"As cold as his mother." Col tossed back the remainder of her drink.

Some of the general rowdiness was returning to the bar by the time they'd finished their drinks. Gabriel reappeared on their side of the counter this time. "Mom's ready to see you. Follow me."

They left their empty glasses on the bar and followed him to a door at the back of the establishment. It looked wooden, but the heaviness with which it swung open and the pneumatic hiss of air spoke of sturdy reinforcement. He pointed down a dim, featureless metal hallway, all pretense of old-time saloons abandoned behind the scenes. "Down there, where Bambi's standing."

"Bambi?" All Maryn could see was a bristling, faceless guard in the dim lighting.

"Yeah. Don't call him that, though. He'll shoot you." Gabriel gave them another winning smile. "It's great to meet you. Mom doesn't have a lot of corps friends who are still alive, for obvious reasons. It's nice to meet the legends."

He slipped back outside the port.

"I guess that means she talks about us," Maryn murmured as they walked down the hallway.

"Apparently," Col whispered.

Bambi the guard opened a second door into a modern reception area, surprising after the utilitarian hallway outside. He motioned them inside. "She'll be with you soon."

Maryn winced as the door slammed shut behind them.

Jac appraised the hand-loomed carpets, floor cushions, and expensive wall hangings concealing the bare metal walls with open wonder. "This is new. War's good for business, I guess."

"Are those blood stains?" Maryn peered at the discolored surface of the freshly scrubbed table.

"Maybe." Col sniffed the air. "Probably. It is Bee we're talking about."

A door opposite the port they'd come in slid aside and slim young being entered, carrying a tray with a teapot and four cups. They set the tray down on the table and fled back the way they'd come. A moment later, the door opened again to reveal a tall, bearded human wearing a scarlet satin gown. Two guards with the same glowering disposition as the one outside followed her in and stood against the wall.

"Maryn! How lovely to see you again. It's been ages." She approached with her hands outstretched. The bare metal of a cybernetic right upper limb gleamed in the harsh overhead light. She clasped Bee's hands and accepted her ceremonial air kisses. Her old comrade's hair had not one gray strand visible in her jet-black locks, but she noted the flowery chemical scent of fresh hair tint wafting from her beard.

Her large, immaculately manicured left hand pressed Maryn's between prosthetic and flesh. "I was so sorry to hear about Primetri Andelek."

"Thank you." Maryn accepted her condolences with caution, not even wondering how Bee had known she was married. Intelligence had been her specialty in the Corps. "You remember Col."

The Boshi exchanged nods with Bee, who chirped, "Of course. My furry friend." Their hostess moved to stand in front of her third guest. "Jacqueline. Where is your wife?" The final word came out edged in frost.

"Scylla's on board the *Girl*, preparing for our acquisitions," Jac answered. "She sends her love, but she is abiding by the conditions of our agreement."

Bee stared her down another few, uncomfortable seconds, then swept her cybernetic hand toward the table. "Sit and we'll spill the tea, as it were."

"Gabriel introduced himself to us. He's a lovely kid," Maryn told her as they moved.

Bee's eyes went large and soft as she lowered herself to the spot in front of the tray. "He's my world. I'm so proud of him. It was his idea to open the bar with a saloon theme. He loves those ancient westerns. You know. Sex. Androids. Murder." She settled on the cushions. "So, Team Huntress is back in business. Why, after so long in the tooth?" Her eyes glinted with hard light as she regarded them, her head tilted, all softness replaced by diamond edges. That was the Bee Maryn remembered. Catty, mean, and cold as ice.

"We've taken an assignment and need to have the appropriate means to protect our clients," Jac replied. "It puts us on the front lines of some nastiness."

Col lowered herself on a pile of brocaded pillows and sank into them, her knees still above the level of the table. Maryn and Jac seated themselves tailor-fashion opposite the arms dealer, who began to pour tea. She handed a cup to Col. The Boshi took the delicate vessel between her forefinger and thumb.

"There's gossip all over the subspace channels this morning about the latest battle for the Pashni. Khepran pilots are talking about a 'golden ship' that came to their aid. She tipped the pot over another cup, her grin sharp and canny. "Know anything about that?"

Jac's face remained a mask, and Maryn fought to match her

dispassionate expression. "Not a clue," Jac said, taking the offered cup. "We haven't been through the Pashni in weeks."

"If you say so. However, gossip says it matches a ship detained a few days ago which carried the Dowager Consort of Primetri Andelek." She looked straight at Maryn as she held out a cup of steaming, fragrant tea.

She took it. Thankful her hand remained steady, she said nothing, though learning of the well-informed gossip made her insides twist into an uncomfortable knot. Bee looked between the three of them before she exploded into unkind laughter.

"Your poker faces are still terrible. You always did have a knack for being in the wrong place at the wrong time," she crowed. "But goddamn, girls! You've got more balls than half the scum out there."

"We had no idea there was a battle going on." Jac sagged in defeat. "It was defensive luck."

"If I had half the luck that you four always did, I would have made it off Peloon with less hardware." Bee sipped at her tea, ice glinting in her eyes. "But let's not dredge up that body. What can I do for you?"

Jac nodded at Maryn. She pulled a PDD out of the pocket inside her coat and slid it across the table to the arms dealer. "You should have received our wish list."

"Oh, I certainly did." Bee took the device and scanned it, one eyebrow rising. "This is going to cost you a pretty penny. That's an awful lot of guns for the four of you, and there's a war on, if you didn't know. I don't think your pension is going to cover this."

"We're good for it." Maryn held up the credit stick, and Bee's eyes narrowed in calculation. She stroked her beard in consideration with the cybernetic hand.

"I can promise you repeat business as long as we're employed by this client," Jac offered.

"If you come out of it alive. Your ship is getting old, and so are you. It was fucking chance you made it out of the Pashni." She leaned forward. "Your luck can't hold forever. Take my advice: you should retire on a boring planet and forget about it."

Before Maryn could process Bee's warning, Jac answered. "We can't sit this out." Her cheeks became flooded with angry color. "Innocent people are being slaughtered."

"Children orphaned," Col said, her voice a growl.

"Ah, so it's the Kheqet resistance, is it?" Bee grinned and sat back. "You *are* in the thick of it. Trying to make a difference." Her smile transformed into something less pleasant. "That kind of idealism got most of us killed on Peloon."

"Will you sell to us or not?" Maryn twirled the credit stick between her fingers. "We can still go down the street and visit the Jackaroo."

"His stuff is shit. Buy at your own risk," she sniffed, offended. "Let me see your credit first."

Maryn handed it to her. The arms dealer plugged it into her own PDD, drawn out of the bodice of her gown. Her lips pursed in interest. She withdrew the stick and returned it to Maryn.

"All right." She named an extortionate figure, but they weren't going to find what they wanted anywhere else.

Without an attempt to bargain or argue, Maryn said, "Done."

Bee transferred the wish list to her device and held it out to Maryn. She pressed her thumb against the glowing square and it registered with a buzz against her skin. One of the guards took the PDD as the dealer held it above her left shoulder, and he went back through the drapery-hidden door.

"One hour. We'll bring it to your pad. Then I would suggest getting your asses off Anubis as fast as possible. Your ship is unique, to say the least. I can't be the only one monitoring what's going on, and there might be a few bounty hunters listening in who don't care whose side you're on. Somebody has a score to settle with you and they pay well." Bee drained her tea.

She and Jac exchanged startled glances, and a low growl rumbled in Col's throat. "Who's looking for us?" Maryn asked.

"Hmm." She made a show of reflection, stroking her beard with her manicured nails. "The information came out over an encrypted channel. There are only a few entities who use it, and fewer people who know how to hack into it."

"How much for the information?" Maryn grated, holding up the credit stick. "We need to know." If they could prove the communication came from a corporation, other planets could intervene on Qet and end the bloodshed.

Bee regarded her with calculating eyes and then shrugged. "I don't know who's after you. I'm not bullshitting, I just didn't care enough to look that hard. But I can ask Gabriel to do some digging. I'll see what he can come up with before you leave. It's on me, for old times' sake."

She stood. Maryn scrambled to her feet, her knees complaining, and gave Jac a hand. Col rose in a graceful flow of fur and muscle.

"Hope your luck holds out." Bee's eyes flashed with a softer light, and she held up her cybernetic hand in a crescent shape. "Comrades."

They returned the answering gesture, raised fists like a full moon.

"In all phases," Maryn finished the pledge.

Bee swept out of the room and the guard gestured at the outer door. They took the hint and left. Instead of leading them back to the saloon, he took them to another exit which led out to the alley door they'd first tried. As they stepped back out into hazy sunlight scattered by dust and thin clouds, the young guard didn't even look at them, his gaze straight ahead.

"We need to warn Scylla," Col said when they were out of earshot.

"Somebody's hunting us?" Maryn hissed as she pulled up her cowl and lowered her goggles. "That means they could be monitoring the jump gates."

Jac held up a warning hand. "Not here. I want to go back to the ship, get everything prepared, and be ready to leave the second we have the weapons on board. I have an idea." She replaced her protective gear. "It might not be the safest one, but we don't have a choice."

Walking back to the ship through the same crowded street and the dusty plain without any cover to speak of became an exercise in pretending to be calm and staying attentive without being suspicious. Maryn's back itched the entire time as if there were a target pasted on it.

They broke the news to Scylla and Dair. Scylla began plotting a course out of the system to avoid high-traffic star lanes and reach the hidden gate in Qet's inner ring, while they handled the incoming purchases. A floater truck appeared at the promised time and Jac pulled back the dust drape to crack open the crates and verify everything was there before Maryn used the hydraulic claws to maneuver the crates into the cargo hold. They would install the missile cradles into the auto feeder once they were under way.

When the mechanical shoulder stuck again, she had a moment of concern that jarring the rack of explosive-filled warheads might be a terrible idea. The hydraulic arms completed their reluctant sweep, and she gingerly deposited the cradle into the hold. Once their explosive cargo was loaded, Jac strapped it in place.

The guard driving the truck handed Maryn a holo card. "From the boss, ma'am." She recognized him as the dismissive little jerk who'd called Jac 'Grandma', but his manner was far more respectful this time. She thanked him and climbed up the tube to the common area to insert the card in the reader on the display table.

"*Girl*, will you float the audio to everybody's headset?"

"Yes, Maryn. Attention: prerecorded message from Beatrice Arturio," the ship announced.

A three-dimensional holo of Bee flashed up. "Gabriel did a more focused scan into the local chatter," her image said. "You girls made quite an impression on him. So far, nobody is talking about your presence. He was able to narrow down the channel broadcasting the APB." She paused dramatically. "But first, you should know things are heating up on Qet."

Dair appeared beside Maryn and listened with a troubled expression as Bee continued, "The old government's last stronghold is under siege. Without reinforcements, they won't be able to hold out much longer." Bee's image frowned. "You girls don't constitute an army, and like I said, you're older than you used to be. So is your ship. You might want to think about it before you fly into another battle where you're outnumbered, orphans be damned." She grinned. "Then again, you made it out alive and whole out of every other situation that should have killed you. Who's to say you won't make it out of this one with your damned luck? Based on the reach of the signal, I'd say it's a corporation on your tail. Gabriel attached the frequency number and some very interesting information to the card."

Her image shredded into particles of light without further comment.

"Of course she's going to make us wait for it," Scylla burst out. "What's on the card?"

"Hold on." Maryn swiped at the display and found the file. Her mouth dropped open when she saw the report. "Holy shit."

"What?" Jac fairly shouted over the headset.

"The transmission putting an APB out on the *Girl* was sent yesterday, but she included … fuck." Maryn gulped, her eyes riveted on another set of data. "Someone has been tracking you for almost three months. Your trips to Qet, the trade hub, Echo Four. Our stop at Zillzanam Station, then the wormhole and Xyri. It's all here."

CHAPTER
NINE

SHOCKED SILENCE FELL for a few heartbeats before everyone started talking at once. "That was after we started working with the agent," Scylla blurted.

"Perhaps the *Raging Fire* let us go at the Pashni because they are in contact with the corporation, and already knew we were lying about where we'd been."

"Did they stick something on the hull?"

"You've already been to the camp twice," Dair whispered in horror.

"Fuck it all!" Scylla ran through a stream of profanity. "Shove those guns from Zillzanam out of the ship. Leave 'em here. What if they're sabotaged or have another tracker?"

"No, we need those guns," Dair snapped.

"We have to find the device," Jac ordered. "Somebody get down here with the sniffer."

"It's in the storage space in the hallway next to the airlock," Scylla informed them over the comm. Col left to retrieve the detecting equipment.

"We have to go back." Dair's young face wore too many crags of responsibility, their dark purple eyes full of anger and fear. "If they know where the camp is, it might already be ..." Their voice failed. Emotions played over their face, too raw to name. Maryn placed a hand on Dair's shoulder, but they shrugged it off and glared at her. "*I'm* not going to fall apart."

The unspoken accusation she thought she heard behind it said, *like you would.* She stared at Dair, her face heating with anger. Col returned with the sniffer. Maryn took it and pushed the tech into the younger being's hands.

"Get down there and help Jac find that fucking bug. Go!"

Dair scrambled down the ladder tube. Col and Maryn stared at each other before she shook herself out of the fugue. "We need to send the APB transmission to Lekere. It might be the proof we need. *Girl,* this is his frequency." She plugged it into the touchscreen on the holo table. "Send the data there. It's his private communication device. Tell him it's from me and give him a summary of what happened."

"Sending now," the ship confirmed.

"It will take some time to transmit through the relays," Col hazarded. "Will it be soon enough?"

"We can only hope. Now that the wormhole is open again, the Kheprans could come through without being attacked. They could be there in two days or less."

Col continued to scan the data Gabriel had gleaned for them. "This information could be useful in my audit. I can compare it to frequencies used to transfer money to colonial accounts. We may be able to identify the corporation that way."

"You don't think it's Zillzanam?"

"Possible, but it is too convenient. Zillzanam does not handle ore, and the mine appears to be the source of the conflict." She ejected the card. "I will enter this in my database and begin researching once we leave Anubis."

"How long before we're ready to leave, Scylla?" Jac over the com.

"Calculations are finalized," the pilot's voice crackled. "Status of cargo and hull?"

"It's clean. There's nothing." Jac's voice held despair. "All secure. I'm closing the bay now. Let's go."

The hum of the ship's engines began to wind up. "Everybody, prepare for takeoff. ETA to gate jump is eighteen hours."

Dair emerged from the tube and headed for the insulated cubicle without a word, their back stiff as they climbed in and shut the partition. Jac came out of the tube after them and sealed the hatch with a thunderous expression.

"You okay?" Maryn asked when she saw her face. "You look mad."

"I know they just found out the ship was being tracked, but Dair and I are going to have to have a chat soon before I punch them in the face. I'm tired of the attitude."

"We were the same way when we joined the corps."

"I know. I can think of a few times I would have punched me in the face, too." Jac sighed, and came to lean beside her, their arms touching.

"What have we gotten ourselves into?" Maryn asked, staring at the message displayed over the table.

"You worried they might be right? That we're too old for this?" Jac asked, her eyes downcast.

"Maybe," Maryn admitted.

"You know what? Me too. But they need our help."

"I'm worried Andelek's parents will take some flak because we went there first, and that whoever is tracking us knows I'm involved. And I'm afraid ..." She shrugged, and amended, "No, I'm terrified. I don't remember being so scared when we were young."

"We've learned a lot of lessons since then, and we can't unlearn them." Jac looked up as Scylla's tunes began to blare from the cockpit. "There's our warning. Let's strap in."

They hurried up the corridor and slid into their seats just as Scylla began to lift off from the dusty pad.

"What did you decide?" Jac asked.

"You're right. I'm going to use Methuselah's Gate," Scylla replied.

"What is a Methuselah's Gate?" Col leaned over in her seat to peer at the pilot.

"It's an unmanned jump ring on the old star lane we use for some of our unofficial cargo. It's unlikely the mercs will be patrolling it."

"And less likely that anybody will be maintaining it." Maryn swallowed against her fear. "They don't have warning systems like the new gates. There's no way to know if anybody is approaching from the other side."

"How does one put in the coordinates if it's unmanned?" Col's brow furrowed.

"Spacewalk," Jac said. "I've done it with this gate several times before. No problem."

A shiver went down Maryn's back at the idea of her friend going outside the ship in deep space. Fear of the void still gnawed at her insides and didn't appear to be going anywhere soon, despite the slow resolution of her aversion to spaceflight she thus far had managed. One step at a time, she reminded herself. It wasn't as if they expected her to go out there.

The ship rose out of the dust storm into clear air. "Scan for other ships that might be following, *Girl*," Jac instructed.

"Negative. No ships are following. However …"

"Speak up. What is it?" Scylla asked.

"I was running maintenance logs during the preflight check, and they are still in my short-term memory space. Maryn said our flight path has been reported for three months. I believe I know where the tracking device is."

"That's great! Where is it?" the pilot exclaimed, relieved. "Did somebody sneak it in when we took on cargo? Or new fuel cells?"

"No, Captain." The AI sounded oddly subdued. "I believe I am the tracking device."

"What?" Confused, Scylla looked to her wife for confirmation. To everyone's surprise, Jac's eyes grew round with comprehension and she slammed her head against the cushioned seat.

"Oh, fuck me."

ONCE THE SHIP rose above Anubis's mottled tan and white atmosphere, Scylla said, "Let me get this straight." Her voice dripped with molten fury. "The new software upgrade we installed in the *Girl* to help me fly is ratting us out?"

"I didn't realize," Jac, stricken, turned her gaze from the tablet in her lap to the pilot. "After we modified it to your specifications I never thought about it. I forgot I gave the codes to Maya so she could keep tabs on us if something happened. She was so worried about you."

"Are you telling me the whole fucking time we've been working with the resistance, we've been under a goddamned *SILVER ALERT*?" Scylla shouted, glaring at her wife.

"No," she reassured her. "I don't see that law enforcement has been notified we're missing. As far as I can tell, it's just … tracking to see where we go, like for vacations, or shopping. It must be programmed to report our flight paths to commercial advertising databases."

"Clearly it was not marketed with senior smugglers in mind," Col muttered.

"I wondered why I was getting a sudden uptick in retirement planet living and laxative ads on the ship's com." Scylla huffed a humorless laugh. "I figured Maya and her dads were behind it, but I didn't expect it to be the *Girl*."

"I am so sorry, Captain," the ship offered. "It was set to run behind my operating system. Would you like me to disable it?"

"YES!" Scylla bellowed. "You traitor."

"All right. Let's all take a breath," Maryn suggested. "Whoever is looking for us may not have access to whatever commercial databases were tracking your movements. If they do, it kind of screams Zillzanam, but Col is starting to think it might be somebody else."

"What did the message say?" Jac wanted to know. "*Girl*, will you read it back?"

"Transmission states: Modified Astradyne cruiser, Caspian registered ship *Golden Girl*, engaged with operatives outside the Pashni Wormhole. All assets be on the lookout for this ship and detain if encountered. Anticipate they are headed for Qet. Should be considered armed and dangerous. Incentives apply."

"Assets. Incentives. Code for mercenaries and bounty, all couched in very corporate language," Col mused. "I would like to start on the audit as soon as possible. But first?" She shook her shaggy head and dust puffed out. "I should vacuum myself."

"ETA to the gate is eighteen hours, forty-six minutes once we go nuclear." Scylla punched a few buttons and the FTL drive began to hum, winding up for transition. Her face scrunched with a wince. "Um. I would like to make a motion we don't tell Dair about the software. They already know we were tracked and the damage is done. They don't need to know how. Just tell them *Girl* located the bug and squashed it. Don't give them any more fuel to consider us old and senile."

Maryn raised her hand. "Seconded."

"All in favor?"

A chorus of 'ayes' rumbled through the cockpit. Jac turned around to peer behind her. "Col, how can we help you with the audit?"

"Someone should talk to Dair," Col suggested. "We need to know more about the element refined on Qet, and its uses. It may allow to us determine what industries are most likely to be interested in the planet's resources and narrow the field of possible corporate interference. If someone is willing to assist me, we will get through it faster."

Jac raised a hand. "Oh, I'll talk to them."

"No punching, no matter how tempting," Maryn reminded her. "I'll help Col. I've gotten good at comparing data, though it's usually biological, not financial." Maryn was relieved to have something to keep her occupied and not think about Jac's upcoming spacewalk.

"At some point we'll need to load those missile cradles," Scylla grumbled. "I'd prefer we do it before we go sub light again, in case somebody's waiting for us out there."

"I'm all yours later," Jac offered. The pilot snorted and flounced in her chair, lips set in a grim, angry line as she knotted her arms over her chest.

"Don't talk to me, old woman. I'm still pissed you and the *Girl* let our daughter track me like a fucking space whale."

"And with that ..." Jac unbuckled her harness. "I will go talk to Dair."

ONCE SCYLLA TURNED on the art-grav and the Boshi took the opportunity to shed her coat of sandy dust, Col and Maryn took over the holo table. Col set up her subspace array, unfolding it from the briefcase into a three-screened workstation. Maryn eyed the overwhelming collection of numbers on the display.

"What are we looking for?"

"These are Qetish accounts gleaned from the last six months. What we want to find are credits transferred into or out of colonial banks via CosBank, perhaps using the same frequency which mentioned us. First, we will need to narrow them down." Col ran the tip of one claw down a column of codes. "These are account numbers. I have already filtered them and removed any transfers too small to be of interest."

"That's still thousands of entries."

"The mining industry is quite successful, as you know. So is their crop production and food processing, though they do not export. The Qet and Kheqet settlements handle all transactions on their planet with as little outside involvement as possible." Col shrugged. "Before we can move on to the transaction data, look for transfers which are immediately moved to some other account either in full or distributed to several other accounts. If there is suspicious activity, it may be hidden in something that contains numerous transactions of large credits." She swept her screen, and the display flickered to life above the holo table in front of Maryn. "You start with this group. I will start another. If you see something, mark it and we will do further research."

"All right." Maryn squinted at the numbers and sighed. "Granny glasses, please, *Girl.*"

"Yes, Maryn," the ship responded. The columns adjusted so she could read them without leaning back. After a minute's silence, the *Girl* inquired over Maryn's headset, "May I speak with you in private?"

"Of course. What's up?"

"I believe Scylla is angry with me."

"Oh." Bemused, she sat up. "I don't think she would ever hold a grudge against you for long." Maryn wondered why the AI would be worried about something so very human. Col looked up, curious, and she held up a finger. "Why does it bother you?"

"She has never been angry with me before." The ship paused again. "Beatrice Arturio said I was getting old. I believe I am deteriorating with age."

"What makes you say that?" Maryn hid a grin behind her hand.

"The piloting software upgrade was for a newer operating system. I did not detect the patch tracking us because it was outside my current parameters. Despite the upgrades, I am in danger of becoming obsolete."

The *Girl* was afraid she was getting old.

Maryn blinked in surprise, not sure how to answer. "We're all dealing with that," she said at last. "Time moves forward whether we want it to or not, and sometimes we don't move as fast as the rest of the universe does. There is nothing wrong with being an older model. You are still able to do your job and do it well. You continue learning new things, just like us. Scylla loves you and trusts you. So do we. I've found it's best to let her be angry. She'll come around."

"Thank you." Another hesitation. "I would appreciate it if this conversation were kept between us."

"You've got it." Maryn ran her hand over her face, still processing that the *Girl* was having a midlife crisis.

"What was that?" Col whispered. "Are Jac and Scylla still fighting?"

"No." She fought the smile tugging at her lips. "It's all good. Just forget you heard it, okay?"

Col's eyes narrowed, then she shrugged and went back to her display. Maryn scrolled through vision-blurring numbers and even more disconcerting sums of credits Col considered 'normal transactions' when she asked if she should flag them.

Half an hour later, Jac climbed out of Dair's cubicle, the younger being close behind her. They appeared to have reached detente, or at least, neither was scowling. "All right. Dair has some insight regarding the elements refined on Qet, but it's not anywhere near conclusive, I'm afraid."

"Qetryllium has dozens of uses," Dair said. "Nuclear power cells. Technology, metallurgy for coloring and strengthening alloys. Weapons, medicine, the manufacture of spaceships. The unrefined crystals have aesthetic value on some worlds. If this is about controlling the mine and its resources, any corporation could be behind it."

"Does Viltrux have any connections to the mining industry?" Col asked.

"No. He was elected by one of the farming communities in the south. He had something to do with the ministry of agriculture, like food distribution and such. That was why the chancellor never saw a coup coming."

"He wouldn't have the kind of money needed to hire a private mercenary army on his own?" Maryn asked.

"I have no idea what that would cost, but I doubt it. His family claimed a large area of land on the first settlement, and their processing business grew up around it. In a capitalist society, he might be considered wealthy, but that isn't how Qet works. Everyone has the same access to food. There are enough stores preserved to last decades."

"Huh." Jac thought about that, her brow wrinkled. "So after the Khepran settlers moved in, surplus may have decreased when population exploded in the north."

"Everyone needs to eat to survive. Why would someone care about that?" Dair's face puckered in confusion. "There's still more than enough."

"Someone with a financial stake in selling the surplus to corporations on the down low would care a lot." Maryn picked up the thread of Jac's unspooling thoughts.

"That's against the colonial charter." Dair looked between them.

"Viltrux's proposed amendments would have allowed it, though," Jac said. "He may have used his arguments about mining profits to fuel his racist dogma, but those changes would have allowed his business to sell it off world. He might already be doing it under the radar."

"There are only a couple of ways they could get it off the planet without being noticed." Maryn held Jac's gaze with a grim certainty. "Smugglers, or someone loading it into the ore leaving Qet."

"His corporate contacts might have offered mercenary troops as an incentive for an exclusive contract," Col suggested. "Food insecure colonies are likely willing to pay anything for fresh produce in stasis. This is all conjecture, but it gives us a place to start looking."

Dair sank into the seat across from Col, pale and angry. "Did you know they bombed the entire city of Tenent? My city, in the north where I grew up." Their voice was near to breaking. "There isn't a building left. But they haven't touched the mines. The refugees hide in the tunnels when there's an alert. The smeltery is still standing, and the qetryllium extraction plant. But people's homes … they're gone. In the south, the outlying communities owned by Viltrux and people like him are untouched. If you're right, they have chosen money over the lives of my family and friends." Their eyes were dry and dull. "What am I fighting for? To return to the planet where I was born, but might never be welcome?"

"I am so sorry, Dair." Col's green eyes softened with empathy. "If we can prove this is not a civil war, there won't be anything stopping the Kheprans or Xyrians and any other galactic force from intervening. The Xyrians are skilled peacemakers. They can help."

"But why hasn't anyone else thought of it?" Dair burst out. "Why doesn't anyone care what's happening?"

Maryn bit her lip to keep from saying anything that would depreciate Dair's pain. Pointing out most beings were self-serving bastards who fought, clawed, and killed to get ahead of their fellows was her own jaded reality. "We care," she said, "and we are going to do everything we can, but our first priority is the safety of the refugees."

"Fucking right," Scylla agreed. She was leaning against the corridor bulkhead, arms still crossed, but her demeanor was less confrontational now. Jac walked toward her with more hip-sway in her step than usual, watching her wife's reaction to her approach through lowered lashes.

"Still mad at me and the *Girl*?" she asked.

"Nah. I just made up with her. I think it's time to make up with you." Scylla reached out and wrapped her arm around Jac's waist, pulling her in close for a kiss. "Time's too short to be pissed off. Wanna take a nap? It's the middle of the night for us."

"Yeah, I think we should." Jac nuzzled her wife's neck, then glanced at Maryn. "You okay to take your usual watch? There's plenty of food if you get hungry."

"I'm good. See you in the morning."

"Good night." The Merrows crossed to their cubicle. Scylla opened the partition and bowed to her wife, kissed her hand, and invited her to go first with a lascivious smile.

Maryn exchanged a knowing look with Col as they climbed into their bunk. The hum of the privacy screen followed the click of the partition.

"Some things never change," Col murmured. "They fight, they make up, they have sex."

"They ... oh." Dair's expression went wide eyed. "I didn't need to know that."

"Lighten up, kid. You should realize by now you need to love the people in your life as hard as you can while they're still here." Maryn rubbed her eyes, blindsided by a fresh wave of grief for Scylla's illness and Andelek's permanent absence from her life. She stood.

"*Girl*, will you transfer this to the PDD in the cockpit? I'll keep looking for numbers."

"Done." The readout over the holo table vanished.

Dair wavered between them, and then offered hesitantly, "Can I help?"

Col motioned for them to take the seat Maryn had vacated. "There is plenty of data to go around," she agreed, flicking another set to the heads-up display. As Col explained to Dair what they were doing, Maryn hit the lavatory before she headed to the cockpit, determined not to cry in front of the younger being.

How long was it going to take to get used to Andelek not *being* anymore? How could she ever get used to the knowledge that Scylla would cease to be as well, her shared memories of their lives erased one after another by dying and damaged cells, maybe long before her body followed?

She allowed herself to sniffle for the time it took to pee and then put herself back together. Stripping the band from the tight braid she'd worn on Anubis, amber-colored dust drifted from her hair and fell deckward with the delayed grace of snowflakes in low gravity while she raked the plaits out with her fingers and rubbed her scalp, sighing with relief. She flipped on the exhaust fan to catch the dirt in the filtration system and combed out her dark hair, pulling it back into a less headache-inducing loose horsetail.

Her thoughts returned to Dair's dead, emotionless eyes, and their growing awareness that evil existed in the galaxy in the form of their own people. Maryn remembered learning this soul-flaying fact so many times in the corps that even the atrocities on Qet didn't shock her or make her as angry as it should anyone with a shred of empathy. She was numbed by repeated proof. It made her ashamed, and other times furious she was this way. Warfare had irrevocably changed them all.

But here was an opportunity to try to make a difference for people struggling to survive on a new world, like she had once pledged to do in the Corps. Bee had called it idealism, but it was the right thing to do.

It was easy to peel back Dr. Alessi's skin and release warrior Maryn. For Andelek, the study of exobiology had been focused on the beauty of life in all its varied, glorious incarnations. But for her, it had always been about a violence she understood; the clawing and killing and fucking for the survival of the species was a savage but cleaner warfare all its own, with fewer casualties and consequence.

And kaiju didn't worship their goddamned bank accounts. She returned to the cockpit and resumed her portion of the audit.

CHAPTER
TEN

"MARYN! GET THE MEDICAL POD READY." Scylla's panicky transmission woke her from the accounting-induced coma she'd fallen into after the night shift. She realized she was floating against her sleep harness as Scylla continued, "Jac's hurt. I turned off art-grav so I can move her up the tube."

"Fuck!" She untangled the webbing and jettisoned from the sleeping cubicle like a rocket, skimmed over the holo table, and slammed her palm against the release on the med bay door. The narrow medical pod's lights began to hum, the lid of the sarcophagus-like exam table lifting to expose the bed. Maryn stabbed the power button with her forefinger and the instrument panel blazed to life.

Scylla emerged from the hatch in the floor and turned to pull her wife out of the tube. Jac was conscious but guarding her ribcage, her face pale and drawn with pain.

"What happened?" Maryn asked. She helped Scylla turn her in midair to a prone position so they could guide her by her feet and shoulders through the narrow port. Jac was stiff as they maneuvered her into the medical pod, her breathing labored and shallow.

"Fucking hydraulic claw arm," Scylla spat. "We were hanging the missile cradles and the shoulder got stuck. When I tried to clear the jam, the cradle came loose and pinned her between it and the bulkhead. Lucky it was only art-grav or she would have been crushed."

"Only a couple of broken ribs, I think," Jac gasped.

"Do you need assistance?" Col inquired over the com from the cockpit.

"Not yet. It's crowded back here." Maryn strapped Jac into the medical pod and brought the scanner down over her chest and abdomen, toggling the radiology program. She peered at the screen, bringing red-highlighted areas into magnification. "Clean breaks of five, six and seven on the left side, but there's no displacement. Is the pod still set up for bone regeneration?"

"Yes," Jac rasped. "But that takes twelve hours. We don't have that much time before we get to the gate."

"You can't do a walk outside in a pressure suit with broken ribs. If you start moving around you run the risk of them coming apart and puncturing your lung," Scylla told her wife, squeezing her ankle. Worry created lines between her eyes as she glanced at Maryn. "*Girl* can fly the ship and I'll do the spacewalk."

"Oh, no you won't. There's rock dodging to do on the other side and you know that gate's touchy," Jac hissed between gritted teeth. Maryn reached into the cabinet overhead and retrieved a hypo spray of strong analgesic. She pressed it against Jac's jugular vein and squeezed the trigger, releasing a dose of pain medication into her friend's bloodstream. She relaxed in increments, her jaw losing some of its tense rigidity, and continued, "Scylla has to be in the cockpit if it deploys too fast, or if there are merc ships patrolling nearby." Despite her discomfort, her steady gaze met Maryn's with a meaningful lift of her brows.

"Oh no." She pulled back as she realized where this was going, but Jac grabbed her by the wrist.

"We don't have a suit big enough for Col, and the gate is redundant Earth tech. Dair has never spacewalked."

Fear condensed on her skin in slippery droplets. "I can't."

"You can," Jac insisted, grabbing her hand. "You'll be tethered to the *Girl* the whole time you're programming. The reel and the thruster pack in the suit will get you back in before the jump deploys."

"But what if I can't?" Her voice was too shrill. "What if the gate goes off and I'm outside? It's a one-way trip. You won't be able to come back for me before my oxygen runs out."

"What happened?" Dair, sleepy-eyed, appeared in the doorway and took in the scene with a glance of dismay. "What's going on?"

Maryn stiffened and clamped her teeth together, busying herself with the bone regeneration settings. She wouldn't give them the satisfaction of falling apart.

"We had an accident in the bay. I need your help loading the last missile cradle." Scylla squeezed in and leaned over to kiss her wife. "Stay put. Do what Maryn tells you."

With another glance at Jac, Dair launched themself toward the ladder tube. Scylla followed.

Maryn's fear came out in irritation, her voice sharp. "Where's the damn growth stimulator?"

"Drawer three." Jac's gaze followed her beneath fluttering eyelids as the pain medication did its work. She found the hypo spray and injected her with the bone factors, then unrolled the flexible pad of tech over Jac's already bruising ribs and plugged it into the pod's frame. Nanos in the medication would direct the bone factors to break sites and repair them, though the bruising and pain would last for days. The radiology scanner showed increased brightness at the site of the fractures already, an indication everything was in the right place. Maryn swung the scanner back against the wall.

"You can do it," Jac slurred. "I know you can."

"Right. You planned this, didn't you?"

"Ha!" Jac winced, her breath catching in a sharp gasp against the laugh. "I can honestly say that's a no."

"Don't move from this pod. If you have to pee, I'll get out the vacuum catheter and shove it down your pants. Don't ask me what I'll do if you have to shit."

"Sadist." Jac's eyes fluttered and closed.

Maryn lowered the sleep harness over her and set the pod's comm to voice activation, then dimmed the lights in the medical bay. She eased out of the portal and pulled herself up the corridor to the cockpit where Col waited, one furry hand clasped around her prayer beads as the other continued to scroll through a dataset of bank transactions.

"Is she alright? How severe are her injuries?"

"Two broken ribs. A lot of bruising but no serious internal injuries according to the scan." She strapped into the seat and attacked the console, punching data screens with more force than necessary.

"May I remind you that my touch-activated displays are newly upgraded and very expensive?" *Girl's* interface said archly in Maryn's headset.

Col studied Maryn. The quick mind behind her furry countenance did the math and came up with the sum of her agitation. "Methuselah's Gate."

"Yep."

"Ah." She nodded.

"*Ah*? What the fuck do you mean by *ah*?" Maryn waved her hands in the air with inarticulate frustration. "Spit it out."

She set the PDD aside. "Just that there is yet another fear to face, about which you will undoubtedly work yourself into a panic attack."

"Thanks. How supportive of you."

Col sat back and cocked her head. "What do you want me to do? Pat you on the head and tell you how brave you are and that we have the utmost faith in you?"

Maryn blinked, stung by her sarcasm. "That's condescending."

"Yes, because you already know these things. You were a warrior before you were a teacher, and neither negate the other. Your nature is bone deep, like mine." Col reached out and clasped her wrist with furry fingers. "I am not dismissing your fear. It is very real, but it cannot differentiate between then and now. You can." She sat back. "How many spacewalks have you done?"

Maryn leaned her head back and looked up with a sigh. "Dozens," she admitted.

"Out of that number, none went wrong, and you could never have prepared for the accidental one. We are planning carefully for this. Logic suggests this will be a routine event despite the reported inconsistencies of this gate, because we already know of them."

"Human brains don't work on logic, Col. They work on rampant chemistry, caffeine, and spite."

"Then rouse that spite. Tell your fear to fuck off and die."

"If it were only that easy." A small smile tugged at Maryn's lips despite her racing heart, and she sighed. "Goddamn. When did I become so whiny?"

"When you have too much time to think. We will stay busy. As soon as Scylla returns, we will go to the cargo bay and prep the suit. That, at least, is a familiar factor with which you can be reacquainted."

IT ENDED UP A TEAM EFFORT, with Col teaching Dair how to connect and disconnect the many valves on the EVA suit. Scylla would need Col's help navigating Qet's treacherous ring system when they emerged from the gate. It would be up to Dair to help Maryn back inside.

Her skin was dripping with fear sweat, and Maryn wiped at her face with a towel to keep the excess moisture from drifting into the bay. The thruster and life support pack pulled at her shoulders even in microgravity, though she knew once the unit was fully pressurized, the bulk would become more negotiable. The bars never wavered, but she still checked the wrist readouts of the battery pack with an obsessive compulsion.

Dair floated at her right side and kept glancing at her with narrowed eyes every time Maryn twitched or mopped her face and neck. It looked as if they were biting back something they wanted to say, a building pressure against her nerves each time they hesitated, inhaled, and then didn't speak. She finally sighed, "Don't hold back, kid. What is it?"

"I still think I should do it," they finally sputtered. "It can't be that difficult."

"She is the most experienced spacewalker," Col stated. "We do not have time to teach you the finer points, nor for a crash course in Earth Standard to read the panels."

"Look at her." Dair waved their hand at Maryn. "She's terrified."

"Yes, *she* is," Maryn growled. "And you are not helping."

"But it isn't appropriate. Elders shouldn't be putting themselves in harm's way when there is someone younger willing to take the risk." They connected the seal for the cooling system to the pack with an aggressive *click*.

"Nor should younglings attempt dangerous activities when they have not been trained to do so." Col's teeth flashed in displeasure. "Would you allow Zeddi to take up a sidearm and defend your camp?"

"Of course not, and that isn't the same thing."

"Then allow me to correct your placement of that hose. You have connected it to the valve for oxygen, not water."

Dair flushed a dark, burnt orange color and disconnected the seal, applying it to the appropriate valve with more care. "I'm not trying to be disrespectful. It isn't our way to … have our elders engaged in war or risky activities. Their knowledge is best utilized behind the lines in a safe environment."

"How boring." Col snorted in derision as she sealed the last hose and began to power up the life support system. A flush of warmth encircled Maryn's body as heated water began to circulate through the layer closest to her skin. They weren't close enough to a star to require cooling, but the warmth made her feel queasy. She raised her left wrist to tap the controls there and bring down the temperature for now. Outside the ship, thermo sensors would control the suit's response to its environment.

"I thought the Boshi treat your elders the same," Dair challenged.

"My culture is similar in the way older beings are viewed, particularly females," Col agreed. She lifted the suit's helmet and checked the faceplate for cracks or damage. "But we are considered unproductive unless we are of use to the younger generation. Such bullshit is why I renounced my citizenship and joined the Artemis Corps when I was still young." Her eyes crinkled in mischief as she met Maryn's gaze. "I was considered quite the suffragist in my village."

She smiled despite her nerves. "You rebel."

"Too fucking right," Col agreed in a sugary tone. "Time to pull up the skullcap."

Maryn stretched the hood over her head and tucked back the sweat-stuck hanks of hair under the tight material.

"Meds." Col handed her the vial of anti-anxiety pastilles. She fumbled one out into her hand, popped it into her mouth, and made a sour face at the flavor as it dissolved under her tongue. Col took the vial back before she lifted the helmet and placed it over Maryn's head, settling it into tracks in the suit's collar.

"There are two clamps. One slides toward you, the other toward me," Col directed Dair, her voice muffled outside the claustrophobic confines of the bubble visor. The younger being slid the clamps closed and locked them in place. Maryn's pulse pounded in her ears, breathing too fast until the cool brush of oxygen touched her face. She took a deep, convulsive inhalation, her exhale fogging the inside of the face shield.

The com in her ear crackled. "Slow your breathing. You are doing well," Col instructed.

Maryn concentrated, her eyes on the readouts inside the helmet. All green, all at full bars, a timer waiting to monitor her exposure to cosmic radiation. "Okay. I'm ready for the gloves."

Col took the sweat-damp towel from her clenched hand and eased the cuff over her left hand while Dair mirrored the process on her right. The Boshi checked all the seals and hoses afterward and nodded in satisfaction. "All systems go. We are prepared."

"Am I tethered?" Maryn's voice went high-pitched as the last of her fear demons began to succumb to the medication.

"You are." Col yanked on the cable, rocking Maryn back on her heels. She pivoted the joystick of the navigational pack beneath the suit's right arm. "Testing controls. Step back, Dair."

Maryn tested each directional thruster, jets of compressed air ruffling Col's fur in the confines of the bay. "All go."

"We are ready when you are, Scylla."

"Copy that. Moving into the gate at impulse."

She lifted her feet heel-to-toe to disengage the boots' magnetic soles and stepped around the crescent-shaped handrail to take her place inside the cylindrical airlock, unwilling to turn and face the tiny porthole yet. Col checked the straps suspending the pack at shoulders, chest, and waist, and gave her a thumbs up. "We will see you in a few minutes."

"Okay." She didn't trust herself to say more. Col punched the controls and the airlock sealed itself from the bay with a thump and a hiss. The suit began to pressurize in response to the decreasing atmosphere in the lock, snugging the fit of the layered materials against her body. The narrow eye-slit port looking out on the bay was eclipsed by Col's jewel-colored eyes, and then she was gone. Maryn was alone.

"We're in position, Mar," Jac said from the medical pod, where she observed the holo feeds on a PDD screen Scylla had rigged up for her. "*Girl* is going to open the outer airlock. The gate control panel is ten meters away on our port side."

"Roger." Her reply was breathless. She closed her eyes and concentrated on her breathing. As she did, she realized the pressure suit carried a faint trace of Jac's perfume. Coupled with her steady, reassuring voice over the helmet com, it was almost if Jac were there beside her, but it didn't lay the irrational storm of lightning in her nerves to rest. Sweat pooled on her forehead, under her arms, and inside the shielded glove where her right hand gripped the joystick of the thruster pack.

Her left hand clutched the rail of the airlock platform as the hatch slid into the hull behind her. She tugged on the retractable tether attached to a ring between her shoulders for the dozenth time and it rattled reassuringly against the bulkhead. All that remained was to face the void, but she couldn't seem to bring herself to move, to look the beast in the eye.

"Okay, love. Scylla's going to move into position so the gate registers our mass. I'll give you the word when it's time to head out."

"Got it." There wasn't time to delay. Maryn turned in slow motion on the platform.

Deep black. Endless spots of light and the clouds and pinwheels of distant galaxies swam in her vision. Her breath came in short gasps as her eyesight tunneled and telescoped. The unsettling perception of this limitless distance registered in her hindbrain as a creature that wanted to swallow her whole.

"Your pulse and breathing are too fast," Jac noted. "In through your nose, out through your mouth. Slow and deep."

She closed her eyes and focused on her breathing, shoulder muscles aching with tension. She tried to relax those, too. The faint, cloying aftertaste of her anti-anxiety medication reminded her it was still in her system, but it wasn't quite as effective while staring into the jaws of a monster.

"How are you feeling?" Maryn asked to distract herself.

"Sore. A few more hours, and the bone regen will be done." Discomfort punctuated Jac's words with tight little grunts at the end of sentences. "I'll take more pain meds once you're back on board. I don't want to be stoned while you're outside."

She huffed a weak chuckle. "Much appreciated."

The pitted steel of the jump gate's triangular frame, streaked with carbon and hundreds of years of exposure to deep space, eased into view as the ship's thrusters fired, matched the drift of the gate's fixed point, and hovered in place.

The panel housing the gate settings, a narrow, grated catwalk on the near side of the gate, blinked sleepy green electronic eyes at Maryn as the *Girl* was scanned. The lights turned yellow.

"All right. Forward thruster, Mar. Slow and easy."

Her hand wouldn't let go of the rail. "This is stupid," she whispered and blinked away the sting as sweat rolled into her eyes. Seconds ticked by.

"You okay?" Scylla asked, concerned. "We can't sit in the gate all day, Mar. It isn't safe."

"I know," she snapped. "Just … give me a second."

"She's not going to do it," Dair's voice sounded over the open com. "You should have let me try."

Heat flared in Maryn's cheeks. *Chemistry and spite,* she thought. Fuck Dair.

She eased the joystick forward, her gaze riveted on the catwalk platform and its baleful yellow glare. Compressed air hissed from the thruster behind her back and propelled her outside the safe, comfortable belly of the ship. In her impatience, she forgot to release the soles of the magnetic boots first. The sudden disconnect sent her into a face-first tumble. Fear engulfed Maryn as the ship and gate passed from her vision and the void threatened to swallow her. Her helmet display glared red, alarms keening in her ears.

"Oh, shit!" She flailed against the nothingness beneath her feet.

"You're okay," Jac said. "Hold still. Let the autopilot gyros in the pack kick in and get you back in position."

She squeezed her eyes shut until the thrusters fired quick, short bursts and corrected her trajectory. The heads-up illumination in her helmet went from red to palest blue outside her eyelids, and she peered between her lashes to find the gate in front of her once more. "Sorry. What a rookie mistake."

"Atta girl. Head for the platform."

With more care this time, she eased the thruster controls forward. The tether created a comforting, gentle tug against her back as the cable played out behind her.

"Eight meters. Seven. Six." She read out the diminishing numbers on the display. The handrail welded beside the control panel was almost in reach of her outstretched left arm. Her boots touched the grated platform and she toggled the eye cursor to bring magnetics back online. Her gloved hands wrapped the rail in a death grip. "In place."

"Look to your right," Scylla instructed. She turned toward the golden hull of the *Girl* and the open cockpit screen where Scylla waved. Col raised a hand from the copilot's seat, and Dair hovered between them. "We're right here. Always. You've got this."

She swallowed and let go of the rail with one hand, fumbled at the lever to release the control panel, and pulled it down. The gritty resistance of time and dust against the hinges vibrated up her arm as it popped free. The panel was a series of ordered chaos: eight rows of cylindrical dials with a flip switch at the end of every row "A fucking dial-up? That's archaic. How old is this thing?"

"Best guess? Predates the Galactic Mining Corporation by a century or so. They were the ones who lobbied for manned gates after one too many ore ships collided and ate into the bottom line ..." Scylla's voice trailed off. "Eh. That wasn't helpful knowledge right now, was it?"

"You think?" she snorted, a twist of sarcasm lifting the corner of her mouth. "Okay. Give me the first coordinates."

Dair rattled off a list of numbers in rapid fire, and Maryn said in exasperation, "Slower, please. These are the most fucking manual of manual controls. One number at a time."

She spun the dials to match the numeric value to the hashmark at the top and pressed. Each cylinder sank flush with the board once the numbers were entered, and a green light blinked at the end of the row when she depressed the final cylinder in the line.

"Next set."

Dair read them off one by one. Maryn kept her gaze focused on the panel and ignored the yawning abyss in her peripheral vision. At the end of the seventh row, she breathed a sigh of relief. "Ready for the last set."

"Before you enter the final coordinates, Mar, listen." Jac's voice said. "The gate is touchy, like we said. We've used it for five jumps and every time, the delay has been different, anywhere between two to six minutes. Release the magnetics in your boots before you push the entry switch. The lights will turn yellow. Slam that panel closed and get back to the ship. *Girl* will reel you in double time if the gate starts to draw us through, so be prepared for a yank."

"Great." She understood why they'd held that information back, but it would have been really fucking convenient to know. "Got it."

She entered the final set of coordinates, toggled off the magnetics, and pushed the button.

The hum of energy started as she closed the panel. Maryn's heart lurched as all the lights went from a brief flicker of waiting yellow, to green, to urgent red. Shimmering waves contorted her vision, the pounding in her chest joined by the pulling sensation of a jump distortion field.

"Oh, no, no, no," Scylla yelled in panic. "*Girl*, get her in—"

Before the word *now* crackled in her helmet, the tether cable snapped taut and Maryn was launched backward. The gate receded against her outstretched, flailing hands, the distance readout between her and the ship dropping so fast she couldn't focus on the numbers.

A wild ride ended with the collision of her hip into the airlock's handrail and forced a cry of pain through her gritted teeth. The port slammed shut as the ship began to pass through the distortion field. Her insides flip-flopped. The jump ricocheted her from aft to stern in the narrow tube.

"Maryn!" Too many voices were echoing in her helmet to make sense. She floated in the suit and breathed in gasping gulps of air for a minute before she answered.

"I'm okay." Adrenaline flooded through her, and she began to laugh. "Holy shit!"

"Bad. Ass," Jac said over the com.

Maryn whooped over the headset in delirious triumph. She peered through the narrow window of the airlock and glimpsed a portion of Qet's rocky ring, so dense the planet below was shadowed by its mass. "We made it."

"We did," Scylla agreed. "Dair, get her out of that suit, then both of you decon and come back up here."

"But I need to contact the government and resistance command," Dair argued.

"She can't do it alone. Scylla and Col have to concentrate on flying right now," Jac's tone was icier than usual. "We'll start scanning from the inner ring and see what's going on planetside. We'll need your and Maryn's input once we have the data. Get her out of the suit, deconned, and back up on deck."

Maryn re-engaged the magnetics and planted the soles of her boots in the foot-shaped depressions on the deck. Her quivering knees wouldn't have held up the weight of the thruster pack if she had been standing in half gravity. Her body vibrated from head to toes with ebbing adrenaline, a dizzy euphoria mixed with *what the FUCK did I just do* pounding a drumbeat behind her sternum. A cramp and a rumble in her intestines signaled that some of her tension was going to come out sooner than later.

Dair's shadow passed by, reflected in the airlock window before the hiss of pressurization began, and the raised dais swiveled to face the cargo bay. The door to the suit's processing compartment rotated to reveal an empty rack waiting for the contaminated gear. When the blinking light turned green, Maryn reached with shaking hands still gloved in heavy, shielded fabric to unseal her helmet.

The cargo bay port moved aside. Dair came in, dressed in disposable hooded coveralls and gloves. They let her fumble for a moment before asking, "Will you let me help you?"

"Yes." She gave up with a sigh. They stepped forward to slide the collar seals of the helmet from ear to ear and lifted it away, placing it on the top rack of the decon chamber. "*Girl*, what was my exposure?"

"Minimal," *Girl* answered. "Standard decon in the bay for you and Dair, plus two radiation tablets."

"Roger that." She glanced at the younger being as they opened the gaskets sealing her gloves to the suit's arms. "Hope you don't mind a cold, naked spin cycle."

"That doesn't sound pleasant," Dair agreed.

Once divested of the thruster pack and space suit, she peeled out of the skullcap and insulated underlayer and put them in the chamber as well. Dair disposed of their protective coveralls and stripped out of their own clothes, leaving the garments clipped to the rail next to the undersuit. They would get deconned with the rest.

Shivering, they faced each other in the round depression next to a set of lockers outside the now-closed airlock. Maryn slipped her feet into the metal stirrups on the floor as a flexible plastic cylinder descended from the bulkhead and sealed itself with magnetic clicks to the metal grate inside the ring.

Dair said nothing during this experience but stared at the story of old wounds on Maryn's abdomen, side, and thigh. Her gaze flickered over Dair's own scars; a palm-sized, concave circle of rough bronze tissue blossomed just below their sternum. It was the wound that sent them away from their family before the purge, she suspected, and chose not to ask about it. Pale, parallel lines slashed the golden skin of their forearms with hash marks. Some were defensive wounds, but some were too neat and too recent to be anything but purposeful. Dair had their own demons.

"Close your eyes," she said. "It's about to get cold and wet."

High-pressure jets attached to coiled tubing descended in a hide-flaying spray, scouring them from crown to toes, the stinging bite of lukewarm water an uncomfortable, invigorating experience. A suction fan switched on below their feet to direct ricocheting water drops with any captured contaminant particles into the drain.

"Turn," Maryn directed as the pipe ascended and reset itself. "It's going to repeat the cycle four more times."

When there wasn't an inch of un-scoured skin left on either of them, the showers rolled back into the bulkhead. They swept clinging drops from their hair and body with their hands to be drawn into the collection fan beneath the drain. The curtain lifted too and Maryn, her teeth chattering, opened the locker to retrieve towels. She handed one to Dair, who wrapped up in it convulsively, and then gave them a smaller one to rub some of the clinging water out of their hair.

She squeezed water out of her braid with another square of cloth and pulled a dry set of coveralls out of the cubby for Dair. She handed them the clothes.

Dair was studying the scar on Maryn's side again when she dropped her towel to dress. "Knife wound?" they asked, nodding to the marks.

"Yeah. Hand to hand with a corporate foot soldier on Gundam

Station during the Steel Union Rebellion." She grabbed the clothes she'd stowed earlier in the locker. "He and his squad opened fire on unarmed strikers at the corporation's orders. The rest of our platoon took out his men. I chased him down into an outer corridor. Neither of us wanted to risk a hull breach, I guess, and we pulled out knives."

"Who won?"

"I'm alive, aren't I?" Maryn answered, gripping a bar on the locker's frame to steady herself while she pulled her boxer briefs up her legs. Her stomach made another unhappy gurgle.

"Do you still fight?" Dair shrugged their shoulders into the coveralls and zipped the front.

"Live combat? No." She pulled her shirt over her head. "But Andelek and I sparred as part of our fitness routine. I could still hold my own."

They had a doubtful expression when Maryn looked up, and she gave rein to the annoyance dampening her sense of pride over the spacewalk. "Listen, Dair. I know I don't pass your muster, but I was very good at what I did for a long time. Give me a fucking break." She yanked on her boots. "You've taken every opportunity to remind me I'm an antique, and I don't appreciate it."

A flush rose from Dair's neck to hairline in a ripple of dark gold. "It isn't that I don't respect what you've done. I told you, we don't ask our elders to fight. It … it isn't seemly. It's a job for the young."

"They have just as much reason to fight as you. Maybe even more. We're at our most dangerous when we have nothing left to lose, and nothing left to prove." She drew on her sweater with wounded dignity and launched herself toward the ladder tube. "Now, if you'll excuse me, this old woman needs to take a shit."

CHAPTER
ELEVEN

WHEN MARYN finally emerged from the head, her ass bore a curved indentation from the toilet seat but she was in a far better mood. She blew a kiss to Jac through the narrow doorway of the medical pod as she floated by and pulled herself into a seat beside Col. *Girl's* high-altitude scan of the mountain range was displayed on the holo table outside the medical pod, so Jac could take part in the briefing while still immobilized. Dair was in the cockpit with Scylla, their voice carrying down corridor in a low murmur.

"Are they talking to the resistance?" she asked.

"Yes. We've noticed movement south of the mines, where the refugees are sheltered." Col circled an area to the south and tapped the display with the pad of her first finger. The image zoomed in. "The city is here."

The metallic shapes of industrial buildings and equipment squatted on a rolling plain in front of a range of craggy peaks. A devastated city spread in a curving moonscape of craters and blackened husks of buildings below the high ground. As the image irised in to show the terrain, Maryn glimpsed debris-filled roads and pulverized residential areas. There appeared to be no activity. Factories lay whole but abandoned, no steam or emissions coming from the stacks. Col trailed one finger to the left and resumed a wider lens.

A rocky valley spread out for hundreds of kilometers between mountains and twisting, narrow canyons. At the northern edge, a paved thoroughfare ran from the city along the foothills to a cluster of more industrial warehouses surrounded by tailings and other mining debris. Behind the processing buildings, the mine was a dark opening in the rocks below a steep mountainside, thick trees making a clear line of demarcation where the peaks rose into thinner air. Col dragged the screen down for some distance before she spread her fingers, enlarging the image.

"And this is approximately 800 kilometers south of the mines." On the edge of the valley lay a road plumed in dust clouds. Bright glints of light reflected off a convoy of vehicles encroaching on the valley in a slow, inexorable march toward conflict. Sunrise shadows created a thin, threatening hand in front of the column.

There were so many.

"It seems Dair's concern about the crew being captured and interrogated was valid, or the tracking data on the *Girl* was somehow accessed by Viltrux's ground forces. They are advancing on the camp. We estimate they'll be in range in eight hours or less. The refugee ship should arrive after sunset per our last known communique."

"Shit." Maryn put on her headset. "Any news from the government, Scyll? Can we expect reinforcements?"

"Dair is getting an update right now, but it doesn't sound likely," Scylla responded in a subdued tone. "They're under siege, like Bee warned us. The weird thing is, Viltrux's unmarked fleet is nowhere to be found right now. We've always seen them orbiting the planet before. We're in the wrong position to know if they're involved in the battle for the capitol, but it's unnerving."

"Where would they be?"

"Maybe the Pashni, trying to take back the wormhole?" Scylla sounded worried. "We still don't know its status."

Maryn pinched the skin between her eyes. "Let's worry about one thing at a time. We'll come up with some alternatives as soon as we know more. How is the audit going, Col? Anything of interest?"

"No smoking guns, but before our brains turned to jelly, Dair and I managed to collect a set of nine transactions that I want to examine further. I have initiated a connection with the local planetary branch to obtain the detailed reports. It is downloading but the satellite connections are sporadic."

A few minutes later, Dair returned to the common area. Their golden skin was pale beneath their controlled expression. "We won't have any help coming. I've confirmed the stronghold is under attack. They aren't even sure how they'd get troops there if they could spare them. I told them what we suspected about corporate mercenaries, but it might be too late to make a difference. We ..." Dair's voice caught in their throat, and they closed their eyes for the space of a few heartbeats. When they opened them again, all emotion had disappeared behind Dair's wall. "My orders are to get to the mine and defend our position as long as needed to get the refugees on that ship."

"What is your troop strength at the mine, and how many civilians?" Maryn wasn't sure she wanted to know the answer.

"When I left, there were two hundred and eighteen refugees still waiting for evacuation, mostly miners and their families."

"And how many trained soldiers?"

Dair paused before answering. "Five now, including me. There are ten civilians we've trained as best we can."

A hollow, sinking dismay filled Maryn's chest. Silence pressed against her eardrums as everyone considered those grim odds, and then, a switch flipped in her head. Calm filled her with a cool, decisive flood as her brain remembered the right cocktail of adrenaline and serotonin it needed and slammed it back in a shot glass.

"Give us a report on the mines and surrounding area. Climate, fortifications, escape routes, weaknesses. Everything." Maryn motioned to the holo table.

"It's high altitude. Dry and cold." The younger being stabbed a finger at the screen where an oblong shadow lay in the lee of the mountain peak. "This is where the refugee ship will land. The only other way in or out of the valley without accessing the main roads are the caverns in the northwest." Their fingers indicated an area near the landing site. "There's an escape route on the western side through a system of caves, but it's a narrow passage that runs for half a kilometer until it opens into a large chamber, and contracts again until you reach the opposite slope of the mountain range. We can't take any large equipment through. The camp is in a heavy forest behind the mine. We have a couple of camouflage emitters to blur the tents so they look like foliage."

Maryn glanced at Dair. "What kind of anti-aircraft weaponry do you have?"

"The big guns are at the edge of the forest. Here." Dair circled the area, their finger leaving a ghost-trail of yellow on the hologram.

"Nothing inside the valley?" She chewed her lip.

"There's a smaller battery at the mouth of the cavern, but it's last resort. We don't want to draw attention to our emergency escape route unless we have no other choice." They lifted their chin. "We need to contact Commander Pasque and notify him of our arrival so he doesn't waste ground to air ammunition. We need to conserve those resources if they do launch an air attack."

Col's tongue poked at one of her upper fangs, considering the suggestion. "Their forces could be monitoring communications. It would be risky to send a communique from orbit. What if they pick up our signature as soon as we enter the atmosphere?"

"Viltrux doesn't have reliable sensors in the northern hemisphere," Jac said from the med bay. "It's how the resistance gets supplies in and refugees out."

"The government crippled the satellites to keep them from using our own defenses against us." Dair explained.

"I guess that's why your data is taking so long to load, Col." Maryn pulled herself against the edge of the table, studying the images.

"It also destroyed our ability to monitor their movements," the Kheqet admitted. "We rely on lookouts in the mountain peaks to report activity. An early warning like this could mean all the difference."

"So, not much risk other than possible friendly fire if we time the communication right." Maryn glanced at Dair for confirmation and received a nod in return.

"We haven't had a problem so far," Scylla said from the cockpit. "We drop in at the north pole where there are no settlements, below the horizon for most radar, then maintain low altitude. The final approach is a thirty-minute flight threading the needle between some pretty narrow canyons at high speed."

"It doesn't have to be fast," Dair corrected.

"But it's more fun that way," *Girl* proclaimed over the interface.

"It's the same path we'll use to escort the refugee ship on the way out." Jac's voice was still strained against the discomfort of her injuries, but she'd insisted on taking part. "It will be at night and their ship won't have our maneuverability. Lower speed, Scyll."

"Yes, dear," the pilot lamented with exaggerated disappointment.

"Killjoy," *Girl* muttered.

"There's only one way for Viltrux's ground troops to mount an assault from the valley." Dair motioned to the image. "It's an unpaved road that comes through the plains and up to the landing pad at the end of the canyon."

"I don't see a landing pad," Col remarked, peering at the holo. "Nor do I see the camp."

"Good. It means the camouflage emitters are still working. It's there, in the tree line." Dair pointed at a notch between two craggy peaks. "We would be able to pick them off easily from the mountainside by daylight, but we've always suspected when an attack came, it would be at night." They drew the image back toward the south and stared in dismay at their approaching enemy. "That's at least a full tactical unit and assault vehicles. They won't risk damaging the mine or its equipment, so they have to be small enough to get up the mountain road for a direct assault."

"But you know they're coming." Jac reminded them.

"I suggest we send a message to Commander Pasque just before we enter the canyon." Maryn glanced at Dair. "How much will the civilians panic if we tell him an attack force is on the way?"

"They've been through a lot. Most of them have already lost family in the purge. They'll be terrified. I can use a code Pasque and I set up. No one else will understand if it's overheard."

"Should we tell him about the corporate mercenaries?" Col's inquiry was met with tense silence, until Dair shook their head in angry negation.

"No. It doesn't matter where they came from. The outcome is the same if the camp is overrun, isn't it?"

"All right. Transmit nothing but Dair's identifier and code, our ETA, and blackout status. As soon as we land, they can brief the commander, then we hit the bay and unload those weapons. We going to need them."

"Yes, Sergeant," Scylla replied over the com.

Maryn found Dair watching her, as if they didn't know who she was anymore. Honestly, she hadn't given this side of herself a voice in a very long time. The adrenaline jolt from the spacewalk hadn't worn off yet. She was vibratingly *alive,* every neuron firing in ways they hadn't for far too long. It was different from the intellectual high of witnessing a struggling student grasp the material. This was far more visceral; a violent joy she'd almost forgotten.

It felt goddamn *good.*

WHEN THE BURN of re-entry faded away and Scylla rolled back the protective plating from the windscreen, Maryn's first impression of Qet was *desolation.* Why would anyone fight over this?

Ice-covered volcanic rock spread out against the vast horizon. Dark fields of smoking fissures blanketed the ground in hazy clouds; a fire-fountain flashed by, spewing molten ejecta into the air as Scylla brought the *Girl* in low to skim over the lava fields.

"This is still undeveloped," Col noted from the co-pilot's seat.

"Yes," Maryn confirmed, glad to know something about it which might impress Dair. "The terraformers concentrated on the south when it was first settled, where it's warmer and they could grow crops right away, but it changed the ecosystem so much it endangered native wildlife. The scientists saw it in time and scrapped ideas to manipulate the northern hemisphere."

"The large number of volcanoes in the north are why the elements we refine here are so close to the surface," Dair added, and gave Maryn an approving nod. "Qetryllium is found in igneous rock and bands of volcanic dust."

"Interesting," Col agreed.

"All I heard was blah, blah, science nerd babble, blah," Scylla quipped.

"Up yours, Merrow," Maryn retorted, grinning.

The flush of vegetation below them began to spot the land in lichen-mottled patches of green and gray tundra, turning to grassland as they traveled farther from the pole. The pilot angled the ship to the southwest toward a mountain range jutting up in the distance as the terrain turned to high-desert scrub below the steep slopes. A fringe of trees darkened the mountainsides, a stark outline beneath bald, frosted peaks.

Then, a group of running animals caught her eye as Scylla banked hard to starboard, and Maryn's excitement escaped in a very unmercenary squeal of delight.

"Lizard elk! Those are lizard elk!" She pointed at the green-hided animals with majestic, curved scimitars of bone atop their heads as they loped across the plains.

"They're still numerous in the mountains," Dair said, leaning over to see. "They come right into camp because there's an outcrop of qetryllium in bands on the cliffside they rub their horns on." Their expression darkened. "They're endangered. Off-worlders poach them for their horns and hides. The southern continent doesn't even have wild herds anymore."

"It's a disgusting practice," Maryn agreed. Sport hunting of alien wildlife was one of the things Andelek hated most, and she had come to loathe it, having dealt with poaching and its bloody, wasteful aftermath.

"We've taken on poachers before," Scylla huffed dismissively. "Bring 'em on. Andelek would have liked that."

Dair's head cocked at Scylla's words and she stared at Maryn. She recognized a question working itself through the furrows between the younger being's eyes.

"Wait. Where did you get the scar on your right calf?" Dair made a raking mark with three fingers across the side of their own leg.

"On Chrekem Seven. I got too close to a nesting female calibotari," Maryn said. "It's a—"

"I know what it is! There was a holo series I loved as a kid. It was …" Comprehension flashed across Dair's face. Maryn recognized an *oh shit* moment when she saw one. "Your mate. That was zem, wasn't it?"

"Yes, it was." A smile lifted the corners of her mouth.

"You're the soldier ze worked with to get the DNA sample. The one who helped prove all the giant lifeforms in Shune sector share DNA with Earth's kaiju."

She huffed a soft laugh. "Are you a hobby exobiologist, or have you studied?"

"No, I just loved giant lifeforms as a kid."

"So did I. It's how I got into the field," Maryn affirmed.

Scylla crooned, "Aww, you two are so cute, finally bonding and everything."

The terrain ahead changed again. Deep, sheer-faced canyons of stone crazed the plain with sharp-sided cracks like a shattered mirror. In the deepest recesses, the white-water turbulence of a river far below was lost in shadows, out of reach from the late-morning light.

The pilot glanced over her shoulder at Dair, who'd strapped into Col's usual place at starboard. "Anything you need to add before I transmit the message? We're just a couple minutes away from being surrounded by rocks."

"No. Send it." Dair's gaze dropped to their hands. Maryn noted they were picking at the golden skin around their fingernails.

"Pre-battle nerves?" she asked. Dair turned their head, startled. She motioned to their raw cuticles, and they clasped their hands into their lap, stilling the motion.

"Yes." Their reply wasn't as defensive as she expected, but Dair raised an eyebrow. "You?"

"Yeah. Of course."

"Wouldn't be alive if we didn't get a little keyed up before action," Scylla commented.

"What do you do to feel calmer?"

"Tunes," Col, Scylla, and the *Girl* said in tandem, and Maryn gave Dair a 'what they said' gesture.

Dair's brow creased. "Do you mean music?"

"Oh, kid, you don't know what you're missing." Scylla put her hand over her heart. "Let me introduce you to some of my favorites. Flying is way better with a soundtrack."

The ship dove into the canyon to an accompaniment of raucous guitars, Scylla's music blaring in the cockpit as sheer rock walls closed around them. Dair winced, hands raised to protect their scalloped ear pinnae, but watched the pilot maneuver the ship through the crevasse at high speed with what Maryn thought was a little bit of awe. The *Girl* danced around curves and the jagged edges of cliffs at Scylla's mere suggestion of movement on the yoke.

"Whoo!" Col exclaimed, and Maryn laughed. She didn't know how much the *Girl* was flying, but for a moment it was a return to the days when it seemed Scylla and the ship were one organism. The knowledge that symbiotic connection might end soon twisted a knife in her gut. The emotional response was overwhelmed by her startled reaction to a portside turn which skimmed so close to the canyon wall she could see cracks in the stone. Despite the turbulent emotions in her heart, Maryn couldn't stop smiling.

"You okay back there, Jac?" she said over the headset.

"Yeah, let her have her fun," Jac replied. "I'm strapped down and full of pain meds."

Scylla throttled down when the gorge narrowed too much to allow showing off for Dair, whose somber countenance had gained a delighted smile during the aerobatic flight. Maryn witnessed the youthful, carefree being they might have been before the war in that moment, unlined and clear-eyed, until tension furrows resketched themselves into the space between Dair's eyebrows, and the shine faded from their eyes the closer they got to the camp.

Scylla guided the ship through a gap between two craggy, snow dusted peaks. They flew over a flat-bottomed basin just above the tree line, the spot Dair had identified from orbit as an apron where the evacuation transport would land that night. Maryn glimpsed individuals looking up in surprise as the *Girl* passed overhead.

The thick, forested mountainside flashed by and seemed difficult to focus on until she remembered Dair had mentioned camouflage emitters protecting the camp. The *Girl* made a wide turn over the mine's industrial center to the east before looping back to the woods. Scylla brought the ship into a hover above a clearing just large enough for them to land down slope from the camp. Maryn caught the edge of dozens of large tents fuzzed by the emitters' mirage of branches and spiny foliage as they sank beneath its coverage.

Scylla landed among the tall, straight-trunked trees. Before the engines began to wind down, Maryn unstrapped and stood, glancing out the windscreen. She spotted movement.

"Welcoming committee," she noted, and Dair craned their neck to look out her side of the cockpit windshield. Armed soldiers slipped through the forest on at least two sides.

"They're ours. I'll bet Commander Pasque was expecting my ship, not Scylla's. He doesn't know what happened. Let me go first so nobody gets excited."

As soon as the engines cooled enough to exit, Maryn operated the boarding ramp controls and opened the airlock. Five beings, a mix of Khepran, Qet, and Kheqet fighters, bristled with a variety of weapons and closed on the ramp with muzzles trained on the port.

"Exit the ship with your hands up!" the squad leader ordered in Gallingua, his words clipped with tension. Dair stepped into the opening with a grim smile and a wave, and the soldiers relaxed, shouting their name.

Shivering against the chill, Maryn drew Jac's leather jacket around her as she and Col followed Dair outside. Morning sunlight hadn't yet made it to the lee-side shadows of the surrounding peaks, and frost cracked under her feet as she stepped off the ramp to the ground. A pungent, pitchy scent from the conifer-like tree species crowding the ship drifted on the cold wind, which invaded the collar of her coat, and seeped up her sleeves. Col appeared comfortable without insulation, her fur shifting in the breeze as she inhaled fresh air, her eyes closed in pleasure.

"Where are Gleb and Revan?" A fair-skinned Qetish soldier in partial body armor trotted up to them and eyed the Boshi with cautious interest before turning his attention to Dair. "Where's your ship?"

"Destroyed." Their voice cracked. The squad shifted, uneasy glances of shock ricocheting between them. Not one of them were any older than Dair, who had recovered their urgency. "I need to talk to Commander Pasque. It's imperative. Are our plans to evacuate the camp still in motion?"

"Tonight." The voice belonged to a tall, black-haired Khepran male who approached the ship. He was perhaps two decades younger than Maryn, his military bearing clear, but his face was lined with exhaustion. His skin echoed the golden tones of Dair's without the ombré fade of dark to pale, and deep, orange discolorations shadowed his eyes. Dair straightened to attention when he reached them. Pasque favored them with a crisp nod and looked up at Scylla as she appeared on the ramp. "Welcome back, Captain Merrow." He raised his voice and spoke to the rest of his soldiers. "Squad dismissed."

The fighters left with uneasy backward glances, and once they were out of earshot, Pasque said, "I received your message. Tell me what's coming."

Dair took a deep breath to steady themself and lowered their voice to avoid being overheard. "There is a strike force entering the plains from the south."

He went still. "How large?"

"At least a company." Dair looked to Scylla for verification.

"We saw five vehicles, probably artillery, but were unable to make a lower pass to gather more intelligence without significant risk. We thought it was better to get here as soon as we could." Scylla's lips made a thin line as she hesitated, then plunged ahead with the worst news. "We estimate they will be here before sunset."

Pasque's dark eyes fluttered closed for a moment, and when he opened them, his tired expression held cold resignation. "They're finally coming for us."

"There's more. The last refugee transport was destroyed by an enemy frigate," Dair told him. This news rocked him back, but Dair gave him no quarter. "It's likely they were boarded and interrogated first. When Gleb, Revan, and I arrived in the system we witnessed their destruction. The frigate turned the guns on our ship as soon as we were detected. Only one of the children and I survived in an escape pod. Captain Merrow and her crew rescued us."

"We learned it's possible our ship was tracked here on a previous supply run," Scylla confessed. "There's no way to know."

Dark anger flickered over the commander's face. The pilot didn't flinch as he glared at her, accepting his silent accusation without excuse. Pasque let out a harsh breath and rested one hand on Dair's shoulder before he cast an appraising glance at the humans and Boshi in front of him. "Thank you for your help. You should leave and get to safety as soon as you can. This isn't your fight."

"We're not going anywhere," Scylla drew herself up. "My wife is still on board, and all four of us are veterans of the Artemis Corps. We want to offer our service and help defend the camp until you can evacuate the refugees. We've got a cargo hold full of weapons: thirty-six long range pulse rifles and a few surprises that might delay the oncoming troops long enough to evac everyone, including your soldiers. My ship is armed to the teeth. We're prepared to escort the refugee transport to Xyri."

Pasque gazed at Col, and his eyes lingered on Maryn. A scratchy sense of irritation tightened her neck and shoulders. She wondered if she was being weighed and discounted as she had by Dair and returned his regard with a hint of challenge.

Pasque blinked first. "Artemis Corps, you say."

"Retired and independent." Maryn straightened her shoulders. "But yes."

"Most didn't live to retire, I heard." His weary eyes flickered over them again, with a little more respect than before. "I am not in a position to turn down experienced fighters," he said at last, "but I can't pay you."

"That's already been covered by a sympathetic benefactor," Maryn assured him.

Pasque's expression fractured into tentative hope. "What benefactor?"

Dair inhaled to respond, but Maryn held up a cautioning hand. "One who prefers to remain anonymous for now."

A grim smile creased Pasque's face, but it didn't reach his eyes. "It couldn't have come at a better time. Dair and I will brief the officers and then break the news to the rest. I do not anticipate it will be received with calm. We will meet at the camp in thirty minutes."

"Send some able bodies to carry crates," Scylla suggested. "It may not be as scary when they see we brought stuff to fight back."

"We have less than a dozen trained fighters," Pasque said.

"And three dozen guns. Are you going to let them sit unused in the crates?" Maryn lifted her head and caught Pasque's gaze. "Some of these refugees must have served in the planetary militia. How many are able to defend their families?"

"Not enough," Pasque shrugged. "The group is primarily elders, and families with children. Anyone young enough to serve in the military is already at the front lines with the true government's troops."

"Have you even asked them?" Maryn glanced at Dair, who stayed quiet and glanced down. "You say you're not in the position to turn down experienced fighters. I understand it's unusual to expect your elders to fight, but this could mean the difference between a slaughter and the chance to evacuate everyone."

Pasque had the grace to pretend to consider it, but never

answered the question. "I will send our people after the crates as soon as they've been briefed. We will see you in camp."

He and Dair walked away, vanishing into the trees.

"He's on the verge of giving up, isn't he?" Maryn had seen the haunted shadows in Pasque's eyes before. "That's the face of somebody who's lost everything."

"Most of them have. Their homes, their careers. Their families, like Dair." Scylla hunched deeper into her coat. "Fuck. I wish there was a way we could find out if Xyri got the message and is riding to the rescue. Maybe it would give them some hope."

"Then it is up to us to provide inspiration." Col shrugged as if the answer was obvious.

"Let's get kitted out." Maryn started up the ramp. "If we look like we know what we're doing, maybe we can give them some reassurance."

"Yeah, but who's going to reassure us?" Scylla was only half joking.

"You can hug your new grenade launcher." Col clapped her on the shoulder.

She brightened. "Oh, yeah. I can't wait to play with that."

MARYN WAS glad for the thermal controls in the skinsuit beneath her body armor and dialed it all the way to maximum as she and Col geared up in the open cargo bay. A full suit in Col's size hadn't been available, but Bee managed to provide a large enough chest plate, backplate, and helmet to protect her most vital organs.

"This armor isn't made for four breasts," the Boshi complained as she helped her strap it on. "It's crushing my lower set."

"It's going to have to do," Maryn apologized, and adjusted clips at the flank. "Better? It leaves a seam, but is it easier to move and breathe?"

"It will serve its purpose unless we devolve into hand-to-hand combat." She went through a set of martial arts forms, testing the constraints of the protective gear. "That's a distressing gap at my waist," she said, as if her whole ass wasn't hanging out. "If we're going to do this often, I will invest in a proper suit."

Maryn stilled. "Are we? Are we going to do this often?"

Col studied her. "I have nothing I cannot leave behind. Given Scylla's progressive illness, I suspect Jac would welcome backup."

"That's true." She fumbled with her tactical gloves. A maelstrom of guilt, grief, self-doubt, and anger spun through her mind, and she swallowed against a rising lump in her throat. She hadn't even thought of offering her assistance to Jac and Scylla. The loss of Andelek was too new and raw to contemplate being strong for anyone else. Shame flushed through her in a scalding wave.

"Maryn." Col's huge, soft-furred hands cradled her red face. "You are a different person now than you were twenty years ago, and you are grieving the loss of your mate. Unlike me, you do have obligations at the university which your ridiculous sense of honor won't let you leave unaddressed. But that honor is what made you the fine soldier I have been proud to follow into battle and beyond. Do not wound yourself further with unnecessary guilt."

"Thank you." She leaned her cheek into the silkiness of Col's palm and blinked back the sting in her eyes. "I needed to hear that, I guess. But part of me wonders if this is the last stand for all of us. We've been lucky, like Bee said. We're horribly outnumbered, and we've made ourselves a target."

"I am not afraid to die with my sisters. My best friends." Col gazed at her. "Nor to fall for a worthy cause rather than as the hired gun of some corporation. If this is what the Universe has decided for me, I could not wish for a more honorable death."

"You'd better not die—any of you. I expect us to be terrorizing the galaxy as cackling old crones." Jac, dressed in an under-armor skin-suit, emerged from the ladder tube and moved into the bay. "Besides, we have a refugee ship to escort."

"Why are you out of the medical pod?" Maryn demanded, stalking to her side.

"Because she's a stubborn brat." Scylla emerged from the tube behind her wife. "Save your breath. We've been arguing for the last fifteen minutes since the re-gen ended."

"Give the meds a few minutes to kick in and I'll be fine. I might need help armoring up, though." Jac stretched and winced, her expression going blank in an attempt to hide the pain.

"No. Those bones aren't fully set." Maryn frowned at her in concern.

"I'll be fine," she repeated. "We need this show of force when they tell the civilians what's coming."

"Okay, you can look the part and then get back on the ship." Maryn planted her hands on her hips. "There is no way you are in fighting shape, Jacqueline Louise. You're staying here. That's an order."

"Oh yeah, *sergeant?*" she hissed with venomous emphasis on the last word.

"Oh, shit, here we go." Scylla pivoted away to sort out her own armor.

"You are not in command anymore, and I am not letting you do this without me," Jac retorted. "I am not going to sit on my ass and worry about Scylla—" she paused in her headlong tirade as Scylla stiffened, her head jerking up, but she didn't turn around. Jac added hastily, "Or you, or Col. Not when I should be out there."

"You can hardly move," Maryn accused. "You won't be able to help us, and we'll be worried about you. Don't be stupid."

"You don't need to worry about me. I'm fine. I took my meds," Scylla mumbled.

"You know those aren't a magic cure." Jac glowered at her wife.

Scylla slammed her hand on top of one of the waiting crates and shouted, "Neither is the damned bone regenerator, but you're acting like it is."

"Enough!" Col stepped into the fray. "We are all stressed. It will do us no good to argue. Jac, you know they are right. You are jeopardizing the bones if you resume normal activity too soon, and if they re-break they will not be so easy to repair."

"But I ..." Jac's face crumpled. "You've never gone into battle without me. I don't think I can stand knowing ..." she gulped back a sob, then burst out, "I won't be there to protect your backs."

"You still can. Someone has to prepare the *Girl* for immediate departure and cover our retreat, if necessary," Col reminded her. "You are just switching roles with Scylla. And we will have each other's backs. We promise."

"I'm sorry, love." Scylla enveloped Jac in a feather-light hug and kissed her forehead. "I didn't mean to yell. I'm gonna be okay today. You're not getting off the hook yet. You're stuck with me."

"Fine. Fine." Jac leaned her forehead against Scylla's shoulder for a moment, then pushed away from her wife and swiped at the tear tracks on her face. She glared at Maryn. "God damn it. It's been twenty-five years since you gave me a direct order."

"And you still argued with me about it." She widened her eyes. "Nothing's changed. Come on, let's get you armored up before they send those kids back to get the crates. At least it will protect your ribs."

CHAPTER
TWELVE

A CITY of tents sprawled beneath the trees. Maryn had known how many hybrid refugees waited here for evacuation but seeing them was another story. Scores of displaced Kheqet huddled in groups around smokeless heating elements and looked up with wary eyes as Maryn and her comrades walked between them, eliciting a stir of commotion with their body armor and weapons. Scylla paraded her favorite beefy gun and new grenade launcher with pride. Col waggled her fingers at children who drew near in curiosity and then ran, giggling, back to their parents.

There were so many kids.

Resolve solidified in her chest, displacing any doubt with an intent to get them to safety off world. Their parents had fled to this mountainside camp in hope of evacuation, and Team Huntress would see it through.

"Why so few trained soldiers?" Scylla muttered. "There's at least a hundred people here who look plenty able-bodied, and old enough to have military experience."

"Dair told me they don't allow their elders to fight. I assume that means everyone middle aged and older." Maryn frowned, taking in the large number of refugees, some with the pinkish streaks of age glinting in their dark hair and others with a glorious, full head of rosy locks. "I wonder if we can recruit some of them. I'd guarantee they haven't even been given a choice."

She spotted Dair drifting among the refugees, speaking to different groups. Everyone seemed to know them; many smiled in greeting and nodded at whatever the young being said. A crowd began to gather around a flat-topped boulder. Trees grew beside it; the trunks angled away from the displaced piece of mountain peak and framed it like a stage. The open crates of weapons lay arrayed before the stone and apprehensive civilians peered into them with wary interest.

Commander Pasque climbed atop the boulder and waited for the crowd's attention to focus on him. Dair stood in front of the rock and their gaze met Maryn's, assessing. Then, to her surprise, Dair motioned for Maryn and the others to stand with them at the front of the crowd.

The apprehensive mutters only grew as they threaded through the gathered refugees to take their place at Dair's side. Pasque raised his hand, and the group quieted.

"The transport ship is on its way," he said from his rocky podium. "We expect it to arrive half an hour after sundown. As a precaution, we will move you to the caverns to await departure. Once there, be prepared to evacuate at a moment's notice."

"Precaution? Why?" someone questioned from the crowd. "Nobody went to the caverns when the last ship left. What are the guns for?"

Pasque's eyes flickered downward, and when he raised his head to speak again, his resigned expression said everything before he uttered a word.

"Have we been discovered?" Another voice rose in hysteria, sending a ripple of alarm through the assembled refugees. "Are those murderers on their way?"

Children began to cry as fear jumped from being to being like a flashfire in pure oxygen, from spark to blaze in a matter of seconds. Pasque raised his hands for order and spoke more forcefully.

"It is imperative you stay calm, listen well, and follow instructions. We received intelligence that forces entered the southern plains earlier today. They will be here by nightfall, maybe sooner."

More cries of terror, shouts ringing through the trees.

"Listen! Listen to me!" Pasque called. He shook his head in disgust as the crowd's attention deteriorated and ricochets of panic claimed more civilians.

"He's losing them," Scylla muttered.

Dair gripped one of the branches framing the boulder and swung up on the rock beside Commander Pasque. They raised their arms. "Please! Please look at me, everyone. You know me and you trust me, right?"

The crowd subsided to fearful murmurs. Dair waited for another moment before speaking. "We've been expecting this. We've practiced it. I know it's different when it's happening, but it's so important not to fall apart now. The enemy is not here yet. The lookouts haven't even spotted them from the southern outpost. We saw them from orbit. There is time to prepare and make certain you're safe."

"I'll be damned. They're a natural leader," Jac marveled as people began to settle.

"I missed that in all the snotty remarks about how old and hysterical I am." Maryn's face scrunched in an over-expressive parody of wonder and she adopted Scylla's accent to say, "Who woulda thunk?"

"We are better prepared than we were a few hours ago thanks to Captain Merrow and her crew. These soldiers"—Dair indicated Maryn, Jac, Col, and Scylla—"brought us some much-needed firepower and are going to help us defend our position during the evacuation. Their craft is well armed and will escort the ship out of orbit and to Xyri. Everyone who has been trained with weapons, please come forward. We will get you armed, and we will be ready for them."

Refugees began to gather around Dair, some of them already carrying the limited rifles the camp possessed, others who had none. They numbered less than a dozen and all were young; some still bore the recent softness of adolescence, while others shifted babies or toddlers to older relatives before they joined the pitifully small group.

"That's not many," Jac said *sotto voce*. "We have three dozen rifles down there. We need to have someone behind every one of them if we're going to have a chance."

"Well, let me see if I can piss anybody off." Maryn squared her shoulders and stepped forward. "Commander Pasque. Dair." She gave them both a courteous nod. "Do you mind if I address your people?"

Dair's mouth opened as if they knew what she was going to say and wanted to protest. Then something shifted in their gaze and they turned to Pasque with a nod. The commander narrowed his eyes, and then stepped off the rock. Maryn swung up to stand beside Dair and raised her voice. Dair translated for those who did not speak Gallingua.

"I'm Sergeant Maryn Alessi, Artemis Corps, retired. I have been told it is not customary for those of you over a certain age to be asked to fight, but I know many of you must have military experience. These are your people, and we have guns to spare. We can't guarantee your safety if you choose to do so, but your future—the future of the children in this camp—will be better assured if we can hold off those incoming troops long enough to get the ship loaded and in the air. Please raise your hand if you have served in the planetary defense corps and are willing and able to fight."

For a moment, Maryn thought she'd made a colossal mistake. People gaped at her with wide eyes, some affronted by her request. Then, an elder male Qet with a full head of rose-pink hair stepped forward with his hand raised. A middle-aged female Khepran followed him, shaking off the grip of a younger Kheqet female with a toddler on her hip. In the end, almost two dozen people raised their hands, most of them in mid-life cycle or older. Maryn breathed a sigh of relief she hadn't fouled up, and continued,

"We have enough guns for anyone with combat training or marksman experience, and we are not about to turn away anyone who wishes to defend their families and friends. Meet us here in a few minutes and we'll get you armed."

Dair raised their voice before anyone could protest. "The rest of you, collect only what you need. Grab as much food and water and blankets as you can carry. Go to the caverns, and you'll receive further instructions there."

The crowd began to disperse with less frantic rumbles than before but urgency gave most of them a nervous energy which was hard to miss. Commander Pasque clapped Dair on the shoulder in approval when they stepped down from the rock. The younger being met Maryn's gaze and gave her a nod of respect but doubt still rode the crease between their eyes. It was the most positive response she'd received from them so far, so she returned the acknowledgement.

Maryn sighed and shifted in discomfort as she allowed Col to help her down from the stone podium. "God damn it. I have to pee again. Thank the universe Bee had two-piece skin suits and I don't have to take all the fucking armor off. I'll be back."

AFTER MARYN WRIGGLED BACK into bottom of the skinsuit and refastened the plates of her leg armor, she hurried down the ramp. She had just hit the last step when she saw the lizard elk.

She froze in wonder. It observed her from the trees with chameleon-like eyes shifting back and forth on their cone shaped lids, its spindly limbs poised to flee. The curved bone horns flashed bronze glints in the filtered, late afternoon sunlight. It turned away and moved on silent, two-clawed feet through the underbrush toward the cliffside rising above the forest.

Maryn glanced over her shoulder toward the camp, knowing she should get back, but followed the lizard elk as silently as possible. She'd never seen one in person, and likely would never have another chance. Picking her way through the trees on what appeared to be a game trail, she emerged in front of the sheer, rocky face and stopped short with a delighted gasp.

On the sunlit face of a pile of scree at the foot of the cliff, a dozen of the creatures sunned themselves on boulders. As she marveled, one of them scraped their horns against the striated rocks with a rasping sound, like a metal file drawn down steel. Where it rubbed, the pale greenish band of qetryllium had a thick crosshatching of discolored marks: red, blue, even purple, a saturation of the red end of the spectrum splashed in abstract art on the sheer stone wall and fallen boulders.

She knew from her studies the lizard elk's bones were rich in metals, the exposed horns containing more than the rest of its skeleton because of its rubbing. The color change was remarkable. Dair had told them qetryllium was used to strengthen and tint alloys. There must have been enough metal in the bone scrapings to discolor the rocks.

She turned her head to see Andelek's reaction and share the experience with zem, confused when her mate wasn't there because zer *presence* was so strong in this moment it was palpable. Her smile wilted when reality crashed down, but the sensation of zem beside her lingered moments longer. The air lightened and emptiness returned to her, but somehow, it wasn't as hollow as before.

"I should have known you'd be here," she whispered with a wobbly smile, her eyes wet. With one last look at the lizard elk herd, she turned back toward camp.

By the time she returned, forty-odd individuals had gathered at the stone podium with Dair and Commander Pasque. It was easy to tell how many of the erstwhile fighters had military training: they accepted the upgraded weapons with sure hands and grim, appreciative smiles as Col, Jac, and Scylla passed them out. The untried volunteers held their rifles like they might bite, and Maryn had to scold a few for placing their fingers on the trigger.

"These people need a class in weapons safety," she griped to Jac, who lifted one of her eyebrows.

"Good thing we have a teacher here, right, Dr. Alessi?"

She groaned. "I set myself up for that one, didn't I?"

"Any training we can manage before those troops are in range is a bonus."

That was how Maryn found herself with six untrained fighters who had never held a military grade weapon before, and a dozen seasoned veterans with florid streaks of age in their hair who wanted a refresher course. In all honesty, she needed a review as well. The new rifles were the latest models, higher tech than she was used to. She approved the smart scope upgrades, which confirmed targeting and had a light-controlled switch between day and night vision.

They got a tutorial on how to not shoot each other. Then she took the group down slope to the edge of the tree line overlooking the plains and taught them to use the scope to aim at specific targets some distance away—without firing at said target to conserve their precious ammunition. After the lesson, with a warning broadcast over the camp's communication system there would be live fire and not to panic, she let them take two shots to check their accuracy and correct for recoil.

From that observation, she separated eight people who hit their target with confidence on each shot and took them aside. Four were from the young, trained soldiers who guarded the camp. The others were among the group of older volunteers, ranging from Maryn's age to the spry, elderly being who had been the first to volunteer.

"I'm looking for snipers," she told them. "If we take out scouts, crews on artillery vehicles, drivers, anything that will delay their advance even by a few minutes, it could be the time we need to load the evacuation ship and get it in the air. But it's unprotected out there. It's dangerous. I won't think less of anyone who decides they'd rather be in the trees than on the forward line with me."

The elderly male stepped forward. "I will do it."

"What's your name?" Maryn asked.

"Elxan." He stood at attention. "Qetish planetary defense forces, retired. I would rather fight the bastards head-on than die penned in a cage like livestock. I will stand in front of that hatred coming for us if it gives my children and grandchildren a chance to survive. No one has come to our defense but you." He turned a scathing gaze on the others. "Will you allow strangers to die for you and yours? I am tired of cowering in a tent waiting for them to arrive."

"As am I." An older Khepran female stepped forward, then the Kheqet mother who'd handed her child off to a relative.

"Your names?"

"Halith," said the older of the two. "I worked in the mines, but I was a gunner in the defense force, once upon a time."

"Oluran." The younger woman cast a proud glance at Halith. "My mother taught me to shoot."

"You're sure you want to do this?" Maryn questioned. "I know you have a child."

"I would die to protect my son," Oluran said.

The others stepped forward and introduced themselves to her one by one. They each had their reasons for volunteering, and Maryn nodded as they shared their stories. In the end, all eight chose to take the forward line with her. She fervently hoped none of them died, herself included. A tightness at the back of her throat threatened to overtake the cool exterior of warrior Maryn, a sun-faded façade brittle with age and stiff from disuse. She cleared her throat.

"Thank you. Let's start. We don't have much time before dark."

The next hour flew by as they scouted for concealed nest sites on the mountainside. The refugees had a familiarity with the area she did not, and provided excellent suggestions where they might dig in —so to speak. There wasn't a foxhole shovel to be found in the camp or in *Golden Girl*'s storage lockers. They'd have to remedy that, Maryn thought, and then shook herself. When would they dig foxholes again?

But once the logical part of her mind where she calculated siege craft was rebooted and running, there was no turning it off. After a strategy meeting with Dair, Pasque, and their five most experienced soldiers, they placed the six novice fighters at the mouth of the cavern behind the anti-aircraft battery to defend their families instead of the front line. If Viltrux's troops made it that far before the evacuation ship arrived, things were already fucked.

The rest of the volunteers were placed in three squads nested in the steep, forested slopes with Scylla and Col commanding the flanks. Four of Pasque's trained soldiers wore headsets and were grouped with civilian snipers. Maryn keyed their coms in the battle helmets to the same frequency.

Throughout the preparations, she found Dair staring at her whenever she spoke, as if they couldn't believe Maryn was the same person who'd broken down on board *Golden Girl*. The younger being contradicted very few suggestions Team Huntress made, and when they did, it was because Dair knew the camp better and they were right. Nor did Commander Pasque override their contributions as they compounded upon his previous defensive plans by adding more firepower.

Cool fire spread across the sky as Qet's star slid down the far side of the peaks, the silver ribbon of the planet's ring a bright slash across the heavens. Maryn began to hope the evacuation ship might arrive before the enemy was on their doorstep, but warning went up from the southward mountain outpost before darkness fell.

"They are coming!"

Standing in a group at the flat boulder which had become the command center, Maryn turned her head and glimpsed of the last orange light on vehicles emerging from hollows in the valley floor. Plumes of dust expanded against the sunless horizon.

Beside her, Jac raised a pair of binoculars. "Track mounted artillery. Awesome," she muttered. "At least two vehicles at the fore."

"Can you see more than that?" the commander inquired.

"Whatever's behind them is hidden by the terrain and dust." Jac passed him the binoculars. Pasque took in the view, then handed the gear to Dair.

"Keep the forward battery hidden until we have clear shots at their siege artillery. It will be their primary target once they know it's here," he ordered his soldiers. "We have a limited opportunity to eliminate the biggest threats. Reserve the battery near the cavern for any airborne attacks."

"Use those rifle scopes to their best advantage," Maryn instructed her civilian snipers. "Go to your protected positions. Once they're in range, start picking them off. Blanket fire will only give away your location and waste ammunition. Remember if you can see them, they can see you. Stay low and change your angle when you can. Keep them guessing. Aim for joint gaps in their armor. Make every shot count and listen for instructions to fall back to the trees."

As the fighters scurried off to their defensive nests, Maryn looked at her friends. The four of them drew together in their tight circle, heads together, arms locked around each other. Ferocious thankfulness for these ride-or-die friends overwhelmed Maryn's heart and spilled out her eyes in a hot flood. "Stupid damn hormones."

"I love you guys," Jac said.

A quiet chorus of affirmation drifted between them.

"We've had worse odds," Scylla murmured. "Couple times. Right?"

"Peloon," Col affirmed.

"What a shitty comparison," Jac scolded.

"Kinzec Five, then."

"Huh." Maryn thought about it. "Didn't we steal a tank from their armory?"

"That was after the battle. We were so fucking drunk." Scylla's giggle-snort made them all start laughing, but Maryn's shoulders never loosened with the strain of tension as Scylla drew back from their circle to passionately kiss her wife.

"You better be careful, Merrow," Jac demanded when they parted. "Status reports from all of you, or I'm going to be gnawing my fingers off the entire time."

"I'm just a com away, darlin'." Scylla kissed her again, and Maryn looked away, her heart aching. The pilot slung the harness of the slender tube launcher over her shoulder and hefted a six pack of rocket powered grenades. "Let's blow things up."

Jac tugged Maryn into another hug and spoke in her ear. "Watch her, Mar. Please. She's fine on board the *Girl*, but good at masking confusion when it hits her outside. She's okay right now, but when things get rolling, I'm worried it might be too much for her to process."

"And she has the fucking grenade launcher?" She rolled her eyes. "As soon as we fall back from the initial assault, I'm stuck to her. Don't worry," she promised. Jac gave her a kiss on the mouth and headed up the slope. She did not look back.

Maryn tugged on her helmet as she took her place within the rocks. Black mountain shadows raced forward in a tidal surge and engulfed the approaching army as the sun passed below the horizon, and night descended on the valley below. The glowing sky faded and took with it the last of the light. The sound of engines rumbled closer, hidden in darkness and dust.

She lay on her belly and peered through her weapon's night scope. "Command, I see four mounted gun vehicles preparing for assault. Unknown number of infantry but at least two troop transports."

"Copy." Pasque replied. "Western flank reports additional motorized assets at the rear but can't identify them due to terrain."

On the plains below, the first creeping scouts emerged like black-armored shadows against the gray topography in her night scope. They were well in range, yet none of her recruited snipers were firing. She understood the visceral reluctance to take a life, even felt it herself. But rediscovering the cold, detached place her mind went when it was necessary to kill was disconcertingly easy, like slipping on an old jacket.

"Here we go, people," she said into her com. She took aim on the lead soldier's neck. Red crosshairs flashed. The shot cracked and echoed across the cliff face, and the soldier crumpled in their tracks.

Whatever hesitation they had evaporated as soon as the advancing forces started shooting back. Weapons fire rang out from all over the mountainside. Maryn dispatched another unlucky scout and low-crawled to her next position, every joint protesting the abuse.

"Oh, fuck, this is not as easy as it used to be!" She dropped into the nest behind an outcrop of boulders and surveyed the scene below through her night scope. She peered closer at the western incline. "Col, somebody's coming up the perimeter, sixty degrees from your position."

But as she spoke, the advancing creeper appeared to fling themselves backward to slide headfirst down the rocky slope. "Not anymore," Col announced with grim satisfaction.

Most of her snipers had taken Maryn's instructions to heart. The volley from their side was controlled compared to what came from below, Viltrux's forces having the luxury of plentiful ammunition. The enemy abandoned the foot assault for now. Maryn thought they were taken by surprise by the unexpected voracity of their defense and falling back, but the throaty bark of a large caliber weapon demonstrated they were only getting out of the way.

She sighted on the gunners crouched behind the armored vehicle's weapons array. One went tumbling over the side, but her second shot went wide and missed the target. The weapons swung in her direction and opened fire, projectiles whining off the rocks beside her. She ducked into the nest as sharp fragments of boulder rained against her armor.

There was a *whump* from the bottom of the hill, followed by a bright explosion in front of the outcrop she hid under. It vibrated the ground in an earthquake jolt and pelted her with clumps of dirt and stones.

"Maryn, sound off!" Scylla screamed.

"Shit. Time to move!" she called back, scrambling out of the nest under the cover of smoke and falling back to the tree line in a crouch, her knees burning in protest all the way. She found the second position she'd scouted earlier and dug in behind the trunk of a gnarled tree.

A streak of fire came from the perimeter to her left, angling downward. The tracked vehicle which had blown up Maryn's previous position erupted with a boom and conflagration. When her vision cleared, all that remained of the guns was twisted metal wreathed in flames. Maryn took aim on the figures fleeing their burning vehicle and dropped the staggering, flame smothered bodies.

Scylla flung herself down beside her, panting and grinning. "Oh, baby." She kissed the grenade launcher. "Where've you been all my life?"

"I'm glad you're having fun." Maryn rolled to her back beside Scylla as projectiles tore hunks of bark from the tree above them. "I forgot how ugly killing people is."

"Just remember they're working for a genocidal maniac and a greedy corporation," Col interjected over the com, the sound of her weapon adding emphasis.

"True." Maryn returned fire from a prone position against the trunk and toggled the camp's frequency. "Dair, where is that transport? It's been dark for thirty minutes."

"They should be coming out of the canyon any minute now," Dair responded.

Another rocket trail spouted from the enemy's forward line and exploded in the trees. Bodies were flung into the air to land in twisted, limp heaps on the ground, the agonized screams of unfortunate resistance fighters caught in its radius echoing above the fragmented, cracking sounds of falling timber and the noise of battle.

Scylla shoved another round into the tube and took aim through the fork in the tree. Maryn was glad for the insulating confines of her helmet, for even with it the roar of the rocket made her ears ring as it streaked out of the launcher.

The vehicle from which the artillery had come disappeared behind the intense upsurge of fire, but she knew it wasn't a direct hit. The next explosive shell from the vehicle detonated too fucking close for comfort. Maryn pulled Scylla down and they crouched together for cover. Once debris stopped raining, they ran for their next defensive position.

"I think it's time to get that siege gun involved, Commander Pasque!" Scylla shouted. "I only have so many grenades."

"I'm there," Pasque responded. "Western flank, fall back to the camp. I'm about to become a target."

"Why are you there?" Dair's voice rose in fear. "Where's Garali?"

"Dead." The word fell in one, chilled syllable. "You're in command, Dair."

For a moment, there was silence, then Dair's impassioned response: "You heard what he said, people! Western flank, retreat to camp! Eastern flank, move in and be ready when it's your turn."

The siege gun's hiding place in the wooded slope erupted in roars of artillery. A tracked vehicle exploded and flipped into the air. Maryn laid down suppressive fire as Scylla loaded another grenade.

"Keep firing downslope!" she instructed her snipers over the com. "Don't give them time to regroup!"

"I'm headed your way, Maryn," Col panted over the helmet's earpiece.

"Be careful! Stay in the trees where they can't see your furry white ass," she cautioned.

"I am well aware of my furry white ass!"

Pasque's siege gun continued to hammer the troops at the foot of the mountain, the enemy visible in strobe-like flashes of weapons fire, scurrying like insects to whatever cover they could find. A smaller vehicle disappeared beneath a flower of orange heat from Scylla's rocket, and then something boomed across the valley floor, echoing off the rock face behind the tree line. A rocket streaked from further back in the plains, headed unerringly for the gun's red maw as it continued to unload Pasque's fury on the troops below.

"What the fuck …" Scylla managed. The hillside erupted in a volcanic explosion. An expanding ball of flame and shroud of smoke swallowed everything. When it cleared, Pasque's gun lay silent, its misshapen bulk illuminated by the burning skeletons of trees snapped by the blast. The enemy was now outlined in the flickering, rusty light from the fire, and at the rear of the valley, the roar of an advancing vehicle rolled over the hilltop. Maryn's heart dropped into her stomach when it came into view.

"Shit, shit, shit. Dair, it's a tank. It was at the rear of their phalanx."

"The evacuation ship just arrived!" Dair's triumphant cry

sounded over Maryn's headset. "The refugees are leaving the cavern. Start falling back! Maryn, I need to direct the evacuation. Take charge of the ground troops and get them to the ship when it's time."

"Yes, Commander," she responded.

"That's our cue!" Scylla said, and spoke into her helmet com. "Jac, fire it up. I'm comin' your way."

"Leave the grenade launcher!" Col roared.

Scylla shrugged out of the strap, deposited it beside them, and shoved the case of grenades closer to Col. "Don't lose her! Her name is Kate and I'm in love. You have three left. Make 'em count."

"Be careful!" Jac said over the com.

"Don't wait too long," the pilot ordered as she rose into a crouch. "Get your asses to the ship, understood?"

"Yes, ma'am." Maryn punctuated each word with the crack of a bullet, leaving two advancing soldiers in limp heaps.

Scylla made her retreat toward the forest clearing where *Golden Girl* lay. Maryn picked off any targets who tried to make a run for the path, but she knew the poor bastards at the front of the enemy lines were nothing more than cannon fodder meant to eat up their ammunition.

What appeared through the dust cloud at the bottom of the slope was the real threat.

"Oh, shit," she said. "Here comes the tank."

Col had already noticed. "This is bad."

"Sergeant! What do we do?" one of the civilian fighters shouted.

"Keep shooting!" Maryn yelled. "Fall back to the rear of the camp. Be ready to head for the evacuation ship. Col, let's try to take out that beast."

The Boshi slid a rocket into the barrel and took aim over the rock. Fire bloomed at the bottom of the hill with a roar; the explosion scattered the advancing troops near the tank in a gory shower of debris and body parts. Col fit another projectile into the launcher and grabbed the last one.

"Cover!" she yelled. Maryn laid down a screen of suppressing fire and followed the Boshi into a grove of scrubby trees fifteen meters away, a rough diagonal from their previous position. Return fire pinged off the rocky soil in her footprints. A shell exploded in the midst of the abandoned tent city, illuminating retreating resistance fighters with a mushroom cloud of flames.

The tank began to climb the final rise to the camp. Emboldened foot soldiers swarmed behind it and fired their weapons. A groan and gurgle sounded over the headset. "They got Elxan!" a panicky voice cried. "They—" the voice ended with a cracking sound, an abrupt gasp, and silence.

"Listen up, squad leaders," Maryn shouted over the com in her helmet. "When this explosion goes off, retreat. Repeat, retreat to the evacuation ship. For the love of the universe, do not shoot us! We're going to try to take this thing down."

"Be ready to run," Col commanded. She hefted the launcher to her shoulder, aimed, and fired. The rocket hit the armored cockpit of the tank and detonated, an inferno which temporarily blinded Maryn's night vision.

"All squads, fall back now," she barked over her com. She and Col hoofed it to their next position. "Nice shot!" Maryn shouted as they ran.

"I was aiming for the treads," she complained. "It won't do enough damage to stop it."

The tracked beast emerged from the cloud of smoke and flame in its inexorable path up the hill. A scorched dent in the armor marked the impact point, but it kept coming.

"Last grenade," Col said. "Buy me time to aim."

Maryn knelt behind a tree as the Boshi prepared to fire between its split upper trunk. She fired off a volley of shots until her magazine was empty, grabbed the last one from her ammo belt and slapped it in.

The crack of a weapon: a wordless snarl of pain snapped Maryn's head toward her friend. Bright crimson bloomed against the pristine white fur of her left thigh as Col stumbled backwards, falling to clutch her leg.

"Col!"

"It's just an insect bite," she growled, though blood dripped between her fingers. "It looks worse than it is. Give me your gun. Take the shot now, before they make it to the top!"

She passed Col the rifle and hefted the grenade launcher, her legs braced to counterbalance. Col hauled herself to her feet and sprayed fire at the advancing troops. Through the haze of dust and smoke, Maryn sighted on the treads of the armored monster, said a silent prayer to the universe, and fired. Her hearing went muffled with the roar of launch.

A blossom of hell lifted the front of the vehicle. She shouted in hoarse victory as it began a slow tumble backwards. It stopped its death roll down the hill midway, sending a ball of flame skyward and illuminating the mountainside.

Another tank rolled past its slaughtered counterpart.

"Oh, you're fucking kidding me," Maryn spat. "There's another goddamn tank! All squads, you'd better be in retreat! Go to the evacuation ship. Dair, they're about to overrun the camp." She toggled her team's private throat mic. "Jac, we're on our way to you. Col's wounded."

She didn't take time to evaluate the new threat, just rotated the launcher on its harness to bang against her back plate, and supported Col as she limped her way through the night-dark forest toward their waiting ship. In the abandoned camp, more artillery exploded, fire racing along the peaks of the tent city.

"All civilians are on board!" Dair cried over the headset. "Anybody in retreat, we'll wait until the last second to close the door. Get here now!"

Relief drenched Maryn in cold rivers when they broke through the clearing where the *Girl* waited. She helped Col up the steps into the belly of the ship, and Jac appeared to assist their friend to the medical pod.

"Where's Scyll?" she asked, looking behind Maryn.

"She's not here?" Maryn's gut dropped, her lips going cold.

"No!" Jac went pale and still.

"She left before we blew up the tank," Col panted, distressed by more than physical pain. "She headed into the trees."

Maryn looked out into the dark forest, muzzle flashes visible on the ridge beyond. Another explosion went up from the camp and rattled the ship.

"Scylla, check in," she said over the helmet com in desperation.

Silence.

"Scylla! Report, goddamn it!"

CHAPTER
THIRTEEN

"FUCK." Maryn dumped the RPG tube in the corridor. "Get Col's bleeding stopped and have the *Girl* prepare us to take off. I'll be back."

"Find her, Mar," Jac begged.

"I will." She pounded down the steps headed back into the dark trees. With each stride, her mind shrieked, *You were supposed to keep an eye on her. You were supposed to watch out for her.*

The last she'd seen her, she was retreating into the forest. She headed for the edge of the tree line and retraced her steps in. She screamed above the battle noise. "Scylla!"

Projectiles ripped bark from the trunks above her head. She returned a volley of fire and retreated deeper into the forest, heading away from the ship. "Scylla! Where are you?"

Another explosion, closer this time, rocked her on her feet. She caught a glint of firelight on something shiny, and she ran in that direction.

A figure in battle armor was standing in a thick grove of trees, looking around with frantic movements. Scylla's helmet was missing, a thread of blood trickling down her face. Her rifle hung limply at her side.

"Scylla!"

The pilot spun and brought up the gun in deadly aim. Maryn read the uncertainty and near panic in Scylla's expression and let her weapon fall against its strap, holding up her hands. "It's me!" She lifted the visor.

"Maryn?" Scylla blinked at her. "I can't find the *Girl*! Did they leave without us?"

"No, she's behind me." She approached her with caution. "Are you good? You hurt?"

"No. I guess I got turned around," Scylla admitted and repeated, on the verge of tears: "I can't find the *Girl*."

"I've got you. She's this way." Maryn guided her to the northwest. "Come on, we need to move."

Girl's engines gained strength as they ran for the clearing. The sound of gunfire behind them thickened into a barrage as bullets whined off the rocks and shattered tree branches flew through the air, pelting them with sharp splinters. She brought her rifle up and sprayed cover as Scylla vaulted up the steps into the airlock.

Maryn spotted two resistance fighters sprinting for the clearing from the direction of the camp. "Come on! Run!" she screamed.

One of them raised a hand, and then both were cut down from behind in a hail of gunfire. Both crumpled into stillness on the forest floor.

"No!" Maryn flinched back into the corridor as bullets whined off the trees in front of her. She fled into the *Girl* and banged her fist against the release in impotent fury. The port slammed shut.

"We're onboard! Do you need me back there?" she shouted to Jac as Scylla dumped her rifle on the deck and pounded down the corridor for the cockpit.

"No, go with Scyll," Jac instructed over the headset, her voice thick with relief. Maryn shoved her helmet and their abandoned weapons into a corridor storage compartment and hurried to the copilot's seat.

"You okay to fly?" Maryn asked.

"Yeah." Scylla didn't look at her as she strapped in. "I just got a little turned around, that's all." She lifted her voice and called, "How's it going? You both in?"

"We're secure," Jac responded over the ship's com. "Get us out of here."

"Hold on to your asses. Let's go, *Girl*."

"Watch for that tank," Maryn warned.

"That's what missiles are for," *Girl* responded with a savage lilt that sounded exactly like Scylla.

The pilot gave her a flash of bared teeth. "Fire at will, Sergeant. Take them out fast and head for the canyon," she commanded. "We don't have time to waste."

"With pleasure."

Golden Girl lifted above the tree line and the pilot swiveled the ship to face the oncoming swarm of enemies. The tank topped the hill and swiveled its guns to take aim on the rising craft.

Maryn fired as the crosshairs converged on her prey. A bright trail emerged from the *Girl's* belly and the target vanished in a white-hot ball of flame.

Another violent explosion rocked them as artillery slammed into their shields. Their hovering vessel lurched to starboard with a heart-stopping brush of its shields against the rocky mountain face above the tree line. Rattled in her seat, Maryn wasn't able to process what happened before the targeting system squealed in impatience, waiting for her to engage. She pressed the trigger.

Another streak of fire launched from the *Girl's* ventral tubes and the artillery vehicle disappeared behind a second magnesium-bright explosion as Scylla wrestled the ship back into control and headed for the pass in front of them.

"I remembered the shields, Captain," *Girl* said.

"You did." Scylla's face was grim, her voice clipped with anger. "Thanks, *Girl*."

Maryn pushed it into the back of her mind for now. The AI was aware something was up with its pilot and was performing its duty. She had her own job to do. She toggled the com. "This is *Golden Girl*, calling the crew of the evacuation transport. Do you copy?"

"Copy, *Golden Girl*. This is Captain Jarad of the *Bright Wing*. We are lifting off and heading for the mountain pass."

"We're right behind you." Scylla headed through the notch in the mountain behind the camp. Maryn glimpsed armored mercenaries swarming into the fire-riddled tent city before they accelerated over the ridgeline.

Below them, the long shape of the evacuation ship pivoted in place and turned toward the narrow pass. The *Girl* followed them and sank into the darkness of the canyon, the near-vertical walls delineated in ghostly green lines as the heads-up display flickered over the windscreen, following the glow of *Bright Wing*'s engine lights ahead of them.

"Cabin lights off," Scylla barked. The display glowed in the gloom. "*Girl*, keep an eye on the sky. We're going to be at a fucking crawl and I'm a little nervous enemy air support hasn't shown up yet."

"Yes, Captain."

"*Bright Wing*, send us your flight plan," Maryn requested. "Once we're clear of Qetish space we'll coordinate. Until then, maintain radio silence unless a threat pops up."

"Understood, *Golden Girl*. Transmitting now."

"Take a gander at their chart, Mar. Let me know what gate they plan to use and how soon we'll be there," Scylla ordered.

Maryn swiveled her chair to the instrument panel and swept the data up to the screen. "Looks like they're heading for the Altroon gate. Only an hour away."

"Like that won't be crawling with corporate ships, at all." Sarcasm dripped from Scylla's voice.

"It's the closest one, so, yeah. It's a straight shot to unclaimed space from there. I wish we could find out the status of the Pashni wormhole. It's a longer trip, but it would get us to Xyri a whole lot faster. I wonder how up to date their intelligence is."

"I'm guessing Lekere's fucking vote didn't go the way he hoped. We haven't heard anything," Scylla snapped. The uncharacteristic impatience in the pilot's voice made Maryn turn back from the screens to regard her friend.

"We knew it would be a long shot." She paused. "You're agitated, Scyll."

"I'm fine."

She wasn't, though. Maryn read it in the tension of her forearms as she gripped the yoke. "How about some tunes?" she suggested.

"Any requests?" the *Girl* chirped.

"Quadra Six playlist," Maryn suggested, and her friend nodded.

"Yeah. Good flying music. Good memories. The bioluminescent beach."

"Wine and chocolate sandwich cookies from the MRE's."

"Not such a good memory." Scylla grimaced, but Maryn's gambit had been successful. The pilot stopped dwelling on the near disaster and focused on the heads-up. Maryn studied the readout of *Girl's* vigilant surveillance, the gentle drift of music surrounding them.

They were ten minutes from the end of the canyon before their luck ran out.

THE FIRST BLIP appeared on the edge of *Girl's* radar at the same time the ship gave a crisp, urgent warning: "Fighter craft approaching from the south."

"How many?" Scylla flicked the radar display to the top of her heads-up screen.

"Two."

"Only two? We're lucky they underestimated how this would go."

"Two is still too many," Maryn argued.

Bright Wing radioed a second later. "*Golden Girl!*" the captain's frantic voice sounded.

"We see them, *Bright Wing*. Maintain your course through the canyon. Stay dark and keep your shields up. We'll go topside to try to draw them away. *Golden Girl* out." Scylla flicked on her ship's headset. "Well, fuck. We'll have company in about two minutes."

"Yeah, I heard," Jac responded. "Bullet passed through Col's leg. It's bandaged and the bleeding is under control. Need me up there?"

"Always," Scylla said softly. "Unless Col needs—"

"I'm coming too," Col interjected.

Maryn slid out of the copilot's seat and back to her familiar port-side station. Jac arrived first, then the Boshi, limping heavily down the corridor, blood-clotted fur below the pressure bandage on her left thigh. Neither had removed their armor.

As they strapped into their seats, seeing all four of them in dirty gear, streaked with blood and dust, sent a giddy frisson of déjà vu through Maryn despite the seriousness of situation. They'd emerged on the other side of a battle alive, yet again. It wasn't over, but she couldn't help grinning at Jac, then at Col, who smiled back with fear-some teeth. Scylla gazed at her wife and they all beamed at each other with ridiculous grins for a few more seconds before the proximity alert began to shriek.

The port behind the cabin sealed with a hiss as the ship entered combat mode, cockpit, engine, and weapons receiving the bulk of life support and power.

"Rock and roll," Scylla announced. "Maryn, port guns. Col, starboard. Jac has missile control."

"Roger, Captain."

The pilot pulled back on the yoke and the *Girl* lifted into the air above the canyon, a steep climb, roll, and level out in front of the oncoming enemy. The crosshairs on Maryn's heads-up converged and she fired a second too late to hit her target head on. The ventral guns spat red-hot tracks of projectiles toward the enemy craft. The attacking ships screamed past them in evasive maneuvers.

"Come on, assholes. Follow the one shooting at you, not them." Scylla banked the ship around to get behind the fighters.

"They're turning!" Jac said.

"Give 'em a little kiss, darlin'." The pilot's spacer accent was back in full force, fierce and musical.

Jac launched a rocket. It left a trail of fire in the darkness and the fighter had plenty of time to dodge. Their wingman fired at the missile and it disappeared in a cloud of bright explosives and shrapnel.

"Now they're pissed." Maryn watched the blips on the heads-up turn back toward the *Girl*. "I hope nothing else comes out because we kicked the nest."

"We should be long gone by then."

"Missiles!" the *Girl* warned. "Launching drone decoys."

The ship banked hard to starboard. Maryn followed on the fast-closing targets on her screen, all focus directed toward the oncoming threats. The lead missile took the bait and slammed into the cloud of drones, detonating on impact. The second kept coming. She trained her ventral guns on the approaching weapon and fired as Jac launched another response from the *Girl*'s belly. Both intercepted the threat in a satisfying conflagration of shrapnel and fire.

"Boom!" Scylla exulted as the explosion rocked their ship.

Maryn swung her gun on the passing fighter and razed it with bullets, striking sparks off the enemy's hull. The craft turned in a rapid arc and came back for more. Most of its own projectiles bounced off the *Girl*'s electromagnetic shields, but plenty got through and she heard them pinging against the hull.

"Fuck! I hate atmospheric battle! I want my energy cannons," she complained.

"Shoot better!" Col said, her voice tight. "Make enough holes in them and they'll go down."

"Make enough holes in us, so will we." Maryn grimaced and kept firing.

"My hull integrity is not compromised yet," the *Girl* assured them. "I'm still a virgin."

"Missile away!" Jac said. The fighter to port came in, strafing them with bullets, and the rocket turned it into a nebula. Scylla pulled up sharply to avoid the storm cloud of fire and debris.

"Great shot, darlin'! Save some of those missiles for later, though. I have a feeling we're gonna need 'em."

The other craft turned and fled. "Chickenshit," Jac taunted the retreating vessel.

"I am not complaining." Col turned away from her console with a sigh of relief.

"*Bright Wing*, this is *Golden Girl*," Scylla announced over the com. "We're coming back to you. The remaining fighter retreated but there's a chance it'll be back with friends. We may not have as much time as we hoped. I think we should break atmosphere and get the hell off the planet."

"Glad to hear you are still in one piece," Dair responded.

"How many civilian fighters made it back?" She both did and did not want to know, a Schrödinger's paradox.

"We have fifteen aboard. Three are wounded but we're doing everything we can for them." Dair paused. "Are any with you?"

"No. I'm sorry." It was a brutal loss of more than half the volunteers, but it could have been so much worse.

"Understood." Their response was hollow. Maryn knew how heavy losses weighed in the scales of command, certain Dair was feeling it too.

"We will follow your instructions, *Golden Girl*," the *Bright Wing*'s captain confirmed.

"All right. Head for these coordinates at FTL." Scylla transmitted the location. "The faster we get out of this system, the safer you'll be. We'll stop there and regroup before proceeding further."

"That's nowhere near Altroon Gate," Captain Jarad's tone was laced with disapproval.

"We need to scout it first, unless you want us to lead you straight into an enemy patrol." Scylla's voice rose into a venomous pitch. "We need to do a sweep and check things out before you go anywhere near sensor range of that gate. You'll hold that position and stand by until you hear from us, or you could die. Do you understand?"

Concerned with Scylla's loss of composure, Maryn exchanged troubled glances with Jac as silence fell between the two ships.

"Yes." Surprisingly, it was Dair who broke the com standoff. "We understand, *Golden Girl*. We'll meet you at those coordinates."

The refugee ship emerged from the canyon and fired her engines in a skyward lunge toward the stars. *Golden Girl* hovered protectively at her stern until both craft broke atmosphere. As soon as *Bright Wing* streaked away, Scylla closed the steel panels over the *Girl's* windscreen.

"Anything on sensors that might be chasing us?" Jac asked their ship.

"Negative. There is no sign of their fleet," *Girl* responded.

"That can't be good." Maryn's reawakened battle sense was still pinging hard. "Where did they go?"

"I don't know, but we're outta here." Scylla throttled up. "*Bright Wing's* slower than you are, *Girl*. Maintain a parallel flight path, close enough to respond if they get into trouble but far enough to scout ahead."

"Yes, Captain."

As the ship took over flight controls, the pilot turned her chair to face her wife. The painful silence stretched between them until Scylla closed her eyes and slammed her gloved fist against the arm of the chair in fury.

"My love," Jac began.

"I almost killed us, Jac!" she shouted, angry tears streaking down her face. "If *Girl* hadn't raised the shields that tank would have blown us out of the air and we'd be dead. You, me. All of us. The refugees too."

"This is why we upgraded her." Jac's eyes glimmered with tears. "So you can continue to fly as long as possible."

"*Girl*, how much flying did you do during the dogfight?" Scylla's bitterness rang against the bulkhead. "You almost yanked the yoke out of my hands half a dozen times. How often did you override or correct my actions to avoid damage?"

There was a pause. "I anticipated the necessary maneuvers twenty-three percent of the time, Captain. Your reaction time was not at peak performance and I ..." The *Girl's* interface sounded almost hesitant, as if the ship were concerned it would hurt her in some way. "I responded as programmed."

"You did, *Girl*. Thank you." Jac's calm wavered at the edges, crumbling like a wall made of sand.

"I don't know what the fuck I was thinking." Scylla began to unravel herself from the five-point harness, fumbling at the latches. "My brain is fried. It's killing me, and I nearly took all of you with me." Her voice broke, quivering with self-directed rage.

"You were thinking of what needed to be done to save as many lives as possible, like you've always done."

"I can't lose this, Jac! I can't!" Scylla shouted, her voice rough and hitched with sobs. "I'm a pilot. I've been a goddamned pilot since I was a kid, and without this, I'm nothing. Nobody. Not with the *Girl* rescuing me from idiotic mistakes. If I can't fly, I might as well take the black nap right now. Just shove me out an airlock."

"Do *not* talk like that," Jac hissed, her tears spilling over. "You are not allowed to leave me that way and you know it. You've had bad times before."

"Not like this. I've never forgotten to put up the fucking shields. Never. The *Girl* never had to yank the controls out of my hands before." She glared at Maryn. "You've never asked her to make sure I didn't fuck up before."

"I've always looked out for you. All of you," Maryn corrected. Scalding tears gathered in her eyes. "She never needed to ask because it's what I've always done. And you didn't fuck up, because you already made certain *Girl* could respond on her own." She lowered her voice but left it edged with steel. "You prepared her for it, and she didn't let you down. You didn't let *us* down. I can't imagine what you're feeling right now, knowing what you know, but we trust you. We have an obligation to that ship in front of us and the two hundred people inside. Beat yourself up later if you want, but do your job now, Merrow."

Scylla wiped at her nose with the back of her glove before shooting a glance at Maryn. "Yes, Sergeant." She sighed heavily, her shoulders relaxing a fraction of an inch, and half laughed, half sobbed. "You did find your damned 'because I said so' voice again."

"Not so different from my 'read the fucking syllabus' voice." Maryn shrugged. "It's all in the presentation." She ran a tired hand over her eyes. "Why don't you guys take a break? I can watch things up here. We have hours before we reach the rendezvous coordinates. *Girl*, will you turn on art-grav, please?"

Weight returned, echoing the heaviness in Maryn's soul. Jac unstrapped herself and stood, holding out her hand to Scylla as the door behind them unsealed itself in a whisper of displaced air. "Come on. I need water and so do you."

"I need more than fucking water," Scylla grumbled, but took her wife's hand and edged out of the cockpit. She roughly patted the top of Maryn's head with her opposite hand when she passed. Maryn winced, but grinned. Jac smiled at her behind Scylla's back as she followed. Her gaze did not reflect the expression, sadness etched in deep, tired furrows around her hazel eyes.

"Do you want me to stay?" Col asked Maryn. "I would like to get the blood out of my fur before it dries."

"No, go ahead. Do you need help?"

"I am fine. I will bring you water as well." Col rose with a groan. "Are you alright?"

"I will be."

Col brushed the back of her hand against Maryn's cheek, and she leaned into it for a second. Then, as the Boshi limped down the corridor, she unstrapped and moved into the pilot's seat, turning it around to face the shuttered windscreen so no one could see her weep for her friends.

It was a long, slow loss they faced. It would not be sudden, like Andelek's, but one that would spool out and stretch them to the breaking point. The battle would be protracted, the casualties high. That hill could never be taken.

They would need reinforcements, and Maryn didn't know if she was strong enough yet.

Guilt gnawed her insides with sharp teeth. She took exactly two minutes to wallow in it, wiped her tears, and got back to business.

"*Girl*." She cleared her throat and mind of the muck. "Let's keep an eye out for their missing fleet."

THE SECTOR of open space they chose for a rendezvous point was a parsec from Qet's sun. The planet and its rings remained visible to the naked eye, deceptively peaceful from a distance. Heavy asteroid activity kept this sector off most charts in favor of the clearer star lanes, but it was still only an hour's flight from Altroon Gate. The slow, drifting chunks of icy rock in this stellar sea could be navigated without much risk here and provided some cover for the *Bright Wing* and her precious travelers.

"We're going in to scout ahead. We'll contact you when it's safe to proceed," Jac told Captain Jarad. "If you don't hear from us within two hours, it means the gate's not secure and you should fly directly to Gaius Station. It's the first gate we know outside Qetish space. You can head for Xyri from there."

"That's almost a week away," Jarad said. "I don't think we have enough food and water on board to last more than two or three days. We weren't able to load everything before we were forced to take off."

Dismay flowed through the cockpit. "Shit," Scylla whispered off mic, glancing at Jac. "There's nothing closer, and we still don't know the status of the Pashni."

"Is Dair listening?" Maryn inquired.

"I'm here."

"Start strict rationing for what supplies you do have based on those numbers, in case we don't come back. You can keep those people calm. We've seen it. They listened to you before, and they will now. If you don't hear from us, I want you to send a message to my father-in-law." She rattled off Lekere's private contact frequency. "Tell him what happened and ask for help. He may not be able to intervene in a military manner but he won't leave you stranded without food and water."

"I understand." Dair's voice was rough. "You fought for us today, and you didn't have to. I want to say thank you for rescuing Zeddi and me. I wasn't very appreciative of everything you did for me, and I'm sorry."

Maryn could not deny the self-satisfied warmth spreading

through her after Dair's apology. "You can buy us the first round the next time we see you."

"Nothing cheap. They like expensive alcohol," the *Girl* finished.

"Synchronize countdown for two hours starting … now. *Golden Girl* out." Scylla sped away from the passenger ship, soon a pinprick of light among millions of others.

"We'd best hope the gate is secure." Col murmured. Her prayer beads clicked through her fingers, a soft, soothing patter like rain.

"Chances of that?" Jac scoffed.

"Slim, unless Col's Universe might be in a giving mood?" Scylla's voice curled upwards in hope.

"I'm praying as hard as I can."

"That energy might be better focused on the *Bright Wing*," Maryn admitted.

Col smiled. "The Universe has an infinite source of energy. It can handle it."

"THERE IS ALREADY a vessel at the gate," *Girl* advised as they closed on their destination. "And surprise, it's *Raging Fire*."

Maryn waited for fear to flood her nerves. It didn't happen, pre-empted by a singing tension along her sinews and bones, a battle rush that brought clarity and calm, just as it had in her youth. "We kind of figured that, didn't we?"

Scylla blew out her breath. "Welp. What's our plan, folks? Run? Trade missiles? Insults? Confound them with dirty limericks?"

Col waved her furry hand. "I vote for missiles."

"Can we write dirty limericks on them first?" Jac mused.

"Sounds like we have a common denominator." Scylla scratched her head. "We go in firing and try to make them chase us. If we can lead them away from the gate, we can send Dair and Jarad straight for it."

"Chances are they expect something like that. *Girl*, is that still the only vessel within sensor range of the gate?" Maryn glanced at the ship's watching eye.

"Yes, Maryn. I detect no other craft in the vicinity. They will have picked us up on their sensors by now as well."

"If they don't chase us?" Col's prayer beads rattled through her fingers.

"Our shields took a beating when that tank hit us, and then the dogfight. No chance of recharging until we're planetside again." Scylla checked her readouts. "Stern shield at maximum with the rest evened out at sixty-five percent power. We've got four missiles left, and the energy cannons."

"Our energy cannons won't make it through military grade shields."

"No, but they can take out any missiles they're firing at us. Or …" Scylla frowned. "They can tax their shields at a strategic point."

"Overload it so a missile penetrates at the same spot?" Jac raised an eyebrow. "That will take some close flying, my love."

"The closer I fly, the less likely they'll use their missiles. I say we deal as much damage as we can and then lead them away from *Bright Wing*'s position." An alarm began to shrill through the cockpit, and the pilot silenced it with a tap on her heads-up. "We're officially out of time. Plan as stands?"

"Go," Maryn said.

"Go," Jac and Col replied in tandem.

"Go." The *Girl* paused, and murmured, "This may void my extended warranty."

"Then we won't tell Manny." Scylla gripped the yoke. "*Girl*, give us some battle tunes."

CHAPTER
FOURTEEN

THE COCKPIT WAS FILLED with high energy music when Scylla dropped out of FTL. The ship in front of the gate got bigger as they approached.

"Holy shit." Scylla peered at the magnified image. "Check out that port side damage! I guess we did more than we thought."

"Limping home from battle?" Maryn wondered. "Where's the rest of the corporate fleet? Do they have an escort?"

"I'm still not picking up any other craft," the *Girl* answered.

"They're going to be pissed as hell to see us." Jac hit a series of panels. "Weapons live. Maryn and Col, you have the ventral cannons. I've got missile control. *Girl*, you'll need to coordinate our fire when we have a viable target."

"Got it," the ship replied.

"Aaaand we're being hailed," Scylla drawled. She switched on the com. "Good to see you again, *Raging Fire*. Where did your friends go?"

"*Golden Girl*." The silky voice of the captain came through over the low hum of music. "You will come to a full stop and prepare for boarding, or you will be destroyed."

"Sorry, that's a negative. Oof, you've got something on your starboard side. Looks like a hole about the size of one of your fighter craft got punched through your shiny black stripe."

"You will be destroyed." His urbane tone gained an unsteady edge.

"You keep saying that." Scylla's words were frosted with glacial ice. "Did you warn the passenger vessel before you killed all those refugees?"

"Like the one you were seen illegally escorting out of Qetish space only hours ago? Your actions are not that of a passenger vessel. We will deal with you and then we will find that transport, and we will eliminate it."

Jac muted the mic. "He's talking a lot. Monologuing, even."

Scylla pursed her lips. "Either the ship is in worse shape than we realize, or he's killing time until his backup arrives."

"Or he's a dick," Col offered, and Maryn snorted in agreement.

"That's a given." Jac lifted her head. "*Girl*, scan the *Raging Fire* and their shield levels when we get up close: engine output, damage, everything. We need an advantage if we're taking on a frigate alone."

"Already in progress. We'll need some close passes before I can estimate shield strength and emissions."

"All right. We're going in hot. We cripple the ship's sensors so they can't find the *Bright Wing*. Then we see if they'll chase us out of range. Target sensor arrays and aft engines." Scylla throttled up. "Watch those missile tubes for action."

Maryn kept her vision fixed on the targeting screen in front of her as the *Girl* barrel-rolled in. The frigate's ventral cannons fired at them. Scylla streaked out of the spin and down the vessel's port side, hugging as close as she could without their shields glancing off each other. The targeting stream grew closer on Maryn's heads-up until it converged. Her thumb depressed the firing mechanism and released a blast of argent energy at the frigate's forward sensor array, a twin arc joining hers from Col's gun.

"It's away!" Jac's cry accompanied the streak of a rocket leaving the *Girl*'s starboard tube. Maryn didn't release her trigger until an explosion blossomed in front of them and Scylla pulled the ship away from the shower of debris.

"Not a direct hit, but very effective," *Girl* reported. "Their forward sensors are no longer functioning."

"We won't get away with it for long. We better make the next one count," Scylla said.

"Incoming!" *Girl* warned. The ship swerved to starboard. The missile followed, and Maryn depressed the trigger before the tracking converged, spraying the rocket's path with energy. Col's beam crossed the back of the rocket and sent the projectile careening off course until it exploded off their bow.

"Second missile closing!"

This one was too close. The weapon evaded the targeted beams of light until it was almost on their ass. The explosion's shockwave rattled the *Girl* as the pilot brought them in for another pass down *Raging Fire's* hull, skirting the ventral gun's aim but taking fire from the main turrets. The ship shuddered.

"Shit!" Scylla maneuvered around the frigate's belly. "That took our shields down another notch. You okay, *Girl?*"

"Shields are holding, but the starboard thruster is misfiring again, and it's getting worse. I am compensating as best I can."

"Just keep flying, baby. Comin' around for a pass at their rear sensor array. Weapons, be ready."

The ship dodged fire from the main guns and Scylla brought them in almost kissing close to the other ship's side. Maryn watched the compressed beams meet in a deadly *V* of energy until Jac's missile went wide of the target, the explosion occurring outside the frigate's shields.

"Shit! I missed!" she yelled.

"We've got one more missile, but I don't know if we can get away with it again. Their guns are getting closer." Scylla checked her display. "Our speed's not the greatest. That sub light thruster is misfiring. It's been a while since I taxed them like this."

"Time to run and see if they chase?" Maryn suggested.

"I'm not sure we can outrun missiles anymore. Listen to that engine." The steady hitch in the thruster was noticeable by vibration and by the lagging lines in the power readouts on the heads-up.

"Scans complete, Captain," *Girl* said. "Their shields are barely holding. Everything is focused on the starboard side damage and their engines are at twenty percent capacity. Their shields won't be able to deflect a low-energy penetration."

"They are not just sitting there guarding the gate. They can hardly move!" Col breathed.

"They got their asses kicked at the Pashni. This is all a bluff." Jac glanced at her wife. "One missile left. Slow encroachment? Like Galaga Three."

"The 'checking for ticks' maneuver?" Maryn gulped. "It was crazy then. Can we do it now?"

The lines in Scylla's face deepened into gleeful fractures as she smiled. "It could work. We come in head on so we can see any missiles and take them out. Then stick tight to their topside." She crowed in triumph. "I'm so glad we got the band back together. We always work best this way. All power to the forward shields, *Girl*."

"Yes, Captain."

The frigate's stern grew large in the canopy. The *Girl* threaded oncoming enemy fire with supernatural ease, a twisting, slippery creature made of stardust and the bright, argent energy spiraling from her ventral side cannons. Maryn watched her heads-up and wondered how much steering control the ship retained, because it moved like a living thing, a melding of Scylla's piloting and the *Girl*'s AI interface. She hadn't seen anything like it since their Corps days. She couldn't see the pilot's face, only her left hand where it moved the yoke with a delicate grip.

An explosion bloomed in front of them and their ship rattled, it's steady forward momentum undaunted.

"Shields are down another ten percent," Jac advised, her voice tight.

"No problem." Scylla's voice was calm. "We're almost there ... *Girl*, be ready to fire the thrusters ... *now!*"

The ship reared like a cobra, engines whining as they crawled up the starboard side of the frigate and topped the deck. The *Girl* settled into a hover above the frigate's hull in front of the conn tower and matched the craft's nearly motionless drift.

"Cue confusion on the bridge in three, two, one—" Scylla pointed at the ceiling. The overhead com hissed with static.

"Fuck you!" spat the *Raging Fire*'s captain, his silky arrogance now threadbare and hoarse. "Only cowards would refuse to confront us."

"May I remind you that we just did that," Jac purred. "*Raging Fire*, your ship is crippled. Your shields won't withstand a direct attack from our current position. We have you by the short hairs. We'll accept your surrender, but given your war crimes, we would also be thrilled to blow your bridge into a million tiny little pieces. Choose wisely."

A collision alarm began to blare over the com from *Raging Fire*, echoed by a blinking red light in the *Girl*'s cockpit.

"There is a ship coming through the gate," *Girl* warned. "We are too close to the distortion field."

Panic leached through Maryn's veins in icy branches of fear, froze her lungs, and made her heart stutter. *No, no, no. Not again.* "We have to get out of here. Now!"

"That will be the rest of our ships returning from the front, and they will find the ship you're protecting," the captain gloated.

"You're just as in the way as we are," Scylla reminded him. "Move away from the distortion field, and we'll tag along."

"We will stay here."

"Now is not the time to play chicken!" Maryn cried. "Fucking move!"

"Ten seconds," *Girl* advised.

Jac glanced at her wife, lines of worry between her eyes. "Scyll? You're cutting it too close."

"If they survive, their fleet will find the *Bright Wing*," Col breathed.

"Last chance," Scylla warned their compromised enemy.

Maryn swallowed hard and turned her chair so she could see the gate through the viewscreen. If she was going to die, she was going to face it head on. Col reached out with soft, furry fingers, and she gripped her friend's hand tightly.

"Your days are numbered, *Golden Girl*," *Raging Fire*'s captain said.

"Shit! Go now!" Maryn pleaded, in tears.

Everything happened at once. The distortion field widened to engulf the *Raging Fire* at the same time the *Girl* pivoted and leapt away from the gate's energy, which pummeled her in its wake and rattled the crew in their seats. Scylla spun the ship around once they were at a safe distance, and Maryn witnessed what emerged from the shimmering aperture of the jump portal.

Four Xyrian fighters flickered into existence and darted out of the distortion wave. The pilots made evasive maneuvers as they caught sight of *Raging Fire.* The gray-alloyed prow of a huge Khepran battleship emerged from the field, materializing from empty, glittering space. Military grade shields rammed into the hull of the frigate on its damaged starboard side.

Raging Fire crumpled and broke in half, drifting away from the gate in a cloud of debris. Maryn turned her face away, breath coming hard and quick through her nose. Cold sweat beaded between her shoulder blades and at her hairline. Col soothed her, wordlessly stroking the back of her hand with her thumb until Jac said with awe, "Maryn. Look!"

She cracked open her eyes. Panic began to transmute to relieved wonder as gray and white hulls came through the jump frame in succession. The battleship. A frigate. Dozens of Khepran fighters, popping into existence like bright stars. Behind the Khepran frigate came enormous silver Xyrian ships in a procession of support vessels.

"Incoming transmission," the *Girl* announced. "It's for Maryn."

She cleared her throat and took a deep breath. "On com."

"Dowager Consort." A familiar, crisp voice greeted her. "This is Flight Leader Katalin. How may we be of assistance?"

"It's good to see you, Flight Leader," she said when she was satisfied her words wouldn't shake. "The Magnus Primetri's emergency session must have been a success."

"He was eloquent," Katalin affirmed. "However, the extended battle at the Pashni dealt a blow to Viltrux's fleet. The Kheprans are talking about a 'fat golden ship' that turned the tide before we arrived." Katalin's tone held a touch of humor, indicating ze knew exactly who ze was talking to.

"This fat golden ship saved their ass," *Girl* muttered.

"Voluptuous," Scylla corrected.

Katalin continued, "The wormhole is under control of united galactic forces and the rest of the unmarked ships have scattered. It is time to end this. Ground troops are landing now to help defend the government stronghold. We are here to ensure the safe transition of power back to the Qetish government in exile and see to the safety of any remaining refugees."

"Did the Khepran battleship take any damage when it rammed the *Raging Fire*?" Scylla inquired.

"Negative, Captain Merrow. We are searching for survivors among the wreckage."

"There is a refugee transport called *Bright Wing* just outside sensor range. They have casualties and limited food and water. They need immediate escort to Xyri. It won't be safe for them to return to Qet for some time, I'm sure," Maryn said. "We will lead you to them, but our shields and sub light engines took extensive damage."

"My squadron will be honored to escort you both to Xyri. Do you require immediate repair? Our service ship is at your disposal."

"Only one person gets in my pants," the *Girl* objected.

"We can make it to Cinderfall on our own, but we've gotta have shields first." Scylla rekeyed the mic. "We'll be heading in a different direction for the rest of the repairs, Flight Leader, but we would welcome a couple of shield batteries if they can spare them before we guide you to the refugee ship."

"Understood, *Golden Girl*. Stand by."

Maryn went limp with the ebb of adrenaline and terror. "God damn it, Scylla," she rasped. "Never do that again."

"I'm sorry, Mar. I didn't see any other options. I knew *Girl* would get us out of there in time." The pilot cleared her throat. "For the record, *Girl*—how much corrective action did you take on my flying in the last twenty minutes?"

"Less than two percent, Captain. I enhanced your escape time at the gate by point-zero-two microseconds, but we would have made it safely out of range as late as point-zero-four microseconds." *Girl's* artificial voice held pride. "You've still got it when it counts."

Scylla closed her eyes for a moment, her lids puckered as if she were going to cry, her voice gravelly. "Thank you, *Girl*."

Jac reached across and took her wife's hand, her gaze gentle and shining with tears. A lump rose in Maryn's throat.

"Is anybody going to talk about how we kicked ass today?" Col broke the silence and her voice rose. "Because we were fucking on point!"

"We were," Maryn agreed with a hysterical laugh. "That grenade launcher was a stroke of brilliance, Scyll. It's the best thing I've ever played with."

"That's what she said," Jac quipped, looking suggestively through her lashes.

Scylla swiveled her pilot's chair around and extended her left hand, curled into crescent shape. "In all phases."

Jac's closed right fist met the palm of Scylla's hand and completed half the pledge. Maryn stretched her right hand to reach them, fist against Scylla's thumb, and from the opposite side Col's curved left hand added the last crescent shape, the palm of her hand resting against the back of Maryn's.

"In all phases." Maryn echoed, her gaze searching the faces of her friends. The odds of finding three other kindred spirits in the vast hollow of the universe who had never wavered when she needed them hadn't seemed so enormous until this moment.

"In all phases." The ship added its voice to the pledge, the amber

eye in the cockpit flaring and receding to its background lumi-
nescence.

Make that four kindred souls, she amended. She smiled, the sting of
gratitude in her eyes. "Goddamn it. Somebody say something or I'm
going to fucking cry again."

"Does anybody else's back hurt like hell, or is it just me?" Scylla
asked.

"God, yes." Maryn sniffled through laughter. "And I have to pee.
I'd better take advantage of the stand-by."

"I'm starving. I'll make a quick snack, and then it's hydration and
pain meds for everybody." Jac released the buckles of her harness and
winced as she pulled herself to a hover over her seat. "You need
anything stronger, Col?"

"It's still numb, but I want to get out of this armor before the anesthetic wears off."

"I can help since we're both going that direction," Maryn offered.
"Scyll, do you want a break first?"

"Nah. I'll take one after we know about the batteries." Scylla's
eyes held a watery line between sadness and pride, but her smile was
happy as her gaze roved around the cockpit. "I'm going to sit here a
while with my *Girl*."

NEWS BEGAN to trickle out of the sector before they reached
Cinderfall. Pitched battles took place both at the Pashni wormhole and
at the capitol between the dictator's mercenary forces, Kheqet resistance fighters, and the Khepran fleet, supported by Xyrian relief ships.

In the end, Viltrux's head rolled at the feet of a Kheqet soldier, and
the government in exile prevailed. The Qetish chancellor broadcast
an impassioned speech of triumph and gratitude for the resistance
fighters and the allies who had arrived in time to prevent the worst.
He promised to make immediate preparations for the safe return of
the refugees in exile on Xyri and vowed to rebuild the city of Tenent.

Rebuilding the trust of Qet's hybrid citizens for their neighbors would be a much more significant task.

Flight Leader Katalin informed Maryn that the remaining unmarked fleet ships fled the system not long after *Raging Fire* was destroyed, abandoning their ground troops to the resistance and their allies. But even with Xyri's help, they still didn't know who was behind the staged coup. The mercenary troops who survived the battle weren't talking, and none of the transactions Col flagged had come from the still-unidentified frequency Bee intercepted on Anubis.

It had taken so little to make a difference. Maryn was proud of their efforts—it was what the Artemis Corps mercenaries once stood for, after all, in its glory days. She was disgusted it had taken so long for other planets—her royal in-laws included—to step in and do the right thing.

Somewhere out there was a corporation willing to engage in genocide to get what they wanted. Galactic authorities had only begun to investigate, and they catalogued their unconfirmed suspicions for Flight Leader Katalin to pass on to those agencies.

CINDERFALL STATION WAS BUILT on a volcanic moon orbiting the aquatic planet of Akebri. Manny's familiar, cephalopodic form met them in the repair bay once the pressurization klaxons stopped blaring and it was safe to exit the ship. The mechanic was indeed larger than the last time Maryn had seen him, the thick trunk of his tentacled body mature and muscled, a change from the scrawny young mechanical prodigy she'd met more than twenty years ago.

"Scylla! What have you done to my baby?" A sharp, dramatic gurgle from his water-filled helmet punctuated Manny's disapproval as he fussed, one curling limb stroking the *Girl's* marred, golden side while more of his appendages plugged one of the ship's com sets into his helmet's collar. "Darling, has the nasty human mistreated you?"

"No, it was the most fun I've had in decades!" *Girl* chirped. "But my starboard sub light engines are unhappy. They need your magic tentacles."

"Poor dear." Manny glared at them through the liquid inside the faceplate, his prismatic eyes magnified into accusatory, saucer-sized orbs. His gaze fell on Maryn and Col. "You are back with these miscreants, I see."

"For now. How are you doing, Manny?" Maryn smiled at him. "You look like a whole different squid."

"I'm maturing at a disastrous rate. Thank you for reminding me." He turned back to the primary recipient of his ire. "What else have you neglected, Scylla?"

"The left hydraulic arm is sticky and it's getting dangerous. Other than that, she's in excellent shape," she bristled.

"Hmm. Yes, well, we'll see, won't we?" The ship's maintenance data filled Manny's heads-up on the helmet's screen. "Not as bad as it could be, but shameful. Give me twenty-six hours. Now go away and let me pamper this glorious ship."

As Manny turned away in regal dismissal the *Girl* cooed, "You always say the nicest things."

Maryn sidestepped to avoid the robotic assistants which zoomed in to begin repairs. She followed Scylla, Jac, and Col to the beltway leading to the commercial parts of the space station: a double-sided walkway, one half a water-filled tunnel, and the other for breathers of less humid mixes of oxygen. Once they were scanned for weapons by bored, helmeted squidfolk, they were allowed passage into the heart of the station catering to travelers.

The outpost wasn't affiliated with any particular corporation. Maryn relaxed as she pulled her baggy cardigan closer against the station's chill, but she didn't forget they might still have a hit on them as they moved into the murky promenade. It was now deserted in the wee hours of galactic standard time followed by cargo ships and star liners. Beyond the dormant robotic ticket agents offering passage on connecting commercial flights, the consumer-facing areas of the station were open and mercifully lacked any riot of flashing lights or holographic advertisements. Merchants here offered the bare necessities of space travel: food and drink, medical care, hotel rooms, clean clothes, fuel, and mechanics.

And booze.

They bypassed the store fronts and went to a set of grated metal stairs taking them to the greasier deck above. The dive bar overlooking the repair bays was familiar to Maryn. Other than a quintet of three casually dressed humans and two Caspian humanoids, their heads bent close over the table as they talked, the bar was empty due to the hour.

"Remember this place?" Jac asked as they claimed a sticky booth in the corner overlooking Manny's bay.

"Hell yes. We got some good drunks on here," Col piped happily. Strands of her fur adhered to the table as she slid into the bench seat.

"I don't think it's been cleaned since then." Maryn ran a hand across the table and rubbed her fingertips together, grimaced at the tacky feeling, then scooted in after her.

Jac signaled the bartender and ordered a round over the din of four different holo screens broadcasting intergalactic sports events, some kind of old Earth holo-drama, and Tertiary sector news. Maryn noticed a story from Xyri about the destruction of the first refugee ship, which included footage of the arrival of the *Bright Wing*. Weary refugees, streaked with blood and dirt, disembarked from the ship into the care of Xyrian medics and personnel. At the foot of the ramp, directing the evacuation of wounded fighters, was a familiar face.

"Holy shit. It's Dair!" She pointed to the screen.

"Will you look at that," Scylla said.

"It is good to see they made it." Col shook the prayer beads looped around her wrist. "The universe came through."

"It sure did." Jac threw her arms around her and Col leaned down so she could kiss her cheek.

Scylla slid a shot and glasses full of beer to each of them when the drinks were delivered. She lifted her shot. "To my best friends. We're still kicking ass."

"And taking naps," Jac added. Laughter passed between them.

"To us," Col seconded. They all threw back the amber liquid. Maryn coughed against the burn of alcohol.

"Oh, that's rough," she managed. It lacked the quality of the Peloonish whiskey Gabriel had served them on Anubis, holding more notes of petroleum than citrus.

"To the *Girl*." Scylla raised her beer. Her eyes glittered with tears as she looked through the window, the golden spread of the ship's rounded dorsal hull visible in the bay below them. Her gruff voice trembled. "Long may she fly."

"To the *Girl*," they repeated, clinked beer glasses, and drank again.

Jac reached out and took Scylla's hand, and they smiled at each other. Love glowed in Jac's eyes, and Scylla's rapt expression reflected the depth of her affection and gratitude for her wife. A wave of bittersweet pain crested in Maryn's chest as she watched, the place at her side where her mate should have been suddenly cold and empty. Andelek was ashes now. She couldn't begrudge Jac and Scylla this moment, but it hurt; oh, it hurt knowing she could never share this kind of connection with Andelek again. Before grief could turn to resentment, she tilted her glass toward them.

"To both of you." She fought to keep her voice steady. "Thank you for getting me back into deep space. Here's to the most fucking memorable girls' trip in history."

"Damn straight." Scylla tapped her beer against Maryn's and Jac and Col followed suit.

Maryn was relieved to hide her trembling lips behind the foamy head and took a deep swallow. The beer was cold and went down easier than the flammable stuff in the shot glass. She looked around the bar and found the Caspian glancing their way with recognition. Her hackles lifted and she carefully set down the glass, clearing her throat.

"Don't look at them, but I think we've got somebody's interest."

"The bunch over there? The shaven heads gave it away." Jac sipped her drink. "You think they're fresh off the Qetish front?"

"Maybe."

"Three bays down," Col said, her height allowing her to look over the back of the booth, "a ship is being repaired. It is black with a shiny black stripe. No other markings, but clear battle damage."

"Their clothes are so new they probably still have price tags on them." Scylla sighed. "Damn it. I was hoping we could just get drunk."

CHAPTER
FIFTEEN

MARYN WATCHED from the corner of her eye. The Caspian had nudged the human female at their table and they were arguing furtively, seeming not to gesture at them, but past their booth. "I think they're looking at the *Girl*."

"Which we were just toasting," Col reminded her. "Is anyone armed?"

"We all went through the same metal detector. Did you hear it beep?" Jac hissed. "I don't even have my knitting needles."

"That means they probably didn't get any weapons through either," Scylla muttered. "Let's wait and see how things turn out before we panic."

The Caspian wrenched himself up from the table, the rest of the group exchanging glances before following their comrade toward the booth.

"Here they come." Maryn took another slug of beer as the young being came right up to their table. Tension quivered in every line of his lanky, gray-green body.

"For fuck's sake, Muto," one of the humans said, casting nervous glances around the empty bar. "Leave them alone."

"That your ship?" the Caspian hissed.

"Yes, it is," Scylla responded like he'd asked if it was her birthday. "We've had her a long time. You like the Astradyne cruisers?"

They were young, Maryn thought. No older than Dair, and all wore the same weary, haunted expression their friend possessed— save for Muto, whose coloring deepened from moss to emerald across the bridge of his shallow nose and cheeks.

"Where are you coming from?" he demanded.

"Heading home from a funeral." Jac added the right amount of bewilderment.

"On what planet?"

"Muto, leave it," the other Caspian barked.

"Shut up, Gualo," Muto exploded. "It's the ship PG is looking for!" Saliva flew from his lips with the consonants. "Look at those tattoos!" He pointed at Scylla's forearm where it rested against the table, beer in her hand. The crescent insignia of the Artemis Corps was sharp and visible against her skin, as was the winged sword on her bicep. "Mercenary."

"They're only somebody's grandmas, goddamn it. Knock it off!" the human female grabbed the Caspian's arm and tried to drag him away.

He jerked free from her and his voice dropped. "Don't you know how much PG is offering in bounty? It would set us up, get us what- ever we need to start over after the repairs and paint job."

"You want that after all we just did?" one of the human men said. He was a tall, muscular kid with arms the size of Maryn's thigh. "You want a hand in killing more people?"

"Why not?" Wild-eyed, the Caspian turned to his friends, greed pulling his mouth up in a wide, hungry smile. "Come on, you cowards."

The woman grabbed his shoulder, spun him around and drove her fist into Muto's chest with a vicious punch, following it with an uppercut that snapped the other being's head back. Muto fell to the floor, unconscious and bleeding from his mouth in slow, green drips.

"Pick him up and take him back to the room before he does anything else stupid." The woman shook out her hand with a grimace. She nodded at them. "Sorry. He's had too much to ..." She trailed off with a tired exhale, rubbing her bruised knuckles. "Too much."

"Fucking right," the smaller male human muttered as he helped the other Caspian lift Muto by the arms to drag him away. The woman kicked the beaten Muto's leg with a satisfied grunt before following them.

"Again, our apologies." The muscular guy had his hands buried in his pockets. He glanced out the window at the golden ship's topside. "I like the old Astradyne cruisers. My grandpa had one."

"Thanks." Scylla gave him a crooked grin. "I like 'em too."

"So. Artemis Corps, right?" he motioned at the tattoo on the pilot's forearm. "How'd you make it out?"

"We had a lot of luck, and the wisdom to know when to quit," Jac said.

He nodded, his eyes downcast.

"What are you going to do when you ... get out?" Maryn asked with a meaningful pause.

"Well. Theoretically, yeah?" He rubbed the stubble on his head. "We might steal a ship. Find somewhere to get it painted. Change its codes and run. Head somewhere there ain't no corporations."

"Look into starting your own security firm," Col suggested.

He smiled faintly at that, but it didn't reach his eyes. "Thanks. We'll give it some thought." His gaze flickered over the bay again and the golden hull of the ship. "What's she called?"

Scylla met each of their gazes in turn before she answered, "*Golden Girl*," with quiet pride.

"Huh." He laughed, a soft sound that almost wasn't there, and then nodded. "Don't worry. We'll keep Muto from doing anything he regrets. Call it professional courtesy."

"Who is PG?" Maryn asked, almost in a whisper. "Help us hold them accountable."

"Not that stupid, lady." He shook his head and was silent for a while, his hand working in his pocket. Maryn stiffened, wondering if he had a weapon after all. "But if you happened to find something on the floor, say, right about where Muto fell?"

A metallic ping sounded as he shifted his hands, still buried in his pockets. "Who knows where it came from. Dropped in the fight, maybe. He was an idiot to keep it on him, right?" He shrugged. "Nothing personal, but I hope we never see you again. Have a nice evening." He turned and followed the dark green trail of blood smears, his broad shoulders slumped in defeat.

Maryn climbed out of the booth and bent over, stifling a groan as her joints complained, and picked up the small item where it had landed.

It was a collar pin, something that might be worn on a uniform. She couldn't place it as she squinted and held it farther away to get a better look. The mirror image design was vaguely familiar, two infinity symbols joined at the outside curves inside a circle. She handed it to Scylla. "Do you recognize it?"

"I sure do." She looked up, her mouth set in a thin, grim line. "That's the PanGemini logo."

"The one that makes those metallic alloy coupes?" Maryn frowned as she slid back into the booth beside Col. "They make expensive short hop spaceships. Why would they have a mercenary unit?"

"Qetryllium makes alloys stronger," Jac mused.

"Yeah, but so do other elements." Scylla shook her head. "What's so special about this element that a fucking luxury spaceship manufacturer would help stage a coup?"

"It might not be about the element at all." Maryn whispered, the ghost of an idea coalescing until it became solid. "Or at least, not completely."

"What is it, Mar?" Jac leaned forward.

"The lizard elk," she said, thinking aloud. "Dair told us they've been poached for their horns and hides so much there aren't any herds left in the south. They rub their horns against ore outcroppings rich in iron, copper, and qetryllium. Before the battle I followed one to the cliffside and saw a group of them. Wherever they rubbed against the qetryllium, they left brightly colored marks. Blue. Red. Purple. It was like a bunch of kids got turned loose with crayons."

"I don't understand." Col, confused, shook her head.

"The new alloy process PanGemini has." Scylla's eyes widened in a flash of insight. "The color doesn't just go skin deep. The whole piece of metal is the same color all the way through."

"It must be a chemical reaction to qetryllium catalyzed by the lizard elk's horns," Maryn breathed. "It doesn't take much. Even scraping against the cliffside imparts some vivid changes. One horn might be able to color an entire manufacturing line's worth of alloy."

"Should I start looking for transactions from PanGemini to Qet?" Col asked.

"It's a good place to start." Maryn frowned. "The study regarding the effects of terraforming on the lizard elk population was most likely funded by a corporation, or even the initial fauna studies of Qet prior to colonization. If we follow the money trail, we might have more evidence to prove our suspicions."

"Or," Scylla suggested in a low voice, "we could give the information to somebody else and let them chase it down."

When they turned their gazes on her, she smiled, her dark eyes filled with peace. "Bee was right. We've got better things to do than take on a corporation ourselves. I don't want to waste what time I've got left on something I probably won't live to see pan out. I'd rather keep doing shady cargo runs on the *Girl* and traveling with Jac. I should spend some quality time with Maya sooner than later." She reached across the table. Col grasped one of her hands, and Maryn claimed the other. Scylla squeezed them with a steady pressure. "There's nothing left for me to prove. I already have it all."

Jac leaned her head against Scylla's shoulder. Maryn nodded, her throat growing tight.

Before things could turn too maudlin, more shots were delivered by the droopy faced Tridarian bartender. "From the human who just left," he droned with a disinterested wave as Scylla protested that they hadn't ordered another round.

"Well, well. I think the kids are all right," Jac muttered.

Maryn watched the bartender unload the glasses, noting he could have been Dr. Globney's less academic twin. Her gaze flicked back to the holo screen where the news had turned to Prime Quadrant stories, and images of protests at the Earthside campus of the Prime Galactic University were being broadcast. The crawl at the bottom of the screen indicated it was a demonstration of outrage over the time it had taken to offer aid to the endangered Kheqet colonists and calling for amendments to galactic law.

It started her thinking about Echo Four.

The idea of going back to a life without Andelek renewed the searing ache in the middle of her chest. What was she going to do there? Pack up the remains of their life and move to a tiny apartment, surrounded by memories? Teach as bloody adjunct to a self-important moron who thought he knew more about Maryn and Andelek's discoveries than she did herself?

And Scylla was going out in a slow fade, poisoned by the vast and sparkling universe she so loved. The thought of leaving Jac alone to deal with the loss of her soulmate, knowing what it was like to lose, made the wound inside her throb with guilty pain.

She realized her friends had gone silent around her, their presence drifting back into her awareness. She looked up and found them all with shot glasses in their hands, watching her with various expressions. Love. Pride. Concern.

"Sorry." She raised her own shot. "What were we drinking to this time?"

"That those kids find their way out," Jac said.

"Hell yes. May others follow." They drank. This whiskey was much better than their earlier shots, still rough, but without the jet fuel overtones of the cheap stuff. She was appreciative of the young mercenary's gesture.

"You okay, Mar?" Jac inquired.

"I got lost in my head for a minute. I'm fine."

"It's been one hell of a month for you, huh?" Scylla's mouth quirked in a sad half-smile.

Had it been nearly four weeks since Andelek's illness and death?

"Yeah. I guess it has." She lifted her hands from the tacky surface of the table to rub her eyes, thought better of it, and instead wrapped them around the glass of beer in front of her.

"What do you want to do now?" Jac cocked her head, her eyes soft. "I glanced at the flight boards on the way over. With the Pashni open again, there are commercial flights listed. We didn't expect any of this to happen, but you met it head on like the bad bitch you are. I'm so sorry we weren't honest from the beginning." She glanced at Col, too. "Truly sorry. Neither of you owe us anything."

"The hell I don't," Col argued. "We've had each other's backs for thirty years. I am rotting at a concierge station performing financial miracles for shitheads who don't deserve it. I will leave nothing behind that I do not wish to. I would like to stay if you will have me. I rather like the thought of doing morally questionable cargo runs."

"That would be ..." Scylla's voice turned rough, and she cleared her throat. "It would be fucking amazing."

Maryn froze, not knowing what to say. Grief and uncertainty competed for dominance while a nagging tone of guilt shouted over everything. Her hands tightened around the glass as she realized she'd fallen into silence again and looked up, shamefaced, to find Jac regarding her with a smile full of gentle sadness. Bright-eyed Col attempted to hide her hope, but it was plain to anyone who could read the Boshi's expression as well as Maryn that she yearned for her to agree.

"You're thinking too hard, Mar. We understand there are things you have to settle back home." Scylla cocked her head at her with a wry grin. "It's okay. Like I said, I have a while before shit gets ugly."

"I don't know what I want," she admitted in a small voice. "What I do know is I will never let go of you three. You are my anchors, my heroes. My best friends."

"And we'll never let go of you," Jac reached across the table, and Maryn met her outstretched hand and gripped it tightly. "We'll take you home. Once you've had time to grieve, and to think, the invitation is always open."

MARYN SENT a communique to the Magnus Primetri and Flight Leader Katalin regarding their encounter with the deserters and her theory regarding the lizard elk. The research data was available at any campus of the galactic University, and exobiologists on Xyri would be able to get to the studies far sooner than she would.

With no outstanding 'business' obligations for Jac and Scylla, the trip from Cinderfall to the nearest commercial gate was less than forty-eight hours away. Once Manny pronounced the *Girl* to be sufficiently pampered, they left.

Time sped by like the blur of stars outside the ship, so much faster on the trip home without the fog of grief and mindless terror of deep space clouding Maryn's perception. The idea of gate jumping still made her palms sweat, but it was negligible now.

Knowing she would have to say goodbye, even temporarily, at the end of this journey weighed on her. She spent as much time as she could with them, sometimes silently, but always listening, memorizing each well-loved face so she could picture them until the next time they were together.

All too soon, the green sphere of Echo Four loomed in the viewport, and she was back, if not home, on another ridiculously perfect afternoon.

"We have a departure time at six," Scylla said, her voice rough with emotion.

Less than two hours, she thought. Just enough time for them to stock up on food and supplies.

They gathered in their four-point hug. "All you have to do is call," Jac whispered, kissing her temple. "We'll be here."

"I know." Maryn swallowed. "Try not to get involved in any more wars, okay?"

"Not without you," Col promised.

"Don't let the bastards cheat you out of your due," Scylla demanded. "We'll come back and kick their fucking asses."

"I might hold you to that."

They exchanged kisses and promises to keep in touch. Maryn strode down the ramp, her feet leaden under the press of Echo Four's gravity and climbed into the waiting shuttle without looking back. She was not going to cry in front of them. She wasn't.

She sobbed in the back of a robotic taxi instead.

As the vehicle she'd taken from the spaceport purred away, Maryn entered the chilly foyer of an empty house full of dead flowers, dust, and silence.

The message center in the hallway blinked an incessant red eye, pausing between every twenty-fourth pulse. She ignored it for now.

In the bedroom she and Andelek shared for two decades, she set her bag on top of the blanket. The white outfit she had forgotten to pack still lay on the bed, so she picked it up and opened the wardrobe. Traces of Andelek wafted through her like an unexpected ghost, the familiar scent of zer body caught in the clothing stored inside. Maryn buried her face in the neat, hanging garments to inhale the cinnamon, citrus, and skin memory of her mate, and wept again. She allowed herself five minutes of helpless, painful acknowledgement before admonishing herself aloud, "We are not doing this all fucking day, Alessi."

She wiped her eyes, blew her nose, and pushed garments aside to make room for the clothes in her bag. Her breath caught at the sight of a jacket hanging on a hook in the back of the wardrobe. Half hidden behind the rest of her and Andelek's clothing, battered black leather creaked against her hand as she grasped the collar and pulled it out of the recesses into the light.

It was her tactical jacket from Team Huntress' privateer days, missing in plain sight for over twenty years. She wiped dust off the shoulders and examined it in wonder, shook it out in case any insects were lurking inside and slipped into it.

It still fit.

She kept it on against the chill of the still-warming house and padded reluctantly to the message center to pull up the list of waiting posts. One was from Malachi Zill, dated a week after the funeral. She deleted it unread. The most recent one was from Globney.

Most of the communiques were condolences from students or academic colleagues. She tabbed through the texts, only stopping to read a particularly favored student or friend's expression of grief. She shunted them all to her personal database to answer later when she was ready.

Interestingly, there was a message from the Earth-side branch of the university inviting her, not Andelek, to be the keynote speaker at an exobiology conference in six months. They wanted to focus on human contributions to the field, lauding her initiative to perform DNA testing in the field on Chrekem Seven and the subsequent bombshell discovery. It was sent the day before Andelek's death and she'd missed its arrival, holding vigil at zer bedside. The request was buried in the avalanche of condolences.

A few weeks ago, she would have deleted the message without answering. She moved the message to her personal database to consider it instead. There was nothing holding her back from traveling now.

She finally opened the one from Globney, received in the last hour. She'd notified him with a courtesy message before they left Cinderfall that she was returning to Echo Four.

"*Hello, my dear Maryn.*" He'd already forgotten she'd asked—rather forcefully, she remembered—to be called Dr. Alessi. "*I am so glad you were able to make it back safely from Xyri. The semester ends in a week and Professor Zill is anxious for you to sign the contract as his adjunct so he can discuss his expectations for next quarter with you. Oh, and if you could please vacate tenured staff housing by the end of this month, he would appreciate it. I have already reserved an apartment for you in the adjunct suites. It's ready for you to move into. Say the word and I will send people to pack and see to your things. It's the least I can do.*"

"It sure fucking is," she muttered, the heat of anger flaring through her.

She was certain that if she saw him again, she would punch him in the face.

It was five-twenty.

It didn't take long to repack the duffel bag, stuffing as many pairs of practical shirts and pants into it as she could fit without regard to wrinkles. She abandoned the shapeless cardigan to hang forlornly in the wardrobe.

Neither she nor Andelek had been materialistic, preferring experiences over collections. There were very few keepsakes she wanted: Andelek's favorite scarf, one she'd bought zem off world when they were first dating. A holo drive full of memories, her personal database, and her digital library fit neatly into the inside pockets of her leather coat. She grabbed a pair of sturdy boots out of the bottom of the wardrobe and changed into them, leaving the sensible pair of flats behind.

Maryn composed a terse resignation for Globney from the back of another taxi, wherein she instructed Malachi Zill should shove the contract up his ass and listed a storage block where Globney could have her belongings stowed. Andelek's personal field equipment was already cached there, and their savings would provide plenty of credits to store her stuff until she was damn good and ready to deal with it.

The whine of engines was already rising when Maryn dived headlong from the shuttle door and hoofed it to the pad where the *Girl* lay berthed, her squid-polished exterior bright against the evening sun. Jac waited outside the open cargo bay, looking smug with her arms crossed over her chest.

"Oh, shut up," Maryn panted, and climbed the ramp.

ACKNOWLEDGMENTS

As always, my books are never completed alone. Huge thanks go out to my editors extraordinaire, Jami Nord of Chimera Edits and Sarah Chorn. You are my heroes.

My beta readers were, once again, incredibly brave and helpful to read the messy early drafts. So much gratitude to J. Scott Coatsworth, Marti Ostrander, Mark Millham, Kayla Dugan, Jessica Smith, and Lilian Zenzi. Thanks to Keith Edwards for encouragement and general cheerleading during the first draft expansion.

JCaleb Designs always blows my mind with his cover art. Thank you, Jake!

To my lifemate Mark and our now grown-up kids, Kylan, Gabriel, and Jayden: Thank you for my office where I can write now that we're empty nesters (but the daybed is always open if and when you need it). And thank you to my furry office assistants, Percy and Aries.

Last but never least, thank *you*, the people who read my books. You rock, and I am ecstatic you like the crazy stories I write for my own amusement.

ABOUT THE AUTHOR

E.M. Hamill writes adult science fiction and fantasy somewhere in the wilds of eastern suburban Kansas. A nurse by day, wordsmith by night, she has sworn never to grow up and get boring.

Frequently under the influence of caffeinated beverages, she also writes as Elisabeth Hamill for young adult readers in fantasy with the award-winning Songmaker series.

She lives with her family, where they fend off flying monkey attacks and prep for the zombie apocalypse.

You can find her website at https://emhamill.wordpress.com/ Bluesky https://bsky.app/profile/emhamill.bsky.social

facebook.com/EMHamill

instagram.com/e.m.hamill

ALSO BY E. M. HAMILL

<u>The Dalí Tamareia Missions</u>

Dalí

Peacemaker

Third Front

Nectar and Ambrosia: An Amaranthine Inheritance Novel

Writing as Elisabeth Hamill:

<u>The Songmaker Series</u>

Song Magick

Truthsong